Alan Sillitoe

was born in 1928, and left school at fourteen to work in various factories until becoming an air traffic control assistant with the Ministry of Aircraft Production in 1945.

He began writing after four years in the RAF, and lived for six years in France and Spain. His first stories were printed in the *Nottinghamshire Weekly Guardian*. In 1958 *Saturday Night and Sunday Morning* was published, and *The Loneliness of the Long Distance Runner*, which won the Hawthornden Prize for literature, came out the following year. Both these books were made into films.

Further works include *Key to the Door*, *The Ragman's Daughter* and *The General* (both also filmed), The William Posters Trilogy, *A Start in Life*, *Raw Material*, *The Widower's Son*, *Her Victory*, *The Lost Flying Boat*, *Down from the Hill*, *Life Goes On*, *The Open Door*, *Last Loves*, *Leonard's War*, *Snowstop*, *Collected Stories*, *Alligator Playground*, and *The Broken Chariot* – as well as eight volumes of poetry, and *Nottinghamshire*, for which David Stillitoe took the photographs. He has also published his autobiography, *Life Without Armour*.

Fiction

Saturday Night and
  Sunday Morning
The Loneliness of the
  Long Distance Runner
The General
Key to the Door
The Ragman's Daughter
The Death of William Posters
A Tree on Fire
Guzman, Go Home
A Start in Life
Travels in Nihilon
Raw Material
Men, Women and Children
The Flame of Life
The Widower's Son
The Storyteller
The Second Chance
  and Other Stories
Her Victory
The Lost Flying Boat
Down From the Hill
Life Goes On
Out of the Whirlpool
The Open Door
Last Loves
Leonard's War
Snowstop
Collected Stories
The Broken Chariot

Non-fiction

Life Without Armour
  (autobiography)

Poetry

The Rats and Other Poems
A Falling Out of Love
  and Other Poems
Love in the Environs of
  Voronezh and Other Poems
Storm and Other Poems
Snow on the North Side
  of Lucifer
Sun Before Departure
Tides and Stone Walls
Collected Poems

Plays

All Citizens are Soldiers
  (*with Ruth Fainlight*)
Three Plays

Essays

Mountains and Caverns

For Children

The City Adventures of
  Marmalade Jim
Big John and the Stars
The Incredible Fencing Fleas
Marmalade Jim on the Farm
Marmalade Jim and the Fox

ALAN SILLITOE

Alligator Playground

A collection of short stories

Flamingo
An Imprint of HarperCollins*Publishers*

Flamingo
An Imprint of HarperCollins*Publishers*
77–85 Fulham Palace Road,
Hammersmith, London W6 8JB

Published by Flamingo 1998
9 8 7 6 5 4 3 2

First published in Great Britain by
HarperCollins*Publishers* 1997

This collection of stories is entirely a work of fiction.
The names, characters and incidents portrayed in it are
the work of the author's imagination. Any resemblance
to actual persons, living or dead, events or localities is
entirely coincidental.

ISBN 0 00 655073 8

Set in Meridien

Printed and bound in Great Britain by
Clays Ltd, St Ives plc

Bibliographical Note

A Respectable Woman published in *Illustrated London News* and
   Paris TransContinental
Beggarland published in *Woman and Home*
Ron Delph and his Fight with King Arthur published by *Clarion
   Books*
Ivy published in *Grant's Bank Magazine* and *Orion River Review*,
   USA
A Matter of Teeth published in *You Magazine*

Contents

Alligator
Playground

ONE

FACING EACH OTHER across the table they took care their eyes wouldn't meet, experienced enough to know that the ley lines of mutual attraction ought not to be played with irresponsibly. When one gaze caught the other the light in both went out, each pretending to show interest only in the remaining half-dozen at the lunch party.

Diana was surprised to note so much detail in a surreptitious glance. A photographer would never achieve the same intensity as her intuition, would at most highlight a face like that of a prisoner of war – static, bewildered, plain – whereas the reality her eyes took in would reinforce her memory, and become part of a floppy disc in the snug case of her brain.

He had the sort of face she would like to deal with in her spare-time painting, but rather than get out her sketch pad she knew that safety lay in listening to Charlotte, whose cigarette ash powdered into her barely touched soup. 'This Tory government's simply got to go.'

'But how?' Norman Bakewell's mischievous call set Charlotte diatribing about housing, education, unemployment, the National Health Service and privatisation. Diana decided to look worried, better to fix on Charlotte's obsessions than be yanked into another ocular contest with the fit man across the table.

Charlotte was a life-long left-winger, grappling such unregenerate views to her bosom as if her existence depended on them which, Diana thought, it probably did, in that she was kept from chewing ivy in the woods, or headmistressing the local coven. She was about fifty, and a little over five feet tall. Grey and meagre hair hung a few inches down her face, but what made the coarse features interesting were lips shaped in the tiniest of bows – a perfect little bow – so perfect yet so out of place in such a grim visage as to give the effect of benign though implacable intolerance. She wore a brown sackcloth garment resembling a gymslip, and no one, except perhaps Henry her husband, had seen her in anything else, as if she had a full wardrobe and took out a clean one every few hours.

The present meal – always called that, never dinner or lunch – was served on a long table in the living-kitchen. No cloth, of course, but the place-mats were distinctive to Charlotte's house, each depicting an episode in the struggles of the working class. Diana's showed 'The Taking of the Winter Palace' and, as far as she saw on another quick eye-shot, the man opposite, whom she'd heard called Tom, was eating off 'The Massacre of Peterloo'. The novelist Norman Bakewell, sitting next to her, had 'The Last Stand of the Paris Commune', and Emmy Brites, across to the left, lifted her plate and with her big blue eyes tried to make sense of 'The Death of Rosa Luxemburg'. Jo Hesborn had been given 'The Strike of the East End Match Girls', while Charlotte, as always, ate her meal off 'The Lord Mayor of London Slaying Wat Tyler'.

Diana was saying something to Charlotte, Tom noted. Every clandestine flash never lessened the attraction of what he saw. The workman type overalls of the best thin cloth buckled over a well cut shirt of pale grey seemed a mite old fashioned, but the way the front came across her bosom made her look absolutely delectable. The face attracted him no less, high cheekbones, and a slightly forward mouth due to her teeth, giving an impression of mischief and availability, which he knew better than to assume was so. Her almond shaped eyes produced a heat in him not experienced since first meeting his wife. A large-stoned ring, not on her marriage finger, could mean anything these days. Fair hair, in a neat line across her forehead, was tied behind. He circled back to her face as if to puzzle out why it was so compelling, then gave up so that he could enjoy it.

Norman Bakewell lit a cigar and puffed so busily between courses that Barbara Whissendine got the full nimbus of his smoke, as if she was the enemy from whom he needed to conceal the industrial capacity of his output as a writer. 'Don't they make you sick?' she asked.

'Not so far, my love,' he said. 'I smoke about seventy a week, and do you know, I was thinking the other day that if you put them end to end for length it'd make over six hundred yards, and since I've been puffing like billy-ho for forty years I've travelled nearly fourteen miles, which is just about right in my slow moving life.'

'I suppose you worked that out when you had writer's block?' Barbara, a rawboned steely-eyed literary agent who hadn't got him on her books for the simple reason that she wouldn't go to bed with such a toad in a million years, felt able to slam him all she liked. 'Doesn't your wife worry that smoking will kill you?'

'Wife?' His roar stopped all other talk. 'What's one of them?'

'It sounds as if she henpecked you.'

Was it the downing of another glass of wine that reddened his face? 'Did you say henpecked?'

'Stop it, Norman.' Charlotte collected the plates, and took the roast meat out of the oven. She knew him as one of those déclassé working-class men who, thinking he had nothing to blame his parents for, or being too sentimental to know where to begin, had reduced one middle-class wife after another to suicidal misery.

'Henpecked?' he crowed. 'You don't know one half. I got carpet bombed from morning till night. Then she came out of the potting shed, thank God, and went off with a woman.'

Jo Hesborn adjusted her collar and tie. 'I can't say I'd blame her for that.'

'The trouble was, she came back.'

Barbara angled away. 'And you let her?'

He paused. 'Wanted to get my own back, didn't I?'

'You mean you picked up with a man?' Jo laughed.

Light from the afternoon sun flashed on his glasses. 'I didn't wear my heart on my sleeve like a patch of snot, or cry into my blotting paper. I had an affair with a girl who was too young to think of becoming a lesbian.'

'So why isn't your wife with you now?' Barbara did her best to smile, and wiped the failure away with a napkin. 'I'm sure she'd love hearing the same old patter.'

Gazing tenderly, he took her hand in his, till she snatched it free. 'I'm glad I didn't bring her, or we'd both been fighting over you, darling. She's finally hopped it, I'm glad to say. Greater love hath no man than this, that he hand over his wife to the tender mercies of a woman.'

Jo Hesborn picked up her empty glass. 'You bastard! You walking gasometer!'

The missile shattered against his forehead, but he stayed calm, not only as if such an event happened every other day, but as if his existence would be without meaning if it didn't take place now and again. Even so, the grin barely lit the middle of his pallid face, thin lips suddenly with more curves in them.

He swabbed the flood, reddening Charlotte's best linen, and patted Jo's wrist as if he had injured her. 'I don't know why you did that. You ought to be grateful for somebody like me. I've probably turned more women into lesbians than any man in London. I thought somebody like you would appreciate the fact.'

Jo was disgruntled at her failure to obliterate – or at least kill – him. 'Thanks for nothing, scum.'

'I confess,' Norman said, fully recovered, 'that I'm looking for another girlfriend, though I can't see myself handing her over to you after I've done with her. Every likely looking candidate I come across gets a written questionnaire, in any case, so's there'll be no misunderstanding. For instance, I want to know whether or not she smokes. I wouldn't like her to live longer than me and burn all my letters and notebooks, though I expect we'd be separated long before that. I want to know if she's married. I don't want to get a dagger in my back from her squash-playing husband. Can she drive? Then I can get drunk at parties and she can take me home. Is she a dab hand at a word processor? That's essential, because I'm bloody hopeless with them. Does she have a sense of humour? She'd certainly need one. Are both her parents dead? Mine are, so it's only fair hers are too. Does she have children? I don't want any of those puking little bastards competing for attention. In any case, little Crispin with the heavenly curls might grow up to be a yobbo and kick me in for hitting his mother. Does she have a job? – preferably with TV or in films, so that she can get my novels put on. Then, of course, will she keep thinking I'm a genius when she hears me fart in bed at night? Does she have a centrally heated flat in the middle of London? I've taken a shine to Pimlico. And does she have a cottage in Dorset, with no neighbours to hear the screams when we start quarrelling and I give her a good hiding? And oh yes – God-Almighty, I nearly forgot – can she unravel the mysteries of VAT? A positive response to such queries might result in a satisfactory relationship for a month or two, but in the meantime,' he ended, with little-boy wistfulness, 'I'll go for any halfway personable woman who takes pity on me. Until the paragon turns up, of course, when I'd throw her aside like an old floorcloth.'

Diana noted the admiration on Tom's face at how Bakewell had ignored the cut from Jo's glass, and now his awe at such a horrid screed. Her face was warm with hatred, and she wanted to say something that would wither all men to pitiable stumps, though

Charlotte came in before her: 'Norman, I shan't buy your next novel if you don't behave to my guests.'

He swabbed his forehead again rather than quarrel with his hostess, and said mildly: 'You'll regret it, if you don't. It's called *The Lovers of Burnt Oak*. Bound to get onto the short list for the Windrush Prize.' He manufactured an expression of repentance. 'I'm sorry, though. I was feeling a bit on the dark side of bilious when I flopped out of bed this morning.' He apologised to Barbara, who responded with silence, so he looked around for another victim. 'Anybody want to talk about modern English literature?'

He lit a cigar when no one did. He was drunk, and Diana hoped everyone would ignore him, but he was malevolent and wouldn't let them. 'I'll tell you about the new novel I'm writing.' He looked at Tom, whose firm had beaten all competitors to get him on its list during an auction at the Groucho Club. 'The hero's a publisher,' he said, beady-eyeing Tom as if to damage him for having bought him like a slave at the market, and hoping that what he was going to say would turn into a prophecy. 'Well, his wife has a relationship – dare I call it, Jo? – with a woman. The husband's quite happy because it takes her attention from a little bit of business he's got on, also with a woman. Even so, the wife carries on in so shameless a way that at times he feels humiliated, but puts her affair in cold storage, as it were, to be dealt with in the future. Well, our hero publisher and his wife have a grown-up son, who he's always suspected to be the result of an early affair of his wife's, though we'll let that pass. This son has an affair with the daughter of the woman his wife is passionately involved with. Are you following me? A real alligator playground, because listen: both affairs tail off, you might say, but as time goes on the husband feels slighted and his thoughts stray towards revenge. A few years later he has a relationship with the woman's daughter that his son has by now finished with, and little by little he blasts her life, as only a swine like him can, to such an extent that she does herself in. The mother then lives unhappily ever after, as a played-out harridan.'

'You're sheer fucking evil,' Jo cried, after the silence. 'I should have pushed this carving knife into your guts.'

'It's a very moral tale,' he huffed. 'I was hoping you'd see something of that sort in it.' He began to cry, head forward over the ashtray, and Diana felt a shameful urge to comfort him.

Jo stood, pushing her chair away. 'The gas-oven's the only place for a snotchops like you.'

They walked with their coffee through the French windows onto a large well-shaved lawn, the grass dry enough for those who couldn't find places on the scattered park bench seats. The softened thump of a cricket ball sounded from the vicarage garden next door as Diana went towards the lilac bushes followed by Jo Hesborn.

Jo worked on lay-out for *Home and Country*. Her grey eyes sparked from behind the smallest of half-moon spectacles which, Diana thought, might be made of plain glass. Her hair was between fair and dark, the androgynous body dressed in a white silk shirt and tie, and checked trousers. She smoked a black papered cigarette from a holder made of bone.

Diana had heard she was a friend of Charlotte's because she had 'impeccable working-class credentials'. It was also put about that as a lesbian she had slept with most of the media women in London, who thought it less of a risk to tangle with the working class through her than get involved with an obese plumber or building worker. Diana considered such slander drummed up by a male chauvinist slob who thought it was witty, because she found Jo likeable, plain and straightforward, and envied her for making the only possible protest against Norman Bakewell. After saying so, she asked: 'Who was that bloke sitting opposite me? Do you know him?'

She spoke with a modified Northumbrian accent. 'He used to be a writer.'

'Why is he here, though?'

'Oh, he did a reportage, for a magazine Charlotte brought out in the eighties called *The New Oppressed*. She thought his piece was wonderful – social realism stuff straight from the front line, to use Charlotte's words, far better than Orwell ever wrote, she said, who she'd always thought a traitor to the working class.

'Tom lived among no-hopers and winos for a month, hung around DHSS offices, talked to kids on housing estates who loved nicking expensive cars and driving them on wasteland to burn. It was a long piece, went through three issues, but the magazine didn't last long. Even Tom's brilliant piece couldn't save it. The chattering classes weren't all that interested, and the unemployed couldn't afford it with their giros. They'd have laughed about it, anyway.

'Tom said that even before finishing it he decided that all he'd met were unhelpable, or just having a marvellous time burning and looting, for which he couldn't blame them. I'm sure he's never said as much to Charlotte, which is why she still likes him. Then he went into publishing, and now he's on the way to becoming a millionaire, or so it's whispered in the trade.'

'What about his love life?'

Jo laughed. 'Don't ask! When he was slumming among the dead-beats he fell in love with a young married woman he got talking to in the DHSS queue. Or maybe he fell for another at the same time, knowing him. Anyway, it all went wrong. She saw through him, I suppose. Then he went down like a ton of bricks for this hardbitten tart from the North called Angela, a coalminer's daughter, who worked at his firm. He married her. Got what he deserved, I suppose.'

'Is he happy?' Diana wanted to know.

Jo scoffed. 'No man can be happy, not even if you got him up in heaven and made him God. I don't know why you're so interested in him, though. Come and have a drink with me sometime, at my place in St John's Wood. I've always got some Bolly in the fridge. We'll have a meal afterwards, then try the Swallow Club for a dance. You'll love it there.'

Diana felt a sudden frisson, but put the hand gently away from her waist, in spite of the steady light in Jo's grey eyes, which she found hard to resist. She wasn't ready for that kind of eating, though might give it a try one day – or night – just as almost every woman wanted to have a baby once in her life. 'It's a bit far to get to from the BBC.'

'If ever you feel like it, let me know.' Wasting no time, she strode between rose bushes and across the lawn to blonde and secretive Emmy Brites, said to be writing her first novel, and whose peach coloured cheeks turned vermilion when the hand went forward.

Languid, dark and late thirtyish, Tom, when chatting at a party (except to a woman) looked continually over the man's shoulder to see who it might be useful to meet next. He did it without shame, on the understanding that since who he was talking to would know what was in his mind, and was probably doing the same anyway, he could leave without either being embarrassed. He also assumed that those under his scrutiny were talking about him, which was sometimes the case. Glad that Diana had given that lesbian the pushoff, he walked across to talk to her, as she had hoped he would.

He leaned on the arbour post. 'I had a lot to say to you, and now I've forgotten it all. At the table I thought the block would vanish as soon as we were face to face.'

'And won't it?'

'I've never felt such an electric connection in my whole life. It was absolutely amazing. It's still there, even more now that you're close and there's nothing between us.'

Fair, for a beginning, especially since he could have been stealing her words. Maybe that was how he had become a millionaire, though these days you could be fab-rich one week and living in Cardboard City the next. 'I thought it was wonderful, the way Jo Hesborn dealt with that emotional cripple.'

'Norman? I suppose he did ask for it. But maybe it's rather admirable, the way he lives like an open wound.'

'Sewer, more like.' His envy of Bakewell foxed her for a second, because she hated his misogynistic novels, and didn't think him worth any talk at all. 'How come you know Charlotte?'

Such a laugh made it hard to know what he thought, as he leaned close and lowered his voice. 'I like her. She's one of the old sort, totally misguided. She can't go to Russia since Perestroika because the planes don't run on time, and she might get mugged. It was the only country she felt safe in, but now she sticks to this old rectory, though she hates the place. Complains all the time to poor old Henry, so that she can seem the calm and all wise earthy hostess to everyone else.'

'I wouldn't like to be *your* wife.' Yet she thought she might, for an hour or two.

Even the overalls didn't hide her figure, the lovely fruity breasts, body going in at the waist and coming out to delectable hips. 'I'll curb my tongue, but if you ask me whether I'd like to be married to you the answer's yes, any time of the week.'

'You sound like the perfect husband. I hope your wife thinks you are.'

'In my experience, only the fatally flawed try to be perfect. I just saw you, and knew we had to talk.'

It was the moment to move on to someone else, easy enough to do. She'd always told herself never to have any truck with a married man, but he had given her no reason to walk away, and she didn't care to think of one. 'I'd love to live in a house like this, on such a marvellous day at least.'

'I'd die here,' he said. 'What's wrong with London?'

'Oh, not much, I agree. But I wake up in the morning plagued by pneumatic drills, or car alarms going off, or a burglar alarm, or a police car screaming to get to the station before the tea gets cold. Then there's the awful smell, and the traffic.'

Charlotte stood at the door. 'Who's going to volunteer for washing up? I only need two.' She thought it educational to make her guests work after a meal. 'When it's done we can go on a nice long walk to the river.'

Tom saw a way to imprison her in talk for the next half-hour. 'Let's do it.'

She used cardboard plates at her flat, and squashed them in the bin afterwards, but was happy to say yes. They put their hands up, like children at school, she thought, then went into the house, applauded by the others.

'Do you know how to get there?' The thatched cottages and front gardens were so neat she imagined people trying for the best kept village of the year. Even the gravestones looked polished and scoured, surrounding the stark grey church whose sinister tower must be visible for miles.

'We turn left along here.' He put a hand on her naked elbow, as if she needed guiding. The others would be left behind, and she liked being near him, though neither could think of much to say after their chatter at the sink. Skylarks and swifts played Battle of Britain in the blue, and the heat wafted an odour of tall wheat from either side of the track.

'I've done this walk quite a few times.' She wondered who with as they turned down a lane of birch trees, treading over hard-rimmed tractor ruts. 'There's a keeper's cottage at the end, then nothing between there and the river.'

Except a band of dark wood. The way opened onto sloping fields of yellow rape, which also patched the rising land across the valley. They stood a moment to enjoy the view. 'I hear Elgar's music when I get to this spot,' he said.

Poppies were worried by wasps of gold and black, and a small aeroplane lazied up from the coast. 'I see what you mean.'

He put an arm around her. 'The "Introduction and Allegro",

13

what else?' – and kissed her, a slow easing of the tongue into her mouth. Her body burned with the heat of the day, and there was sweat on her upper lip. The kiss was brief, could have lasted longer it was so delicious. She held his hand as they walked, breath quickened and not altogether from exertion. A rabbit zig-zagged out of their way. 'I know a short cut through the wood.'

Thistles and stubble slowed them down, then she detoured trying to avoid tall nettles, but they brushed her thin overalls and the vague tingle of stings came through, increasing her desire for him. 'Won't we be seen from the keeper's cottage?'

He waited for her to catch up. 'I expect he's too busy with Lady C. – if you see what I mean.'

They clambered over a ruinous stile, Tom scuffing a chocolate-looking stag beetle from a beam before handing her across. Unnecessary, but it was fun to let him think he could help. The way down levelled under foliage of clustering elms, brambles and small bushes almost covering the track. He stopped at a clearing.

Collared doves warbled, flapping at the disturbance. There was nothing to be said, hadn't been since eyeing each other across the table, her hands as forward as his as she drew him down, seeing his glazed eyes and still lips, and sweat on him also. An aroma of damp undergrowth played around the cool wood as she undid the straps of her overalls, and pulled at the buttons of her shirt. The crack of a twig sounded from some animal, or a disturbed branch, and she hoped there'd be no unseen audience.

She had never made love in a wood, while he obviously had, and she wondered at the unfamiliar air so cool to her nakedness. When he took off his shirt and trousers she could hardly bear to wait. The heat went back into her, and they seemed a thousand miles from the nearest human. He knew what he was doing, in ways she hadn't thought of before, but passion took care of them in any case.

*

Unexpectedly discovered love put them into a state of indolent stupefaction. She hoped there would be no wet patch on her overalls for the others to notice when they got to the river. His instinct was good, for he passed her a newly ironed handkerchief from his back pocket. 'Use this.'

'You came prepared.'

'Be unforgivable if I didn't.' He never felt better than after a good long fuck, and hoped she did too, complimenting himself that it hadn't been for want of plying the old skill if she didn't. 'The idea of sadness after sex must have been a liberal middle-class invention, like socialism or anti-smoking, or not eating meat. Anything to stop people enjoying life.' Gratified at her laughter, he lit a cigarette. 'This is the first weekend I've had off in months. I get up at six, and am never in bed before midnight.'

'It certainly keeps you fit,' she said languidly.

He flicked his ash towards a butterfly. 'I spend an hour at the gym every day. Otherwise, I'd scize up.'

'You certainly didn't get anywhere near it then.' She wanted to sleep in a big white bed with him, but stood to smooth the aches in her hips.

He straightened his collar. 'We'd better go, I suppose, or they'll wonder where we've got to.'

He wasn't there when she next went to Charlotte's, and she had almost grovelled to get invited. She had to push aside foul Norman Bakewell, who ragged her all through a lunch that would only have been good if you were peasant-hungry. He taunted her at Tom's absence, as if his wormy novelist's mind guessed every detail of their encounter.

Walking towards the wood made the distance seem twice as long. She was depressed and chilled in the damp glade, rain trickling from the foliage. The half-hour with Tom had been so perfect, she might have known it was too good to recall. Her mac was like wet muslin on getting back to the house. Luckily, Norman Bakewell was asleep in the lounge, though sending up vinous fumes and the stink of foul cigars.

Home dead beat from work, she picked up the phone to hear Tom's unmistakably nasal tone. 'It's been a long time, far too long, but can I come and see you?'

A month had gone by, and while knowing his number she had waited rather than do him the honour. The stab of wishing they had never met came now and again, but their idyllic summer's day would return in smell and touch, visual detail flooding in so that the innermost part of her belly yearned.

'When?' she asked.

'Now.'

He came out of the lift wearing Reeboks, jeans, and a Gap shirt. A copy of *The Big Issue* showed from one pocket of his blue cashmere overcoat, and a bottle of White Horse stuck its neck out of the other.

'I'm serious.' He sat by her on the couch, a drink cupped in his free hand. 'I can't ever forget you. I love you, and want to see you all I can. The trouble is, I've been rushing here there and every-where these last weeks, and couldn't find a minute to get in touch.'

She was glad, having been too often on the point of ringing him. 'Is your wife away tonight?'

'Nothing like that. I'm working late. I always am.'

She sipped whisky and Evian, and fought away laughter at noting that Evian backwards spelled 'naive'. She felt mischievous. 'Does *she* have a lover?'

'She could, for all I know.'

'Would you mind?'

He laughed. 'I'd kill him, maybe.'

'Suppose *he* played squash as well? But would your wife kill you?'

'I'd expect her to try, even if only to prove she loved me, or because I'd made the elementary mistake of letting her find out. It's never an accident when someone does. There's malice in it, you can bet. If you really care for each other – I mean, beyond love – you make sure the other never knows. Carelessness in that situation is sheer stupidity, maybe even hatred, or to get revenge.'

Men are all the same, she thought, though she'd never had a lover with the wit to speak so openly, which threw her so much off balance that she could only join in, and give up wondering what he meant by caring for somebody beyond love. 'What about those who have affairs by mutual agreement?'

He followed her into the kitchen. 'It ends in disaster, which must have been what they wanted.'

She put two pizzas in the microwave. 'Hungry?'

'Starving,' as befitted, she thought, someone who spoke in such a way. 'You seem to have had plenty of experience.'

'It's all speculation. Or intelligent observation, if you like.' He leaned across and kissed her. 'Most of it comes from reading Norman Bakewell.'

'I do hope not,' she said into his ear.

Her parents had sold their house in France two years ago, and bought a flat in Sevenoaks. Having too much furniture from that rambling old mill, they had given her a double bed, and because they or their guests had slept on it Diana was put off when sporting with her lovers. Another thing was it took up too much room: all right to stretch out on in summer, but hard to warm with her own heat in winter. With Tom as a lover she didn't care who had humped on it before.

A call of once a month was hardly sufficient to serve someone like her. She wanted to have an affair, and this was more like a treat from heaven whenever he cornered a spare hour. Time that dragged into a month had a ball and chain to its feet, though as soon as she heard the bell it was as if he had called only days ago. Out of chagrin she would greet him as if he were a stranger, forcing him into his most charming mode to get them back into high romantic style. Not until after the meal and bottle of wine, when she was lying naked on the bed, and he was leaning over in a very satisfactory state, did this feeling come about.

After they had made love she said: 'I'd like a phone number, in case there's a need to get in touch with you.'

'You have the office one already.'

'The home number, if you don't mind.'

'I'm hardly ever there. It would be a million to one if I were to answer it. And I shouldn't like Angela to.'

She wasn't so stupid as to go on if anybody but he lifted the receiver.

'I know,' he said, 'but I wouldn't even want her to suspect – not one little bit.'

He thought of everything.

'It would be unforgivable if I didn't.'

'You like to keep everybody happy?'

'It's the best way of keeping myself happy.'

He wondered why she laughed, unable to understand.

Perhaps she was being unreasonable, and couldn't think why, not especially wanting to call him at home. Nor, feeling his equal, did she need to test him, or put herself through such futile emotional hoops.

He fastened his shirt almost to the neck, and she pointed out that the buttons were in the wrong place, perversely wishing she hadn't told him.

'Christ!' He rapidly undid them, remembering how he had once got home and, while undressing, Angela noticed his pants back to front, though she was satisfied when he told her he had been playing squash and in a hurry to have a drink. He looked around at windows and doors, as if planning a quick escape, though there was no need. Probably instinct, and in any case it was three floors up. 'What's in there?'

'My spare room.'

'Full of junk, I suppose?'

'It's where I do my painting.' Daddy had walked into Winsor & Newton's, and bought a great box for her birthday.

'Painting?'

She laughed. 'Therapy I call it.'

'Look, Diana, I'm off to Rome next week. Can you sham illness at the Beeb, and get time off? I'd love to have you with me.'

Nothing easier. She could see some wonderful paintings. 'How long for?'

'Three days, say.'

'Could swing it. We're between projects at the moment.' Which was half a lie, but she didn't want him to think she was doing any favours.

'Marvellous. I'll bell you.'

'Oh, right.'

'I'll never stop loving you.'

'I know, darling. Love you, too.'

TWO

Angela, back with a hundred quid's worth of grub and cleaning stuff from Sainsbury's, hadn't realised she had left her natty little Japanese tape recorder on. It wasn't in her to be so witless. But she hadn't left it on: the cunning little devil started at the sound of a voice.

Operating such technological gimmicks was complicated enough to give a feeling of achievement. The manuals were easier to memorise if you read them aloud and, noting each movement phase by phase, she set the timing mechanisms of the video if a programme on television needed taping while they were out. Tom was baffled by such mysterious gew-gaws, and thought it strange that a woman should be so competent.

As a kid she had wanted to be an engineer and build bridges; he may have praised only to flatter, but it was pleasing to have her skill acknowledged, and flattery harmed no one, as long as you didn't take it seriously. In any case, she flattered him, being as how he was so juvenile. She laughed at his failures, and said he couldn't be a genius at his job and understand modern technology as well, a remark that soothed the abrasions of a seven-year marriage.

'It's just small enough to get into your handbag.' He handed it over after his trip to Rome, and thought it useful as a notebook for dictating shopping lists into, or reminding her of something while driving the car.

She sat on the bed, holding the unobtrusive recorder which

usually lay in the hairpin basket by the bedroom telephone. The playback mechanism reproduced a door clicking, drifts of music from the kitchen, a police siren, or the roarpast of a souped up van along the normally quiet Holland Park street. When traffic was thick around Shepherds Bush a few rogue vehicles, or reps handy with the map, used it as a slip road.

The black box was something of a miracle, and one day soon an invention would let you talk into a recorder and, at the touch of a switch, after attaching it to a word processor, a printer would bang the text neatly out. Bang also would go the secretary's job, and if such a thing had been possible ten years ago she might not have been a rich man's wife with a very des res in Holland Park.

Whatever she was she had never stopped being herself, because if she hadn't always been as much of herself as possible she wouldn't have become Tom's wife. She supposed the process began by the sudden revelation at school that she was of better quality than anybody around her, and that O Levels could be passed if she tried.

She dropped a few pegs in her self esteem when no office in Wakefield would set her on. 'You've got a long way to go before you're any good to us,' every smarmy personnel manager seemed to say. She was given work at a meat pie processing firm and, despite rock bottom wages, saved enough to buy a typewriter, and went to night classes to learn shorthand. It was hard to say whether the worst part of her year was being at home, or having to sweat with a row of foulmouths at the factory. The woman in charge of the conveyor belt was as much of a bully and even more dirty minded than her father, while the others were on the same mental level as her mother and sister. Maybe the combination had been invaluable in giving the energy to flee from both.

Angela supposed she came from the sort of place in Yorkshire which journalists referred to as 'a close-knit community'. The phrase made her want to throw up. Those who used it would never live in such a place, not in a million years, though she could see them shivering with almost sexual pleasure while tapping the phrase out. Even her father, getting it from television, had used it with pride before cursing her as a fool on hearing she was going to live in London.

She couldn't wait to get out of the village. London next stop, she said to herself, sniffing the odour of the carriage at Doncaster. They could stuff their close-knit community where a monkey stuffed its nuts.

It wasn't hard to land a job, and she was soon able to mimic posh talk because of splitting a flat with Debbie and Fiona in Putney. They thought her patois charming, but when she began to sound more or less like everyone else, found her less agreeable, so she rented a room in West Ken, happy to be on her own.

Anyone who asked where she'd come from and deserved an answer was told Leicester, a safe bet, but a few months later she would mention Luton, and after a year she fobbed off whoever asked with the request that they mind their own business or, if they were trying to get at her, and if she was at a party and sufficient drink had put her into an awkward mood, she would revert to what she had once been and tell them – as she had from time to time fishwifed back as a girl to one or two collier slobs calling some funny business from the doorway of a chippy, or from the bus shelter on a windy night – to fuck off, which she was gratified to find worked marvels at a London party.

Such a whiplash rejoinder, from someone who could talk the Queen's English with the best of them, did not reveal that such language was a basic part of her. In any case there was enough on television for any gently brought up girl to pick out for use.

She didn't care what they thought, but if she had realised that Tom was close when she let fly a mouthful at the party she would have folded with horror. She didn't approve of such talk – oh dear no, she laughed in recollection, of course I fucking well didn't –

but on falling into it had been consoled by imagining there were two people inside her instead of one and that, she liked to assume, was where whatever strength she had came from.

She singled Tom out on her first day at the firm. He was one of the directors in charge of the editorial division, and she recognised him as the sort of man who often appeared in her erotic and romantic dreams. He was said to be clever, the only person in the place with any imagination. The combination of charm and ruthlessness was carried with confidence, and his self-assured handsomeness was hard to deny, even for London where there were so many fit men, though his personality alone would have attracted her. You could tell by his face and manner that in a few years he would be at the top.

He was tall, with dark curly hair, and thin curving lips always on the point of saying something which would either burn you into the ground or make you fall on your back and open your legs – though she didn't feel herself a candidate for either fate. She rarely heard him talk, he just walked into the department, spoke to someone in the distance about schedules or book jackets – as if he owned the building and could manage the mortgage with no trouble at all, thank you very much – then went back to his office where, she imagined, a nice thick sheepskin rug lay in front of his desk.

His nicely shaped ears picked out every word within radius, that was for sure, and though she couldn't tell what he had heard exactly, her vile language got him talking and, being too pissed to know what about, she listened in such a way as to make him think she wasn't interested, which caused him to go on longer than he thought worthwhile to this pert office runabout from somewhere north of Potters Bar. Her look of glazed indifference offended yet intrigued him, for she was amazed at him wanting to flirt with her, while asking herself who the blinding hell he thought he was?

Knowing she was as good if not better than everybody else, she paid as much to have her hair cut before the party as her father earned for a fair week's slog down the pit. The mirror showed how attractive she was on getting into her wine-dark dress, though she didn't need a flattering glass to confirm it. Full lips and a small firm chin, straight slim nose, and sufficient expanse of forehead, gave the impression that she could be efficient and intelligent, which she knew she must be compared to most other girls at the firm. She'd had too much of a struggle getting there to act as conceited as them.

Lots of famous people were at the party, mostly writers the firm published, but she wasn't good at picking them out, and anyway so what if they were famous? She supposed those who were there and didn't work in the office must be writers, except that there were so many unknowns from other departments that as far as she was concerned a lot of them might be writers as well. You couldn't tell. Writers, she found, dressed like everybody else, and other people got so togged up that they might also be writers.

A man in a three-piece gravy brown suit and a cravat for a tie, crinkly grey hair, and stinking of whisky and aftershave, pinned her against the door. He told her he was a novelist, with the sort of leer not beamed in her direction since living in Yorkshire.

'My name's Norman Bakewell. I'm sure you've heard of me.'

The titles he ran off reminded her of the names her mother used to read aloud before going up the street to put bets on them at the bookies. Glittering eyeballs winked through heavy glasses that must have cost a bomb but looked dirt cheap.

'I've read every one of them,' she lied.

His lips were too close. 'I only came to this firm because they said I could go to bed with any lovely woman who worked here.'

'Written in your contract, is it?'

'I insisted: a fat advance, twelve free copies, and any girl I fancied.'

'And what part of the world do you come from, crumb?'

He winced. 'Norman, if you please. A place near Wakefield. The name's on the jacket of my latest bestseller.'

The village wasn't far from hers, so he didn't need an interpreter to understand the argot telling him to put his head in a bucket of cold water and keep it there for fifteen minutes. He moved to another girl, who had been at the firm long enough not to shove him away so abruptly.

She was getting undressed for bed, and couldn't understand why Tom had been so attracted as not only to blab for half an hour, though mostly about himself and what a big shot he was, but even to fetch her another drink and, later in the evening, ask if he could see her home. Her no to this bumped his self confidence into paralysis, but she couldn't bear him to see the slummy house at 24 Dustbin Grove where she lived.

Her put-down hadn't been unpleasant, though however well she behaved she was always aware that her inborn mannerisms might give her away. The split drained her, but now she could feel the beautiful all-powerful woman because even Tom was interested in her. While settling into bed she was sorry not to have come back in his car instead of by the packed Tube. He was sure to be good at making love, certainly better than the deadbeats she'd so far tried it with.

She had held him off for so long that he became dead set on marriage, though not more keenly than she. He had made as good a husband as he was capable of, and while that seemed all right most of the time for both, it didn't entirely come up to par for her. Something was missing which he was incapable of giving, a limit he couldn't pass, unless what she sensed lacking wasn't really there. Perhaps it was something in herself, though she didn't see how.

He thought the fact that he could fuck well covered a multitude of sins, and much of the time it did, but at her most discontented she wondered whether the deadness in him was what stopped the uxorious devotion she craved from coming out. Even so, she supposed she was as much in love with him as she could be with any man, his only fault being that he gave too much time to his work.

A year after marrying she had a miscarriage. No, they had a miscarriage. For no known reason, the great event of their lives never happened. Did he wish it on her because he wondered if he was the father? He had no reason to, but every insane notion came to mind, to such stony country had the loss driven her. All talk was loving while she was expecting: Saul for him and John for her, or Rebecca for her and Mary for him. They discussed the matter for days and weeks, filling a chest of drawers with clothes for either sex and any age up to ten.

Her laugh was acidic. Toys and trinkets, tuckers and bibs, cups and a silver spoon, stashed and no longer looked at, the trunk locked. Lavender was powdered between cot blankets and cot sheets, as her mother had shown. The stupefaction lasted months. Maybe it was still going on, when she thought about it. She'd had tests but nothing was wrong – fuck-nothing was her anguished cry. Tom's ebullience reasserted itself, telling her they could only exist and let the pain evaporate, and that nothing could part two people who had suffered such a blow.

She sat on the bed, and the sad resonances of Elgar's music put her in mind of a motor excursion up the Wye Valley and into the Malvern Hills. Tom had arranged the trip to divert her from the miscarriage, but it only expanded the wilderness of loss, for how could anything other than going deeper into yourself find a solution as to what had gone wrong?

Such music indicated that she had done well for herself since leaving Yorkshire with a cheap and overfull suitcase, all that time ago. She had often thought of slinging the case away – a treasured memento in the attic – but pictured the dustbin men footballing it into the van with a laugh, wondering how such a shoddy item came to be in her opulent house.

Tom soon had a firm of his own, and travelled the world for business, a big man in it, youngish though he still was. She gave up her job, since more money was available from his gaudy books than they could throw about on everyday expenses. Habits of thrift from Yorkshire made her unwilling to spend unless for something essential.

To be lavish with his money would make her feel unequal, parsimony a counterweight to remaining herself, and not being completely taken in by a man who could give himself more cash in a week than many earned in a year.

And what an efficient little wifey I've turned into, she thought, grooming and mooning, entertaining and chatelaining. She supposed she'd hoped for it on running away from home, because didn't you always achieve what you dreamed of in your ignorance, and even get that bit of romantic extra you never quite admitted to wanting for fear it wouldn't happen?

Twice a year she loaded the Volvo with whatever pressies her parents might like, and ferried them up to Yorkshire: a hamper from Selfridges, a video and some James Cagney movies for her father; a camcorder in case they felt like making a memento of them staring at each other and saying nothing week after week.

Tom told her he loved Fred and Janice, and Angela laughed at how they behaved with their language and fussed to make him comfortable. He was too busy to go more than twice, but liked to choose their gifts, once sending a box of chocolates so big they joked about roping it to the luggage rack.

On the Great North Road she always stopped for lunch at The George in Stamford. She liked the old fashioned place, because Tom once booked them a room on their way to the Edinburgh Festival. She sat in the lounge afterwards for coffee. Feeling herself to be a woman of mystery and elegance, she surprised herself when, seeing a man come in who she fancied, she wondered whether she would go away with him for the weekend if he asked.

'Fell off the back of a lorry, did they?' her father said, seeing the gifts. 'I hope the police won't be round in the morning. We don't want to upset your mother, do we? Do we, Janice?' he bawled.

'Don't be daft,' her mother said. 'We should be glad we've got such a nice son-in-law.'

Her father grumbled, no gracious corpuscles in his blood. 'I like to look life in the eye.' The first time he met Tom he said to Angela on the QT that such a man would end up either as a millionaire or in prison. A real judge of character, but that was his way, and she could never stand being at home for more than seventy-two hours.

The first day was tolerable because she took from her parents all that had been useful in her early life. Not much, but it served, though she was irritated at feeling sentimental about it. People gawped as she walked around the village, wondering what she was up to in the call box by the main road trying to get through to Tom. She strode to the stone-walled fields, and remembered running across them as a kid. Now she wore trousers, and laughed at the fact that she was too tall to graze her crotch anymore.

On the second day in the terraced house the silence was even thicker than the walls she had clambered over, and an effort was needed to stand up and go outside. But after the midday dinner of overcooked lamb, potatoes and cabbage, her father took his jacket from the back of the door and said: 'Come on, Angie, let's walk down the road to the pit. The men have been laid off, and the women have set up a protest camp outside gates. You'll need a scarf and hat, though.'

Maintenance men kept the mine humming so that seams wouldn't collapse or water pour in. Pits were closing all over the coalfield, he said, but the miners wanted jobs not redundancy money. 'The government's playing arsy-versy one minute, and changing its tactics the next, just to unnerve everybody. They treat people like bloody schoolkids.'

28

Three women were warming themselves at a coalfired brazier, all dressed in various styles of anoraks, rainbow scarves and woolly hats. One young woman sat on a plank between two barrels, helping a young boy to drink out of a titty-bottle filled with warm tea.

An elderly grey-haired woman in a duffel coat, tall and thin, came out of the headquarters caravan. 'Up from London, are yer?' she said, when Fred had introduced Angela. 'My name's Enid. You don't talk like us anymore.'

'I can't help that, can I?' The woman had spoken with humour perhaps, but Angela had never liked that kind because whoever used it only wanted to put one over on you. She regretted her sharp tone, and even having opened her mouth.

'Well, here *we* are,' Enid went on, 'doing the only thing we can to mek the buggers see sense. I'm not sure how far we'll get, though. They're doing their best to shift us. Last week they set the bulldozers on us, but the drivers refused to do it, bless 'em. The media and TV was here, and the powers that be didn't like that, so they 'ad to call 'em off.'

A young woman came out of the caravan with mugs of coffee and gave one to Angela. 'We was at school together, don't you remember?' The wind blew the flaps of her headscarf this way and that. 'We was in Miss Griffin's class.'

She said yes, now I do, and knew she would have been here as well if she had stayed and married a man whose only hope of work was down the pit – being bossed about by this woman who had set herself up as their leader.

'The men are used to the work, and get good money,' Enid said. 'It's the only job they can do, and there's no other. If many more pits close it'll be a disaster. Even now, all these villages are dying, and the crime rate's soared. At one time you could go out without locking your door. We used to police the place ourselves, you might say, but nowadays the young lads break in and tek everything. It goes on all the time.'

'Enid's one o' the best,' her father whispered. 'None better. The salt o' the earth.' Such phrases suggested matiness, and bigotry, yet she listened, asking the right questions, with words and gestures natural to her. Still feeling a fraud, yet knowing they had more of a case than anybody else, she signed the petition, and gave a tenner for the fighting fund.

Enid told her father he had a lovely daughter, and there were tears of pride in his eyes. He held her hand affectionately by the back door, but let it fall as they went in, for fear her mother would see.

On the third day she said she had to go home and look after Tom, and was as happy to get away as the first time, unable to smile till reaching Doncaster and heading south. To have stayed longer might have turned her back into someone she had always had a horror of being, only feeling what she assumed to be her real self when a tea tray was brought to her table at the hotel in Stamford.

Tom was away in Frankfurt again – or was it Bologna – conferring with publishers about translations, reprints and bestsellers. He was all over the place these days, but would shine in tomorrow, merry and bright before burying himself back in the office.

The melancholy notes of Elgar stopped, and Tom's voice vibrated at her ribs, as if he had been dead a year and was talking from the other side of heaven or hell, if there were such places, which she wouldn't believe till she had been there and seen for herself. His tone was low-pitched, and eerily confidential in case someone who shouldn't be was pressing an ear to the other side of the door.

'Diana? Tom. It'll be marvellous. Can't bear to wait. I know. Have to, won't I? We both will.' He gave a sneaky laugh, new to Angela. 'It'll be worth it, I know.'

She sat in an armchair, and his voice was clearer. Her flesh felt as if coated with ice. Last night she had been to see a play at Notting Hill Gate. He had come in before her, and complained of exhaustion when she got into bed with nothing on and laid lovingly by him.

'No, I won't pick you up. Get a taxi, or a minicab, if you like. All right, a proper black cab. Safer these days. I'll see you at the check-in. Oh, don't worry, I'll be there. Who? Norman Bakewell? How did his interview go? Yes, he's always very good. I've never known him not to be, providing he's interviewed by an attractive woman. You saw him afterwards? What did he say? No, he doesn't know about us. Nobody does. He *is* a vile old gossip. Angela? Glad to get rid of me, I expect. How do I know what she does? Of course she doesn't, so don't get nervous. I must hang up, though. See you at the check-in. You've got your ticket and passport?' Another sneaky laugh. 'You'd look a right charlie getting there and finding it was out of date. I've heard of it happening. Mine? I check it every morning before brushing my teeth. Can't wait, either, my darling. Love you. Yes, a lot. Love you, then. 'Bye. All right. 'Bye, love.'

No more voice. She knew she should laugh, but her lips wouldn't untwist. Like an episode from one of Bakewell's gloating and cynical books. Well, the next chapter would be hers. The heating was on full but her hands and feet were cold. Maybe an unknown voice would come out of the hissing tape with the gen on how to kill herself. Better still if it told her the best way of doing him in without being found out.

She couldn't think, so neither was likely, head blocked solid till her eyes were sore. At the end of the Elgar she had needed to go into the bathroom and pee, but didn't want to anymore. When she did she might squat over those lovely bespoke frilly fronted shirts he was fond of poncing around in.

Diana, he had called her. 'Diana,' she said aloud, 'I'll fucking Diana her. I'll dish him, as well. I'll make the bastards spit tacks.' The only time he had shed tears was once when she asked him to peel some onions before a dinner party.

THREE

Tom took into account only the surface features of life, and never went properly into the depths to try and make sense of the turmoil, and bring it under some form of control. In any case, to imagine it would be beneficial or worthwhile or – more important – cost-effective, was futile. Wasn't the dazzle of the surface more attractive than trawling for significance in the stinking slime? Such nit-picking was the work of novelists like Norman Bakewell who, in their hit or miss fashion, manage it fairly well, and make it amusing to read about.

Any answers might be too gloomy to endure, or too bland to respect, and only those without a satisfying life deceived themselves into thinking an explanation could be dragged out of the sub-conscious (whatever *that* was) or that any good was to be had from fruitless revelations. And suppose you were telling someone about yourself, who would be interested in self pitying maunderings rather than hearing of bizarre and manly events that made a fasci-nating story?

Only pathetic and inferior people got involved with the therapy of analysis, or took drugs to blast a way through the obfuscations to a mind that was still as puerile when the dust had blown away. Tom thought that the less he knew about himself the more of a puzzle he would seem to everyone else, and there was much advan-tage to be gained from that.

After three days of unmitigated sex he travelled back on a different plane to Diana, thus avoiding any taint of suspicion. He left nothing to chance, yet his unthreaded spirit plagued him as he stretched both legs in first-class and poured from a half-bottle of champagne. The stewardess wondered why he laughed, and why he drank so obviously to himself by holding the glass up to her. Poor slob, she thought, he's put his girlfriend on another flight, and now he has to go home and face his wife.

Tom found it encouraging to believe that whenever he had been to bed with Diana – or whoever else – any young woman within range would be curious about him. It could be that his marriage to Angela had made him an interesting if not near perfect man for other women who, being clever and intuitive, felt it – which thought made him smile as he fastened his safety belt.

Yet things didn't seem as right as they ought to be, and there were times when he felt timid and insignificant, having nothing, deserving nothing, and existing in an aura of boring mediocrity, an utterly dissatisfied state of mind which no one else was allowed to suspect. To lift himself out of this near fatal fit of corroding worthlessness needed such energy as, when he succeeded, gave him a shark-like and not unsubtle advantage in dealing with anyone at work (and elsewhere) who stood in his way. He never knew the reason for this sudden descent into a bleak landscape, had no indication as to where it was or where it had come from. God-given and God-smitten, was all he could say. Maybe it was the curse of the black dog, which resulted from too much good living, too much hard work, and too much sex.

A glimpse of Hyde Park between the cumulus helped him back to an awareness of the world, making him feel as if London and everyone in it belonged to him. He never travelled with enough luggage to put on the conveyor, so could go through the nothing to declare – but not too quickly in case the Customs people suspected his briefcase to be bulging with crack – and take a taxi straight to the office.

The M4 was blocked as usual, by a lorry that had shed its load – or was it a burst water main, or a chemical spill, or one of those common accidents involving a half blind non smoking teetotal vegetarian of eighty hurrying for his (or her) insulin shot? Well, whatever was wrong with Tom, he knew he was in love with Diana, and that their liaison was worth all he put into it, because the more you did the better it would get, which was better for both and so, ultimately, best of all for him.

Walking up the path at dusk, a raddled tiredness made every limb ache, but he forced a brisk pace, because for some reason it annoyed Angela when his behaviour suggested he'd had a hard day at the office. He supposed that even signs of a back-breaking slog down the coalmine would have put a curve of disapproval on her lips.

Leaves blowing erratically against the background of a lighted window made it look as if the house was on fire. She usually sat in the living room with her evening vodka and orange, but she wasn't there. An empty bottle and glass lay on the low table, and every light from the entrance hall to the attic had been left on.

Not in the dazzling white kitchen, either, two plates on the floor overflowing with bits of something gone crispy and black. Upstairs two at a time, he found her by the uncurtained window of their bedroom, holding the little black tape recorder he had been so good as to bring her back from – where the hell was it?

She wore the dress in which he had first noticed her at the office party, the line of small gold buttons on the plum coloured material moulding her bosom to a good figure still. The white lace collar set off her face, though her normally wavy dark hair was as straight as if she had just walked in from a monsoon, which he thought strange, for the hair drier was of the latest powerful make. Even the strongest of men would have been alarmed at her pallid cheeks, as if she had been poisoned by a long afternoon sleep.

'What is it, love?'

At the press of a switch the sound of his voice couldn't be denied. He'd heard it before, but is that what it's like? Scrape, scrape, mumble and snigger. Well, it would be, for something like that, wouldn't it? Hoping he wasn't betrayed by the pallor of his own skin brought a laugh up from his ribs when she pressed the machine off.

'Oh, that!' he said, 'I was reading a bit of Norman Bakewell's latest while getting dressed, sort of acting it out. And you thought I was up to something else! What a beautiful, suspicious and adorable person you are! I love you more and more for thinking that, because it shows how much you love me. You don't need to flatter me to that extent, sweetheart.'

An ominous sensation told him that his patter wasn't convincing, not even to himself. You bet it wasn't. But he went forward to embrace her.

She stepped away. 'Who's Diana, you two-timing fucking rat?' The tape recorder shed pieces after bouncing against his forehead and hitting the floor.

He hoped the liquid was sweat rather than blood, recalling Bakewell's noble stance at Charlotte's lunch party when Jo Hesborn had clobbered him for far less than this. 'She's a character in Norman's novel. It was so enthralling I took it to Germany with me. Looks like we've got another bestseller on our hands. I left it at the office, but I'll finish it tomorrow. I wouldn't have put it down, but I wanted to be with you for the evening.'

'Oh, did you?'

'Thought we could go out for a meal.' He put a hand over his face. 'God, that really hurt. What did you do it for?'

There was something to be said for not saying very much, but there was even more to be said for saying so much that she wouldn't be able to disbelieve the lies he was forced to tell. Failing that, she would be mystified by what she thought he was trying to say – the verbal equivalent of drowning a treaty in ink. All the same, this was life on the Heaviside layer. He would have to take even more care, knowing by her blow what a pity it was that technology hadn't stopped at the bicycle, the battery-run wireless set, and the wind-up gramophone, but had progressed, if you could call it that, to the diabolical invention of a tape recorder set going by the human voice.

'I asked you who she was, you lying deceiving gett.'

He was disappointed by how easily she went back to her origins, and she could sense him thinking it, which pained her so much that she angled a heavy glass ashtray halfway upwards. 'Who is she?'

He flinched. 'Throw that, and I'll phone the police.'

'Will you?' she raged.

He certainly would. 'I'd rather them handle you than me kill you. I've no intention of running the firm from a prison cell.'

She lowered it, not her plan to kill him – yet. He would die by a thousand cuts. 'Why don't you call mummy and daddy, and tell them what a pathetic fix you're in?'

'They're dead, and you know it.'

'I expect you broke their hearts.'

Better and better. Talking was all she wanted, no one could resist it, proof of his recognition that she was alive, and he was fulfilling his obligations towards her as a human being. 'They died of old age. I was a late birth, the only son. They loved me, and I loved them. Oh, you know all that.'

She sat, hands on her knees, skirt rucked up. It excited him, the bastard. She pulled it down. From now on I wear nothing but trousers. 'And they spoiled you rotten. You've allus seen yourself as God's gift to humanity, but you're not to me anymore.'

'I never thought I was any of that. But I loved you and still love you.' Shame she yanked her skirt down. 'I love you more than ever. I'll always love you.'

'You won't if I know it.'

'I will. You can't stop me. I adore the ground you walk on.'

'Oh, do you, then?'

'Yes, I do.' They were bickering. Better than ever. But he was angry with himself because stupidity was unforgivable, and bad luck frightening, which made him want comforting, so he became tender towards her in the hope that she would provide it. She mistook his attitude for contrition, and for the moment regretted her violence, almost willing to put aside the enormity of what he had done, because really there was no point when the only thing to do was walk away from this state of five-star humiliation.

Gradually she was soothed and, after kisses that sealed a lightning-charged truce, he put on the suit in which he too had been at the party – thinking it a nice touch – and walked her to a restaurant across Holland Park Road.

A bottle of champagne and the best food on the card would bring her round, though between each lovey-dovey clinking of glasses he reminded himself that in the morning he must go through his wallet and fax book to make sure there were no clues as to Diana or her whereabouts.

He doesn't know me. They had made very satisfactory love and now he had gone to sleep. He thinks an orgasm makes up for everything, and I'm going to say no more, when he's been doing it on me ever since we got married. I see now why my body threw out his rotten kid. And all those times I went to Yorkshire on my own he was pushing his filthy cock up all the scruffy tuppences he could find.

No wonder he's always had so much work to do at the office and been so knackered when he got home. I could go on the razz myself but I wouldn't do it just to get back on him. I don't see any men I fancy these days, and if I did I don't suppose they'd fancy me, but if ever I do do it I'll do it in my own good time.

He'd be easy to deceive because the only person he knows about is himself. All the times I've gone through the gamut of a bad cold or the flu without him being aware, but when he caught it, whining about who had passed it on at the office, he moaned in bed for at least three days. When they both had colds she had to deny hers because two people could no more have one at the same time than they could complain of a common misfortune – and he'd never noticed.

The issue stopped her getting to sleep, when up to now she had fallen off the ledge and felt nothing till morning. Whoever robbed her of slumber was guilty of murdering her dreams. Her language lapsed again, something else to destroy him for: I'll fucking kill 'er. I've had the sort of upbringing where I would never let anybody put one over on me. I've been spoiled by having it that easy, spoiled even rottener than him with his pampering, which is something he'll never understand.

Changing position didn't help. His snoring, as always after he had swined and dined, was like a lawnmower going over rocky ground, but she was bothered more than before because he had set on a stoat to eat up her brain. The shit-nosed little animal was halfway through the front lobes and getting on very well towards the back, thank you very much, but soon there would be nothing left so it would turn round and start again at the front, hoping a few scraps remained from the first time through. The more it stoated back and forth the more determined she was to clock Tom and his moll who had let it loose. First of all – getting out of bed – I'll go through his things and find out just who that bitch Diana is, because she's not going to be like herself much longer.

Diana often swore she would never have an affair with a married man, not realising till too late that whoever said never would sooner or later be inveigled into doing whatever they'd said they would never do never about. In the first place, the hole and corner complications would drive her spare, and in the second, if the other woman found out, she might be miserable, which Diana was too humane, or too loyal to her own sex, to gloat over. In the third place she didn't want to get close enough to another woman to the extent of sharing her through her husband.

And now here was Tom phoning to say that his wife had pulled the big whistle from her bloomers and blown it long and loud after their time in Rome. He wouldn't be seeing her for a while, he said, though there was nothing he wanted more in the world. He could be lying, of course, because what more appropriate time was there to end an affair than after a wonderful few days on the Mainland? His tone was so adoring that she had to believe his spiel, though her faith in his abilities went down a notch or two at his wife finding out. Had he done it deliberately? Shit-headed Norman Bakewell said that people only let their opposite know of their entanglements when they wanted a bit more excitement; and that sort she could well live without.

She opened a half-bottle of Beaujolais and threw the cork in the bin. Such a sexy weekend made her want to see him next day, tonight, this minute, instead of waiting the fortnight he implied she might have to. She tore off the plastic and put a steak under the grill. His pleading tone was something new. He was afraid of his wife. It was worth a laugh, because most men were. A programme arranged in Sheffield would keep her away for a week, and if her craving didn't diminish she would see who might be possible among the camera crew. Tom was sleeping with his wife, so she had a right to a diversion as well.

The first message on the ansaphone was from who else? 'All I know is I'm in love with you,' he said, and it felt as if a hand were already reaching across her breasts, 'totally, passionately, irreversibly. Can I see you on Wednesday evening?'

'You certainly can,' she said, phoning his office.

Then came six calls from the same heavy breathing person who, not finding her home, wouldn't commit a voice to tape, but was trying to get her with eerie persistence. Well, you got all sorts in the world, meaning London, so it wasn't worth thinking about. After the usual hellos from parents and friends she went to the twenty-four-hour shop and stocked up the larder. Supper done, she would stand with brush and palette in the spare room, finishing her notion of a female nude.

Instead of his usual month at a time Tom came every few days, as if the new situation fired his libido. Diana kept the interpretation to herself, but was glad at his visits, couldn't have enough of them, because a higher intensity came into their affair for her as well. Some evenings the phone sounded several times while they were in the bedroom, most of the callers – or caller, she was sure – did not go on to talk.

'Someone's phoning me,' she said. 'And I don't know who.'

He sloped in the best armchair, blowing rings from his long thin cigar. 'Probably wrong number.'

'It happens too often.'

'Any theories?' He sounded uninterested.

She had picked up the phone once and, expecting a call about work, had stupidly given her name. 'No, have you?'

'Could be an old boyfriend trying to get in touch.'

'I never went with slobs like that.'

'People do funny things,' he said.

'They say them, as well.'

Ash showered onto her carpet. 'It won't do any harm. Could be Angela, I suppose.'

'I wondered that.'

'Hard to find out without giving us away. I told her we weren't seeing each other anymore.'

'Was that wise?'

'It was easy. You don't know Angela,' he said, at the contempt on her lips. 'Oh, hell, I wonder how she got the number?'

He sounded petulant, but who wouldn't? 'You should know.'
'I don't, though.'

'Anyway,' Diana said, 'as long as she doesn't find out where I live.'

At the back of his address book was a seven-group, unlike any other, and she altered each digit a number ahead. Didn't make sense. Changing them for the one behind produced a recognisable London number which, when dialled, got this posh trollop on the ansaphone. Naturally, she gave no name, but it must have been her.

She had to laugh at how simple it was. He was piss poor at making codes, and that was a fact. In another part of the book Diana's address was made plain by similar deciphering.

He had promised, oh so easily, but she knew he wouldn't stop seeing his Diana because if she had been in love no one would have spoiled her affair, certainly not him. In one way she couldn't care less whether they broke it up or not, because if it weren't the whore Diana he would be having somebody else.

She would never trust or love him again, but tired herself to do the job nevertheless, because without much thought he had kicked her so brutally in the guts that the pain still brought tears and such a bumping of the heart that she wanted to vomit. It hadn't been exciting enough for him to just have the woman but he had to plant the tape recorder where she was bound to play it back.

He came home, and Angela wasn't there. She so habitually was that the fact worried him. He sat in the kitchen eating bread and salami, a glass of red by his elbow. Diana had been too upset to feed him. And at the office he'd had Norman Bakewell haranguing him in the most obscene language about the jacket of his next paperback.

Angela came in with an expression of satisfying superiority, and a shine of dislike for him in her eyes. The curve to her lips discouraged friendliness, at a time when, not long out of his girlfriend's bed, it was vital for him to show it, even if only to diminish the guilt which harried him since she had found out.

He stood. 'Hello, darling!'

Scales at the gym told him his weight had gone down in the last weeks. Hers had, as well, so that both looked raddled and mean. She had put herself on the machine, and laughed at the notion of selling the idea of an adulterous affair to Weight Droppers Anonymous. If a couple wanted to economise, only one need do it.

'What's funny, love?'

She sat facing – looking, she assumed, right through him. 'You.'

'How come?'

'You said you'd packed her in.'

'Who?'

'There's more than one? I'm not surprised. London's full of 'em waiting to fall on their backs and open their legs for a walking cock like you.'

'Oh, don't let's go into all that again.' Again? She hadn't stopped since that fateful day nor, he supposed, would she ever. Did she want a divorce?

She didn't. 'I'll let you know when I do.'

Nor did he. It would disturb his life too much.

'I know,' she said. 'You want everything.'

He wondered whether silence wouldn't be better, but his mouth took control again. 'Who doesn't? You can have a divorce, if you like.'

'When I feel like one I won't ask you.' She didn't want to swim around in the slime of the alligator playground for the rest of her life. But she was in it, couldn't help herself. He'd pushed her under and she was drowning. 'I don't need permission how to run my life from a scumbag like you.'

Back into the maelstrom, and who needs it? A divorce might be the only way, but would mean defeat, and more trouble than he wanted to face. Men were often too busy having affairs, Norman once said, to have time for a divorce.

'I want you to give her up,' and then she would leave him.

'I've told you. I have.' He'd never be able to, apart from not wanting to surrender on principle. Women who were easy to get were hard to let go of.

'You haven't.'

'You've got to believe me.' She had played the spoiler with Diana's phone all evening, belled the number ten times and stultified both in mid-pleasure. Knowing who it was infected them with despair, compounded by each being aware that the other knew but was trying not to say. He couldn't even manage twice, and Diana had only half come. In her edgy mood she had puffed a cigarette, after giving them up a month ago.

Angela's smile alarmed him, and he wondered if she was sane. If she had followed him to Diana's his lies would have to be more convincing, but he had hit the limits of his ingenuity.

Even so; he decided to give his artistry one more try, but with no warning she leaned across the table and battered his face with the whole weight of her left fist. He told himself later he had seen it coming and could have dodged, but a malignant imp far down in his psyche – and he couldn't say better than that – hadn't let him. Nor did he avoid another ferocious knuckling to the other side.

'You can't shit on me, you bastard.' She crashed him again, caught up in a heady mix of despair and enjoyment.

He retreated to the sink, and slid around the table, but only felt safe when halfway up the stairs. Well, almost, because she pursued him to give more of the same, telling herself, when he ran into the bedroom, that she wasn't a coalminer's daughter for nothing. She sat on the stairs to exult, because he wouldn't like what he saw after locking the door against her.

*

Diana looked on the white Ford Escort parked outside her flat on Primrose Hill as an additional room that she could travel around in if she had to. Daddy had bought it for her when she landed a job at the BBC, proud of her working there, because he had lapped up the ritual of the nine o'clock news throughout the War, while doing his duty at the Food Office.

Nippy as a devil in town, the car was good for long distance too. A cardboard box in the boot contained plastic bottles of water, oil, brake fluid and antifreeze, as well as spare bulbs, fan belt and jump leads, and an entrenching tool in case she got caught in snow, put there on her father's advice, whose favourite refrain had always been that you must prepare for every eventuality.

In the glove box was a torch and a tub of sweets should flood or pestilence strand her. She'd added a box of tampons and a packet of Mates, leaving nothing to chance. On the empty seat was a box of Kleenex, an A to Z of London, and a road atlas of Great Britain so that she could go anywhere at no notice.

A long day's stint in Guildford made her glad to slot into a convenient space by the door. She needed a hot drink, then to bed, whacked utterly after the twenty mile slog-and-jog through jams and traffic lights. Tom's eager presence would be too much this evening, and even a bit of therapeutic painting wouldn't soothe her strange mood.

All the way back she had wondered whether their liaison hadn't gone on too long. Boredom and emptiness had replaced the excitement, and she wasn't born to put up with an affair once its first passionate flowering was spent. Though never to be forgotten, maybe it was time to be free again, and she couldn't imagine him unhappy at being released to flash his talent at someone else. Life was too short to stick with one man. She might just as well be married, and who would go into that kind of death?

She supposed the woman who bent at her window wanted directions, London crawling with idiots unfamiliar with a street atlas.

Dark, even attractive, but there was something manic about the eyes, nothing strange, after all the loonies had been kicked out of the hospitals, poor things. 'Yes?'

'Are you Diana?'

Rain trickled over the windscreen, and she hoped for a downpour to run off the dust and pigeon shit. She reached for her handbag to stow the key. 'Yes, why?'

'Tek this!'

Thinking of a photograph, she would never forget that visage painted with an aspect of insanity and wrath, and justice about to be done. Eyes unfathomable with vacancy made one blink of the shutter, exultance another – Diana named many sorts – except they flashed across too quickly, everything vivid, then forgotten as one shutter-smash after another compounded the blows that seemed to come from every direction.

She put a cold towel to her head, hoping to decrease the swellings and pain. 'I'm calling the police.'

Tom was at the office. 'No, don't do that.'

'Fuck you!' She wanted everyone around him to hear. 'Your fucking wife came and beat me up.'

'Please,' he said, 'I'm coming right over.'

Diana couldn't understand why she hadn't got out of the car and plastered her back, except that the concatenation of righteous blows only stopped when she put the ignition on and closed the windows, at which Angela kicked a tyre and was halfway up Primrose Hill before Diana could get out and reach for the entrenching tool with which to do murder.

She hated herself for crying, and giving him a reason to hold her close. Full of rage, his false concern was too much to bear. 'She ran away. She was raving mad. She didn't care what she did.'

He held her shaking body, so warm and pathetically trembling he wanted to make love on the spot. 'It's all over with me and

Angela,' he said, 'and she knows it. I can't tell you the disgusting things she did with my clothes.' He stood aside. 'Look at me! This is how I went to the office today.'

A flowered shirt, pale unseasonal trousers, and a bomber jacket. 'That's how you often dress.'

'Yes, but I usually have a choice.'

She sat. 'I'm terrified. She might come back. I'll have to triple lock the doors.'

'So you should.'

She laughed, hoping not too hysterically. 'Yes, but look at this,' and reached behind the sofa. 'I brought it up from the car.'

'For God's sake, don't use that.'

'If she gets in here I will.'

And he could see that she would. 'I put a chest of drawers against my bedroom door last night. She'd cut my exercise bike to pieces with a hacksaw.'

Diana laughed. 'Top marks for malice,' then groaned from her bruises.

'It's not funny.' There had been no long lunch today, and famishment made him hollow, which put him in a state to announce: 'We've agreed on a separation at least. She's leaving in the morning, and I'm not going back tonight.'

'You can book a room at Claridge's, then, though I don't suppose they'll let you in looking like that. But there's the phone if you want to use it.'

'Oh, come on, you don't think I'm afraid of her, do you? If I start to hit back I might get into even more trouble than you with that entrenching tool.'

A man would think that, wouldn't he? He could shack up in Cardboard City for all she cared.

'I'll be glad when she's left, though. She's been putting things in the Volvo since yesterday. I'll give her an income. She'll be able to live fairly modestly up North.'

'Maybe she'll find a nice big expensive flat in Nice.'

His squash playing shoulders were no longer taut, nor his features so cock-a-hoop. Something had cracked, though she wasn't dim enough to imagine it would last very long. Unregenerate, he would get back to the same old ways as soon as he was married again.

'I don't care where she lives, as long as it's a long way from me.' He didn't love Angela anymore because she wasn't the same person as when he had married her. Then again, in the early days he hadn't had time to get into his own stride. Even so, what she had changed into now that he had, wasn't to his taste. Love at first sight hadn't been solid enough for him to endure her recent fits of shark-ripping violence. She could go her own way, though he wasn't sure enough of the justice of his conclusion to mention his thoughts to Diana, who waited for him to say something while he faced her from the sofa. 'She can go to hell for all I care,' he said.

'I still think I should let the police know. She's not fit to be on the loose. She should be in the loony bin.'

He thought the same, but tried to smile. 'They'd only laugh at you.'

'Not at me, they wouldn't.'

'After all, it's just a domestic tiff.'

'Oh, is that what you bloody well call it? Well, I don't. I really think I ought to bell them, even if only to stop her doing the same to anyone else.'

'It would get in the papers.'

So that was it. 'You'd better go,' she said, 'before I start throwing things as well.'

The car was overloaded, so she would check the tyre pressures at the next garage. Then she could look forward to lunch at The George in Stamford. Surprising what few things were her own, though she had filled the old suitcase which had come down with her in the first place. Whatever was left could go to Oxfam. Maybe she would click with a very fit man in the restaurant.

She had been gratified at her strength on manoeuvring the trunk into the car, that they had maniacally filled before her miscarriage. Lifting it onto the tailgate had been a job, Tom looking on but not offering assistance. If he had she would have spat in his eye, and he knew it, so he was too cowed to take the risk. He thought her barmy as she worked it slowly in like a coffin. She didn't altogether know why she wanted to, except it was impossible to leave such a cargo to someone like him.

Nor was she driving north for the last time. None of that end of the world dramatic stuff for her. She would come up shopping or to see a play whenever she felt inclined. 'I'll never go back up there,' had often been her cry, but in those days it would have meant a defeat whereas now it was better than hanging around in the hope that Tom would wave his cock in her direction now and again.

He was free, so she supposed he would install one of those numbered ticket machines on the outside of the house. They used to have them at the deli counter in the supermarket, and people would pull out a little tongue of paper with their number on it so that they could just stand around and not look like they were queueing. The women waiting to go in and let him fuck them wouldn't fight as to who was first.

Wherever she was going or would end up she'd get back to being herself before deciding what to do with her life. At least she had learned that nothing was forever. As for him, let him laugh, and go on with the only existence he was fit for. In any case, who cared for adventures when the discovering of her true self would be as much of one as she could attend to? She would screw enough money out of him to pay for a three-year stint at whatever university would take her, never mind that she would have gone by such a roundabout way to get there. Maybe she'd even do something in mechanics or engineering.

A man who couldn't be true to you, and was only happy doing the dog-paddle in the turdy waters of the alligator playground, wasn't worth the shoes he stood in. She would rather be on her own than know anyone like that. Whatever world you lived in was as big and as rich as you made it, and hers, she could only hope, would be bigger and richer than the one fading in the rearward mirror.

FOUR

Tom remembered Charlotte saying – during dinner table chit-chat at her house in the country, on a night when hail was driving almost horizontally against the windows, and Charlotte was waiting for a power cut so that she could set out candles and let them sample the lives of workers and peasants of seventy years ago – that a man who left his wife, and took up with a girl young enough to be his daughter, would soon repeat the mistakes which had destroyed the previous liaison.

Henry agreed. He had to. But Tom replied, pushing his cup forward for more coffee, that making the same irreparable gaffes with a new spouse was more interesting than staying with a woman to whom there was no more of your bad side to show. In any case, some years must elapse before boredom or acrimony crippled the new union, and by that time you might be dead.

Another disadvantage of not enduring the first ordeal, Barbara Whissendine suggested, was that a man never really got to know himself, and there was surely some value in that.

Tom, under scrutiny, retorted – and he was of course backed up by Norman Bakewell in this – that even supposing there was no more for a man to discover (and he may even so be well aware of all that there was) to remain in one emotionally arid gridlock would nullify all that experience had taught him up to that point, rather than illuminate the mind in any way – or words to that effect, after the prose was honed up in Bakewell's ever-working brain.

A third point, perhaps more perceptive, not to say provocative, was that the gadabout was incapable of reasoning along such lines. Tom threw this in free. He was a man of action, he went on, not a vegetable deadbeat languishing at his fireside, like Henry, who may, he thought, for all anybody could tell, be a deeply philosophical character, though the only effect was to keep him securely under Charlotte's thumb, and what kind of philosophy was that?

Too much reflection was often more useless, and demoralising, than too little, and made action difficult if not impossible. Norman Bakewell, who was at his most acute when cogging into others' thoughts, went on to comment that whatever move one makes, even if it does little good, or even if it exacerbates the situation, must be better than the abandoned marital state of ongoing bitterness and eternal inertia – he concluded, reaching for his glass and then becoming too drunk to come out with anything that was either sensible or readable.

'To stay in one marriage for life under any conditions deadens a man,' Tom said, riding roughshod through Charlotte's silence, 'and argues deadness even in a woman' – a nod to Barbara and Emmy Brites, who were holding hands – 'but a man who gets hitched two or three times may have done so in order to try and rectify genuine errors.'

Nearly everyone around the table chipped in at this point, Emmy Brites coming up with the barb that a man has to be diabolically flawed to marry a third or a fourth time, an inference which Tom absolutely disagreed with, considering himself the opposite of a failure in life.

'Men are blest who marry often,' he said, and stood up to say it. 'Those who don't try more than once could be said to lack energy or, let's face it, money, or confidence, or the good fortune to pick 'em and the know-how to have them fall in love with him. Most men, like most women I suppose, whether due to love, loyalty, or the inanition brought about by the inborn ability to put up with ongoing turmoil, stay with the same partner for life.'

'Don't talk such rubbish.' Charlotte filled his glass in the hope that he would get too drunk to speak, a mistake, because he swigged it off, looking at Emmy Brites and hoping, that since Norman sat boggle-eyed and out for the night, she would put his words if not into her present novel then plough them into the next. 'Men who go from one woman to another must be more interesting and attractive than those who don't because they can't. Those who can't look on those who can and do as amoral villains, or lucky dogs, according to the way they feel about their own marriage.'

Recalling such an evening did Tom little good as he sat by himself in the club with his bottle three-quarters empty. To say his fourth marriage was going badly was, as a negative exaggeration, the understatement of the decade. He was unable to understand why a man like himself, who knew so much about women, and loved them more than any other creatures in the world, couldn't keep a marriage going for life (though on his own terms) and so give more time to his work.

The first try with Angela lasted seven years, and he justified its ending by saying he had never really loved her but had been trapped into marriage by her spiderish act of keeping him for too long at a distance. What held them together was at best infatuation rather than love, luckily broken on her taking umbrage – a real North Country set-to there – at his affair with Diana.

Calling for another bottle, he remembered that his love for Diana began with crashing sexual magnetism at one of dear old Charlotte's lunch parties. What love didn't start in a similar manner, he would like to know. Unhappily for both, his affair with Diana turned into something they mistook for love. In those heady days he prided himself that, like Bismarck, he was able to learn from other people's mistakes, with the result that he never saw the big ones coming.

Unable to be apart from each other, in those dangerous weeks after Angela had gone, and when their affair seemed to be ending, he made the biggest blunder of his life and, as soon as the divorce came through, asked her to marry him.

Fireworks, he recalled, Catherine wheels and exploding rockets replaced the umbrella of nuptial starshells. Who would have realised that their allotted bliss had been used up already during their passionate affair? In little time at all they were unable to tolerate each other. They endured for a while through misplaced pride or obstinacy, so that after a year they were like siamese twins and couldn't live without each other. Neither could they live with each other, which galled them so much that they could only sit back appalled and hope the other would leave first.

Because the other – whoever it was at some vindictive Jason and Medea moment – was unable to act due to the potency of the original infatuation, their sterile marriage went on for almost three years. Tom hoped to find her gone on getting back from the office. After he had left for work Diana prayed he wouldn't come home again. Tom knew that if he returned exhausted from work to find she had flitted he would cut his throat. Diana realised that if he didn't show up at the expected time she would hang herself.

Tom was aware that such a perfectly balanced emotional pendulum was diabolically organised by something more powerful than either, and might keep them close forever. Diana assumed that, though able to walk out at any moment, she couldn't unless he went first.

The hour Tom felt most able to light off was between eleven o'clock and midnight, but by then he was too half seas over to crawl on hands and knees to the car. He could do nothing more than find the route to bed, though mumbling his absolute determination to scarper at the first blink of dawn. He would be at Heathrow in no time, and a few hours later Diana would get a telephone call from as far off as Lisbon or St Petersburg. Before being released on his alcoholic decline into sleep he would even pencil a reminder and leave it under the alarm clock on the bedside table, telling himself: 'Leave her definitely today,' but on waking with a fuddled mind, and hollow for breakfast, his only thought was to eat and get away early for work.

He surmised that such a marriage must have been brewed up in Antarctica, while Diana placed the destructively spewing volcano of Krakatoa at the geographical centre. The fact of their mismatch was all they could agree on, though to say so was unnecessary. Foreseeing far more anguish if they separated, it was only possible to stay together as if observing someone else's marriage, while realising too late that they were looking in on their own, and were humiliatingly bound by it. Whatever emotional profit there was in being taken beyond the limits of a tolerable existence, which someone like Norman Bakewell might have seen as a positive advantage for his writing, was not enjoyed by either.

The wineskin of torment burst for Diana when Tom made the situation remorselessly clear to her one evening, after the meal, of course. She ran from the house in a fit of the miseries which even her paintbox and easel could not dilute.

Crossing against the lights at Notting Hill Gate, she was sorry not to have been flattened into the asphalt, but immediately felt better on being comfortably installed in a taxi, and telling the driver to drop her at the Swallow Club in Soho.

She somnambulated to a space near the bar, and saw Jo Hesborn, who was halfway through a bottle of champagne.

'Now why did *you* have to turn up?' Jo said.

'Why shouldn't I?' Diana snapped, though noting there were no men in the place.

'Have a drink of this, anyway.' Jo called for another glass. 'I can't believe my luck, that's why I sounded a bit sharp.' She held Diana's hand, who felt thrillingly at ease, and not willing to withdraw it. 'I've been madly in love with you ever since that lousy lunch party at Charlotte's,' Jo said. 'And to say I've been repining for you would be putting it mildly, but I have. So come on, love, knock that back, and let's have a dance.'

For Diana it was more of a *coup de foudre* than the first encounter with Tom. 'So,' he sneered, when she took no trouble to hide the fact that she had stayed the night with Jo, 'you chose freedom by falling in love with a woman.' He wanted to find Jo, and crush her dry hard body to bone and gristle but, recalling her vicious attack on Norman Bakewell at Charlotte's, thought better to leave her alone. 'Anyway, you can clear out.'

'I don't see why.' Jo had told her she shouldn't, at least not in a hurry. 'Marriage ought to be able to contain me having a relationship with a woman. Ours ought to, certainly.'

Oh, ho, tell that to Tom. He couldn't bear the thought of touching her sexually from then on, without imagining he was with a woman he had picked up at a party, though he conceded, in order to have peace, that she might have a point about staying on, because when she brought Jo to dinner he didn't dislike the situation, to his surprise and Diana's chagrin. They were both women, after all.

At such cosy get-togethers he was uxoriously polite to Diana so as to make Jo jealous, but put on his maximum charm to Jo, who had a certain louche pull (though she was too thin in form and somewhat outspoken) until Diana thought his behaviour was working even on Jo in the same old way, so that Diana who, he couldn't help noticing, was more in thrall to Jo than she had ever been to him, fell into a discussion with Jo about buying a chocolate-box cottage in deepest Wales, in which they could live much like the 'Two Ladies of Llangollen'. Tom was glad to note that Jo thought more of her job in London than this promise of eternal clitoral bliss.

Tom was embarrassed when he and Diana went out together, because she looked at young women with the same famished intensity as himself. Neither liked the competition, but should have been happy to know that after years with nothing in common they now had one in which both hungered after the same sex.

Tom was more jealous than if she'd had affairs with men, or so he claimed during arguments stoked up with even more bitterness than before. With a woman the odds were piled too high. Maybe it was envy. It certainly was. She lusted after the women he fancied which, after the amusement had worn off, he didn't like it at all. Such tackiness was undignified.

At a party one night, while Jo was visiting her family in Northumberland, Diana purloined a girl from under his nose. On another occasion, when he saw her smitten by a very good-looking middle-aged woman, he sidled in and worked his charm, so that Diana didn't get her – the sex war to end sex wars.

Such argy-bargy – or was it hanky-panky? – led him to observe that any woman he reckoned he could get into bed within half an hour was invariably an easy conquest for Diana as well.

Perhaps Diana's way with women was a final attempt to prove her love for him, stunts he had not previously imagined and certainly not wanted. Maybe she thinks I'll turn queer, he thought, so that we'll be a devoted couple into old age. 'Fat chance, mamma,' he snarled, in their last bout of cat and dog fury.

Assuming that almost every woman was drawn to the lesbian condition as they became older, he took Norman Bakewell's advice and found a young one before she'd had time to think it worth a try. Nineteen-year-old Debbie worked as a waitress. Wearing a caramel coloured shirt and a tie, she had a shapely bottom but not much bosom, hands lightly clasped behind her back, waist nearly reached by her rope of dark hair. Pale-faced and with a somewhat pinched and distant expression, she brought Tom's soup to the table as if it was the last thing on earth she wanted to do, or to be seen doing, then stood by the wall to stare contemptuously in turn at everyone else who was eating. When she came with his steak au poivre he asked if she liked working here.

'I don't like working anywhere.'

He laughed. 'Then why do it?'

'My father just died, and my mother threw me out.'

He was fascinated by the inch of white ankle between the top of her boots and the bottom of her brown trousers. 'We ought to talk about it sometime.'

'You can if you like.'

He ate there the following week, surprised she still had her job. 'Thanks for that tip,' she smiled. 'Nobody's dropped me a tenner before.'

As a device for being remembered it was worth every penny. 'What part of the world do you come from?'

'A little semi in South East Ninety Eight. Shitville.'

At least it wasn't Yorkshire. Or Sevenoaks. 'That's not far away.'

'It's too close for me, though. I might as well still be there, having to work in this pig-dump, and living in a squat.'

'It sounds all right,' he said, wanting to hear more of her fairly basic lingo, which he assumed covered a profundity of unexplored emotion – and love.

The head waiter, or maybe he was the boss, came close. 'Haven't I told you not to talk so much to the customers?'

She stood so high Tom thought she would break her toes. Nobody was going to show *her* up in front of a man who'd left a ten pound tip. 'Well, you know what you can do, don't you?'

'And what's that?'

'You can fuck off.'

Nor was anybody going to humiliate him on such a busy night. 'I rather think that's what you're going to do, my dear, and this minute – *if* you don't mind.'

Tom, ready to get up should the man give her that smack in the chops which she certainly merited, enjoyed being in a real life situation. She let a napkin drop to the floor as if it was a dead rat, and stepped on it. 'You don't need to tell me twice.'

'Oh, I shan't. Out, out, out,' he said, walking away with Tom's plate.

She lit a cigarette, and made sure the smoke clouded over the next table until a woman waved it irritably away. 'He thinks he's the fucking cat's whiskers because he can't fancy me.'

Tom had fallen in love with her by succumbing to a so-called general truth from Norman Bakewell, a fatal way to behave, but what way was not? 'Let's meet outside,' he said. 'I shan't be long.'

He took her to the best pubs and clubs, feeling in the prime of youth when older men saw them as so apparently happy. He installed her in the house which, for a while, she kept scrupulously ordered and clean, scrubbing and polishing (in stiff checked aprons Tom lasciviously provided) as if it was a big new toy unwrapped for her birthday.

Even before marrying her he ought to have guessed that such a sloppy proletarian underlip dripping tea into the saucer, or onto herself if the cup was at too much of a slope, meant trouble. What he had assumed to be an endearing pout was the shape of her mouth that had not evolved since birth. It was even more emphasized now that she was transmogrified into a grown-up married woman.

After a few months of wedlock Daddy's little darling became, as she put it, too bored to live, and took to going out on her own. She came home in the middle of the night, usually on the back of a motorbike ridden by a leather jacketed, well-studded and bearded land pirate.

Tom shouted that it had to stop, as she walked upstairs looking worn and well used in her harlequin shirt of yellow hearts and red stars. She had taken to sweeping her hair up into a bun, which seemed always in danger of crumbling but didn't until now, when he slapped her.

He had caught her on the rebound from her dead father, though what two lovers didn't meet in that way, if he thought about it.

As an unregenerate specimen she was even more determined in her behaviour than he. Her fixed smile of half-open mouth was too disturbing to look at for more than a moment, so he slapped her harder this time, and she fought back with the violence of a demented cat.

Angela's departure had been like a loving wartime sendoff compared to hers. A biker gang must have held an all day rave before helping to do the house over, and the professional firm called in to clean up the squalor charged five hundred pounds.

He wondered if he were choosing the wrong sort of woman, or whether the wrong sort of woman was singling him out for special treatment, and if so why? He had spoiled Debbie by keeping her in a style to which he now hoped she would never again have the possibility of becoming accustomed. Norman Bakewell said he shouldn't have done it, while listening with set mouth and appreciative wide-awake eyes to the sad narrative of his troubles.

A year after being divorced from Debbie he met Diana at a hotel in Leeds. She had come down from a disastrous visit to Northumberland with Jo, and he was there to talk at a publishers' conference. He asked her to eat at his table and, in a calm, adult and deliberate manner they fell in love again, she missing coffee and he his cigar in the scramble to get up to his room.

He couldn't hold back from asking what had happened to Jo Hesborn, whispered the query into an ear never known to be of such a warmly beautiful and exquisite shape.

'That's all finished. Maybe she went back to her father, or maybe her mother, I don't know, but I've come back to you.'

He stood behind, undoing her blouse while looking over her shoulder into the full length mirror, till she stood naked and half fainting with a sharp and unfamiliar lust as if from the first stirrings of puberty, turning so that they could kiss each other step by step towards the bed.

He couldn't understand, didn't care to, and in any case, wasn't able to because they were fired beyond the limits of reason due to knowing so much about each other, a resurgence of all their previous intimacies fuelling them into a mutual delirium that reminded him of his first lubricious affair with an older woman at sixteen.

They had no option. This time it would be different, and forever – they decided, on marrying again. They went through days and nights of infatuated madness. Why did they leave each other before? She was the only woman for him. Tom was still the same man for her, whom she had been so intoxicated with at Charlotte's lunch party. She would do anything for him, and he would do whatever his beloved wanted.

She gave up her job at the BBC so as to paint all the time at home, sculpt when she tired of painting. 'All I want is to be in the house and make sure you're taken care of,' she said, 'but I also need somewhere to paint.' They sold the place in Holland Park and bought a manor house in Hertfordshire with a suitably spacious barn that could be made into a studio. It cost him an extra twenty K, but his love had never been so intense, genuine and satisfying, which made it easy to be generous.

On reflection – and it had to come sooner or later – he had ricochetted out of his disaster with Debbie, and Diana had ricochetted from the slime of her long affair with Jo Hesborn, and when two ricochets clash in interstellar space the rate of burnout as they fall in the direction of Planet Earth, though not phenomenal to the naked eye, certainly becomes fast when they reach the pull towards gravity. And where do the star-struck lovers hit the deck, except on the lush banks of the alligator playground?

Marrying her again was another worst fatal move he had ever made. The two year itch excoriated, sooner perhaps than could have been expected, but no less sure for that, and he wondered how and when the split would come.

Itch? St Vitus didn't know he was born. Diana bored and harried him more than he could remember, the complications of their reunion making a Black Forest clock seem like Stonehenge. Why had he been such a fool as to give her a second chance, which she took as an opportunity to spill out all the unresolved grievances saved from the first time? Her muted way of tormenting him, honed by the mill of her abnormal existence with Jo, generated more pain than in their first, which even so had been unendurable.

She declared herself to be an artist, obviously a road which Jo had set her on, but he could make no sense of her splashy style, and hardly knew whether he liked it or not. On a wet Saturday afternoon, which he'd hoped they would spend in bed, she unveiled her latest vast painting in the barn and asked what he thought.

'Wonderful,' he said. 'I like it. What colour! What composition! What do you call it?'

'"Witch Doing Widdershins Under the Great Oak". I thought you'd have more specific comments, though.'

'Well, you could take that head out of the tree, and put it closer to the ground.'

'You don't know anything, do you? It's not a head, it's a ball of mistletoe.'

He looked closer, hoping to make some sense of the bullshit. 'Ah, so it is. Sorry. I do like it, though. You're very talented, darling.'

He wasn't being serious, but she had to talk to somebody about her work. 'In that case, why don't you get me a commission from the firm to do a few book jackets?'

And get his head kicked in by Norman Bakewell? 'The head of the art department likes to choose his own people. He's very cantankerous, and I wouldn't like to get rid of him, he's so good.'

He tried to make up for this festering issue by arranging her first one man (Christ! *Woman*, you nit!) show. At the vernissage he heard a critic say how profoundly interesting her technique and subjects were, though that may have been due to the top class champagne and food, because even while harried by someone Tom had the capacity to act generously towards them.

Half the paintings and two pieces of sculpture were thumbed with little red sales tabs, and he noted with no resentment that the money went into her piggy-bank account. She would soon have enough saved not to starve when he kicked her out for the final final time.

But how to do it? There were several ways of telling your wife you were fundamentally unsuited to putting up with her volatile moods, cosmic doubts, and too frequent manic depressions, which at the best she assumed went with the artistic temperament, and at the worst blamed on you.

Riffling all possible options deadened the guilt which he felt too delicate and privileged to tolerate in middle age. If they had been living in the sixties he could have paid a rogue psychiatrist to put her in a halfway house and shoot her full of LSD, or to lay the blame on her parents and really drive her mad.

More mercifully, he could inform her that he wanted a divorce when she was miserably out of sorts, one more hurt that would be hardly noticeable – if hurt it turned out to be.

Perhaps better would be to say he wanted out when she was feeling so good that his decision couldn't possibly be upsetting or, gallant and kind, he could soften her up with a couple of bottles of champagne over dinner, so that she would be too fuzzed to let his announcement worry her.

Another tactic was to persuade Denise, his girlfriend, to telephone and own up to their affair. No, he would lose her as well, because Diana could be very amiable with anybody but him, and he knew what might happen if she got into a confessional mood with another woman.

He straightened his back with a laugh of self congratulation, ingenuity at last coming up with the very *it* of everything, his gesture almost knocking the bottle off the table. To strike free of the marriage with the maximum drama and satisfaction he would arrange to be moving his clobber into the car while a dozen guests were arriving for a dinner party that Diana had planned for weeks and sweated hard to make a success. Everybody would expect him to greet them, smiling at Diana's side, even her crumbly old folks from Sevenoaks. Tom however would pass each person as they came in with: 'Hello, how are you? So glad to see you,' but adding with contemptible brightness: 'I'm not able to shake hands because we've just decided to split up, and I'm taking my stuff out of the house before she burns it.'

Norman Bakewell, wearing a Greek fisherman's sweater and a sea captain's hat, glass in one hand and a steaming cigar in the other, swayed over from the bar. 'Why don't you just clear off, clandestinely, as it were, and take a flat somewhere? Don't contact her for a few weeks so that she'll be worried to death about the housekeeping money. I did it once. Works wonders.'

Whatever Tom decided, he had been too long in the waters of the alligator playground to let Norman influence him anymore. 'Oh, belt up, you cherry-headed old fart.'

'Do it, though,' Bakewell insisted. He wanted to understand peoples' anguish, as a writer must, and see into the heart of everyone, especially when halfway through a chapter. All the same, he existed in a fog of comprehension, his barbed advice coming from concentrated pain, which he described in such language as he hoped would be amusing to read. 'Put my finger on it, did I? A man is only thinking of one thing if he lingers so long over his grog.'

'Why don't you fall down,' Tom said, 'and leave me alone?'

'I can't. Won't, rather. And you know why? It's because I like to see a real live publisher suffer. Most of them I can't, because they're just a computer stuck in an airtight underground bunker, clicking and flicking in different coloured lights, and I'm no longer strong enough to lift a sledge hammer.' He put down a lily-white hand to support himself at the table. 'I hope you don't mind if I let a fart tickle its way out, as even the Devil must.'

Tom decided to laugh rather than throw up. 'Go home to your little wifey and wash the dishes. Then she'll let you write me a novel, you old fraud.'

Barbara Whissendine at the next table was talking to Emmy Brites about her new novel, and Norman's blast of wind brought a glare of disgust from both.

'I wrote one last night,' he said, 'and burned it this morning. I'd got as far as the third draft, but it wasn't wicked enough.'

Tom laughed. 'Too kind to me, was it? Tell me, though, Norman, why are you such a dreadful old sinner?'

He finished drinking, and jelly-rolled his words. 'Don't know, old boy. Suppose it's I want to come across God one day and see how someone does it who's better at it than me.'

'Got to go, anyhow.' Tom didn't want to strike a match for his cigarette in case he and his most profitable author blew up in a composite explosion that destroyed the club. He just hoped he would have the necessary sleight of hand to get his key in the car door.

'Marriage is the best system yet devised that halfway works,' Norman went on, as if he had been wound up and still had some distance to go. 'It's a factory for suffering, the only heavy industry left in the country after Thatcher. The alternative would be too frequent visits to St Onan's Well. So don't despair. Just remember that the first forty years are the worst.'

A shadow crossed. Thought it was a man, poor chap – or a cow from the field. Corned beef for breakfast. If a meal was waiting (make me laugh again) he would thumbs it down because the chops from lunch were still heavy in his stomach. The wash of booze in his system had fogged the difficulties of his drive, so he would relish an argument about that. On the other hand he dreaded it, but dread was the emotion that brought them on. Stamping on the brakes sent him into a fifty-mile skid along gravel into a flowerbed. She won't like that, either. Planted them herself, playing Mummy in the garden.

The porch was illuminated by an automatic alarm system against predators, and Diana, stout and desirable under the floodlight, stood with a levelled twin-barrel twelve bore as if to confirm that he hadn't exaggerated the extent of their marital difficulties.

He weaved towards her. 'I'm Captain Skylight on the nightshift.' She should be so lucky. 'So go on, do me a favour.'

Was it loaded and primed? It was. She had found the keys to the filing cabinet where the shells were stored, but he was too head in the air from drink to be alarmed. If a woman couldn't scare her husband with a gunful of death what love was left between them?

She took the cartridges out and put them in her smock pocket – His and Hers.

His gestures towards her were always abrupt, as if to intimidate and keep her on edge, but among other people he moved with ease and rhythm. In the beamed dining-kitchen he flipped a pair of free-range eggs from their slots in the fridge. Not hungry, but he needed her to feel guilty – or at least remiss – and jerked up the lid of the Aga. 'A fry-up for you as well?' Recalling the loaded firearm he added: 'My love?'

If she didn't say what was on her mind the words were wasted, and though on this occasion (as on most, these days) there was much to be said for saying as little as possible, she knew that if she didn't hear the sound of her own voice she would be dead. 'I'm not hungry.'

For two years he had been doing his best to drive her mad, while she had tried to make him sane and responsible. Could anyone get more cross-purposed than that? He had turned her into a mouse by tormenting her with the malice of a cat, knowing that to send someone loopy all you had to do was push them into a state they had never imagined living in.

The innards of the eggshells slopped onto the hotplate instead of into the pan, causing a necrophiliac stench. She regretted not having squeezed both triggers.

'Sorry, darling.' He hoped she would respond, with venom or without. Either would be soothing, any words preferable to silence but, when none seemed in the offing, he closed the lid.

Looking at her with a resentment he couldn't seriously admit to feeling he ran across the hall and up the stairs, darting from side to side as if, should the malignant part of her stand like magic and point the gun from the landing, he would have a chance of avoiding the lethal spray.

Seconds after getting into the spare room he was launched down the slipway into an uneasy oblivion.

Malice was his hunchbacked playmate, and jingle bells his music. He had planned his theatrical set piece all the way back from town, but how much longer could she let the two of them curdle her life? To blame others signified something flawed in oneself, so it was time to pull the chocks clear and run.

She lit a cigarette and flicked on the kettle to coffee herself up for a couple of precious hours alone. No use trying to sleep. She had loved him from the moment they had crossed glances at Charlotte's lunch party, but had never imagined that, of the two people he had become, the worst would one day stay in the ascendant. He was on top form as an unkillable romantic whose aim in life was to stifle all that was human in everyone else, and as the closest person to him as far as she knew, she was most in danger from the knives of his Scythian chariot.

The coffee was good in being bitter, and strong enough to keep her alert. Nothing could wake him, not even the television yackering away, two newsreaders mouthing instead of one because she had worried her way through three large whiskies waiting for him to come home, or waiting to hear from the police that he had spiralled the car and himself round a tree. How otherwise could she have been so insane as to load the gun, when she'd had no intention of turning it on herself?

You can work when I'm not here, he often said, but it was impossible because she didn't know where he was when he wasn't. His fanciful existence stopped her painting, which was why she'd been tempted to squeeze both triggers. Let someone else do him the favour. Maybe he craved it to avoid turning into an object of pity or hilarity when he took to groping young girls at bus stops in his old age.

He no longer tried to hide his affairs, the ultimate contempt of the bachelor-husband who lacked the finesse to do as he liked, and at the same time show he cared for whoever he lived with. He needed an absolute dictator to bring him to order, which would mean giving up all her waking and sleeping minutes, and becoming someone else entirely.

Soil and trees gave off a healthy smell, clean and refreshing in the drizzle. She crossed to the barn – he'd be dead for eight hours so wouldn't hear the double doors squeak open. She backed in the big old Peugeot, and put down the midway division so as to load all that was hidden under a heap of canvases. He would enjoy the victory of waking up and finding her gone like a thief in the night, but she had come by day and would go by day, not shred the place while he was at the office, like that bitch Angela, or poor pathetic Debbie.

Back in the kitchen, she swallowed some pills to make sure of a few hours sleep.

Curtains rattled along the rail, lightening the room enough for her to set a tray by his bed. 'Darling! It's nine o'clock, and time to get up.'

She had checked everything: oranges freshly juiced, a pot of coffee just ground, the last two croissants warm from the bottom oven, a plate of wholemeal toast, home-made apricot jam from the Women's Institute bazaar, and a block of his favourite Danish unsalted butter. All the way upstairs she had imagined crashing back down with the tray.

Of course he was suspicious. He was no fool. 'I was horribly drunk last night. I don't think my legs stopped till they reached Australia.'

Her laugh was familiar and friendly, so life was good. 'I was rather sloshed as well, come to that.'

He looked all of his late forties, and gaunt while guzzling the juice at one go. 'I hope we didn't do or say anything too bad.'

He was always at his best when recovering from a frightful binge. 'Not that I remember.'

'That's good, then.' Crumbs of toast sprayed the duvet. 'What day is it?'

'Saturday,' as he was well aware. His bile continually drip-fed towards another bout of spite. 'We must do the provisioning this morning,' she said. 'We've eaten ourselves to the bone.'

The one human activity he allowed himself was an occasional call at the supermarket. 'Keeps me in touch with reality,' he smiled, 'to see what the poor have to pay for food.' He enjoyed doing something halfway companionable, such as pushing the trolley, choosing goodies to eat and, of course, eyeing the women shopping on their own. Dashing back for a few overlooked items she once saw him talking to one at the checkout, though he generally behaved while helping Mummy.

'Ready in half an hour, then.' He chopped a corner off the butter and laid it on the toast. 'Is that all right?'

'Yes, darling. See you downstairs.'

*

He had shaved, and looked his best in jeans, dark blue shirt and cowboy boots, lithe and fit as he walked to the Volvo. Better to leave a bastard, she supposed, than a grovelling wimp who whined every minute about how much he loved you. He sweated out his debaucheries twice a week at the gym, or played squash at the Lansdowne. 'When I kick the bucket,' he said, 'I hope it'll be sudden. That's how I want it. A massive no nonsense cardiac arrest in the middle of nowhere, such as a wood, wearing a camouflage jacket so that no one will find me and rush me off to hospital for a quintuple bypass, and give me another six months of miserable life in a wheelchair.'

Whether he felt such an end in his guts, or was weaving another fantasy, she couldn't care less. She agreed with the sentiments, but didn't want to hang around for the big day, preferring to let someone else get kitted out in black.

Sitting beside her in the car, and fastening the safety belt with care, he wished he hadn't talked about dying. Last night's dreams, of serpentine horrors in blood-dripping caverns – not unusual after so much indulgence – swamped over him in spite of the delicious breakfast and Diana's surprisingly good temper.

As the cow-speckled fields sleeved by he wondered for the first time in his life whether he ought to make a genuine effort to keep his marriage going, and grow up like she had often implored him to do. They knew each other so well it ought to be easy, and it would certainly be worthwhile. He remembered that after two or three watered whiskies at Christmas her pompous old daddy would maunder with moist eyes about the frugality of wartime living. Well, maybe he was right, and that by comparison she and Tom had everything to eat and drink they could want.

The house was a monument to ease and convenience, and they had two cars to trundle around in, so should be able to exist without the torment he continually hatched for his apparent amusement, and without all that she brewed up out of a mistaken idea that he didn't love her. What was the use of being on earth if two people couldn't make each other happy? 'You drive, my sweet,' he said, as if his thoughts had turned into reality, and their new life had already started.

He was enjoying her affection only by planning to steep her in misery when he found out it was a sham. Perhaps she was wrong, but his behaviour of the last months had reduced her to living his conclusions even before he rammed in the daggers.

He let her out at the automatic doors and went to top up at the filling station. She hummed a tune and pulled a trolley from the pack. Tom at the pumps felt top of the world enough to let a woman slot in before him. The black attendant smiled when he went to pay. Back at main base, he parked as near the exit as possible. Inside it was easy to pick Diana from the weekend crowds: ultra white shirt, black skirt, cropped hair. The beacon of compatibility beamed him onto her with no problem.

She had got beyond the veg section for the basics of spuds, and the silage of salad stuff, greens and fruit before he arrived. When the trolley was heaped almost full Tom rearranged it pathologically to order, though it still overflowed. 'Go and get another from the entrance, darling.'

'I've often wondered how many weeks we'd last in a siege,' he said, 'or a white-out, after one of these mammoth provisionings.'

'More than most, I expect, with the freezer full.'

He manoeuvered both trolleys to the fish counter. 'That's what I like to think.' He kissed her on the cheek as if, she thought, knowing what she intended doing, and hoping she wouldn't. 'I'd be glad if we got snowed up together this winter,' he said, 'with no possibility of me getting to the office. We'd have nothing to do but make love, eat our fill, and drink.' He scampered forward. 'Oh, let's have some of these fat prawns. They look delicious.'

'Be lovely, wouldn't it?' A seductive situation, to be snowed in, but she walked on, reaching for rice, farinacery, tins of beans and tomatoes. 'Don't make a list,' he always said. 'Just get everything.' But she had come with two or three sheets in her small neat writing, leading as if at the head of a convoy and ticking items off through preserves and cereals, butters and yoghurts and creams, then on to cheeses and bacons, sardines and pickles, Tom following dutifully with both trolleys almost too laden to manage. 'Station yourself here, love,' she said, 'while I go and get soap powders and bleach.'

He hardened his grip on both handlebars, and positioned himself at the top of an aisle by the cake and bread counter. Alone a few moments, though Diana was still quite close, he found it hard not to take pleasure in looking over the woman in a tight mauve skirt, and a red blouse buttoned over a bosom which moved sublimely (albeit subtly) as she reached up for two packets of brown rolls. He wondered whether they would fall in love and be happy if she were the last woman on earth. She caught his interest and smiled as he put back the fruit scones which Diana would say they didn't need if only because he had chosen them.

She saw from a distance what they wouldn't have to quarrel about anymore. Imagine finding her attractive, in such garish clothes. He had no colour sense at all. At parties his flirtations brought out stabs of rejection and jealousy, she envying the women, as well as him. She once lied that she was having an affair, hoping he would be stricken, but he smiled and wished her luck. Even a letter on the hall table, as if from a boyfriend, didn't rile him, and only after three months did he taunt her with having read it.

Jinking through the crowd made her thighs ache, but she was soon several alleys away. A coagulation of trolleys at all checkouts blocked her escape, till she found one that was closed, and stepped over the chain.

Since he was still smiling and gesturing to the youngish woman, who was now holding a loaf, she wanted to go back and stay for as long as it took to torment him into the grave. On the other hand it wouldn't be worthwhile if she had to be with him to make sure he got there.

The Volvo, easy to pick out by length and luggage rack, started up with the spare key, and she threaded a way to the road between cars still coming in.

Oh what a beautiful morning to be leaving the valley of salt. No more rain, she yanked the visor down to stop the dazzle on the five miles home. An aunt in Cornwall would give her a room while she found a cottage to rent. Winter was about to begin, with plenty of cheap places for the next six months, and then she would buy a house for herself. Today she'd do the three hundred miles, since tomorrow the inanity of shorter days began, and she didn't relish the fatigue and peril of driving in the dark.

A future of living alone glowed like paradise, no longer listening to his sneers about her painting, which he had encouraged her to work at full time so as to take the pressure off himself, though he had always denied it. Tyres crunched gently into a layby, and she switched off the engine to lower her head to the wheel.

The scene of going back brought hot tears that were cold when they hit her wrist. Nobody deserved leaving more than Tom, and the picture of him searching the aisles would be one to smile about while getting used to living without the pall of his closeness. Not that the vision would do anything for her self-esteem if he was still so much in her thoughts.

She checked for money, passport and address book, fingers shaking through her satchel, the uncertainty another step towards strengthening of the will. He had given her a small photo in case she forgot to whom she was shackled and, pulling it from the wallet, her fingers couldn't rip beyond four pieces. They skimmed satisfactorily out of the window, caught up by the wind, a large crow chasing in case they were food. Poor thing would choke.

A surge of energy drove her on, short-cutting along lanes where speed, and she used one of his favourite clichés, was of the essence.

No need to go into the wonderful house, the best she'd ever lived in. She set the Volvo by the barn, couldn't say whether the phone was tinkling from the kitchen, or a bird family in the great elm was arguing about what to pack for the migration.

In minutes she was out of the gate and up the track in her faithful Peugeot paid for by money from her paintings, wipers dealing with a flush of rain, no tears anymore, not even a thumping heart, only a childish lightness of spirit that set her singing. If he came towards her in a taxi, 'I'd ram the bastard,' she shouted, winding down the window to see the way clear.

A cigarette tasted fine and was good for a meal. When he found the house empty he wouldn't know which way she had gone, and even if guessing he would only sit with a bottle of booze waiting for her to come back. Nothing is forever, he had often said, but now it was. Hard to know why she hadn't flitted months ago, but she had made up her mind in a dark mood when unable to put any life into one of her paintings, and had asked herself what was the point of being on earth and at the same time miserable. She'd never know, but could now ponder the matter without him distorting her reason.

Take time, drive well, don't bump the verge – she forked by a pub towards the main road, the punch-button radio playing 'The Dead March From Saul'. Gloomy music and she soon knew why. The newsreader said that the death had occurred of, due to. My God! A loss to the literary world because. Electricity pylons snaffled the reception. Had he gone into a despairing spin on finding that Mummy had left him without a bucket and spade? Luck was fickle. He hadn't had time.

'The death has occurred of Mr Norman Bakewell, the eminent novelist, who collapsed last night at his club, and died in hospital this morning.'

The titles of bestsellers were trotted out, and she pictured Tom, sombre and handsome in his black at the graveside, annoyed by the clayey soil on his shoes as he glanced around to see what writers he could poach into the place of slimy old Bakewell who, she now knew, had put a curse on them at Charlotte's lunch party all those years ago.

FIVE

NEVER WITHOUT A credit card, Tom paid for his loaded trolleys and laughed at the idea of pushing them the whole way home. He parked them by the toilets, hoping they wouldn't get looted while he went searching for Diana, and made a phone call to the house telling her to come and collect him or he would go on a berserker's spin with a knife through her studio.

He got her prim voice on the ansaphone, and gave it a good talking to in case she picked it up in the next few minutes. He could only assume that, seeing him once too often trying to get acquainted with a personable woman, she had thrown a spectacular nervous breakdown and gone home to sulk, or to put more splashes on her trashy therapeutic paintings. All the same, he was nagged with distrust at this explanation, thinking that maybe the tension of treating him like a normal human being at breakfast had brought on a heart attack by the bleach and soap shelves, and she'd been stretchered away in an ambulance. But when he looked around there was no sign of piss or vomit, and business seemed normal.

The woman he'd chatted up laughed at his story of an au pair from Eastern Europe, whose morbid fit at seeing such masses of varied and marvellous goods had driven her from the supermarket. Once started, his tale spun on. In panic and despair she had driven off in the car he had taught her so patiently to drive. 'I suppose she'll turn up later, probably this evening when her suicidal misery has worn off. Meanwhile, she's left me to get all these groceries home, so I'd better call a taxi.'

Tina said she would give him a lift. It wasn't far out of her way.

'That's wonderfully kind.' He smiled at the thought of landing once more with his bum in butter, as Norman Bakewell put it in one of his books. 'My name's Tom.'

If Diana was there to see him come home with his new friend it would serve her right, and certainly make him happy. It occurred to him that when he was married to a dark-haired woman his affairs were with blondes, and that when hitched to someone with fairish hair he went for lovely dark-haired women like Tina. 'Are you sure, though?'

'If I stow my lot in the boot, you can put yours on the back seats.'

'What sort of a car do you have?'

'It's that BMW over there.'

Life was good, just when you felt a tremor that it might not be. Diana could go to hell, playing a trick like that. Tina joked about his predicament on the way back to the house, especially after he admitted, angling for more advantage out of the situation: 'It's my wife, really, who left me in the lurch. We've been on about splitting for months, and this is the way she chose to do it.'

'I suspected it,' Tina said. 'My husband does that sort of thing a bit better, though, and it suits us both. He's an aeronautical engineer, and he's away most of the time in Saudi Arabia. He fixes up planes, and writes off as many as he can so that they'll go on buying more from us.'

'Very patriotic,' Tom said.

She touched his wrist. 'Isn't it?'

Unloading the stuff, after noting that the Peugeot had gone, he called Tina into the kitchen for a cup of coffee, jet-grinding the beans to give her the best. He kept up an amusing spate of talk as if to show that any wife who abandoned someone of his quality could only be a wayward spoiler.

Saying goodbye, they clung to each other at the door like the positive ends of two magnets. The first kiss with a new woman was always the best ever. 'Sure you can't stay a while?'

'I'd love to, but it's not possible. Must get back and feed my two children. They're home from boarding school this weekend.'

'Pity.'

Her brown eyes sparkled. 'They go back on Monday.'

'Can I have your phone number?'

She wrote it on a bit of card from her wallet.

'I'll call you,' he said.

'Do.'

Another kiss, as well as one blown from the car window. He danced around the kitchen in expectation, so randy after pulling the lubricious encounter out of the future that he called for Diana, and realised she wasn't there.

His spirit slumped further when the one o'clock news gave out that Norman Bakewell had been topped by the grim reaper. The way he lived should have set Tom waiting for it, but the evidence against Norman living forever – more or less – never had much weight. His death was also a bang to the system because, though sales of his books would be good for a while, they would drain out to zilch within a year, which made it the worst of news.

He spread an island of cornflakes over the table and shaped a narrow bay on the south side while thinking of Tina: 'She loves me, she loves me not; she loves me, she loves me not,' then stopped because he didn't know whether he meant Tina or Diana.

At three o'clock he brushed uneaten cornflakes onto the floor with his sleeve and, crunching over them, walked out and into each room, downstairs and up, over to the barn and storehouses, truffling for indications as to why she had bolted and where she had gone. The beams of the long two-roomed lounge were a bit low for a rope, but he was too spongy in the brain to be serious, and by the time his curiosity had been swamped with the truth he wouldn't care to hang himself. In any case, hanging could be a slow business. The shotgun might be quicker, but that was strictly for the rabbits. There had never been a clearer case for giving Norman a bell and talking about the matter, but the crazy piss artist had kicked the bucket.

If she had really gone – and maybe she had, not denying a flicker of relief at the thought – it was unforgivable that she hadn't left him the consolation of a fiery anathema in red ink on the back of their marriage certificate. And yet, where could she go? Probably to that batty old aunt who lived in clotted cream and pasty land, and made shit-coloured pots. Maybe Diana expected him to go after her so as to give proof of his love. Fat chance of that, as well.

He stretched his long legs from an armchair, troubled to realise, at long last, that in personal relationships his mind wasn't subtle or wary enough to detect in advance the schemes being laid for his downfall, while those he wove himself were useless because they were only for his amusement and never led to action.

The central heating was at full crack, but he shuddered in the chill gloom. He put on another sweater, hoping he wasn't marked for the flu. The temperature seemed ten degrees lower with a single body in the house, but the thermometer read normal. He couldn't understand why Diana's absence made the house feel so different. How would he be able to work the washing machine, and figure out the time clock for the central heating system, not to mention the various burglar alarms?

Sleep was getting the better of him, as it never had during the day. To stay awake he dialled Denise. Her ansaphone came on, and he had no real message to leave. Saturday afternoon wasn't their time, and whose it was he couldn't know. Where was she, anyway?

Was the world suddenly without women? He should have been more forceful with Tina and got her to stay, or at least to come back in the evening.

When he reached Denise on her mobile she sounded as if just back from a bout of tennis – or love.

'Diana's gone,' he said.

She laughed. 'Gone where?'

'Not to the bathroom, that's for sure.'

'To see a boyfriend, I should hope.'

'It's not funny.'

'Oh well, if she comes to my place I'll let you know. But thanks for telling me. She might try the same as one of your ex's did to her.'

'She's not that sort, so relax.'

'Even so, you'd better not show up at my flat.'

'I know. I'll hang on here, in case she comes back.'

He didn't like her way of avoiding trouble: 'Yes, that's best.'

'Where are you?'

'Not up your way, if that's what you mean.'

He hadn't expected her to be any help, but why was it that the women he took up with, so compliant at first, soon became too hard to handle? He put the phone down and lay on his bed, the question putting him to sleep.

Waking, something had shifted and he didn't know what. His chin was smooth but he felt in need of a shave. There was too much on his tectonic plate, though nothing around him seemed solid or real. Having a wife run out on you was one thing, but to be left high and dry in the middle of a supermarket with two trolleys of provisions was so original an idea as to be unforgivable. Of all the ways he had mulled on to leave her, his well-dug imagination had never thought of that, and the sense of gall was destabilising. Devilishly planned and done, it showed she wouldn't come back,

---

which made it futile to chew on the miseries he would put her through when she did.

All lights on, no curtains drawn, he set Sibelius's 'Finlandia' to play full blast on the Bang & Olufsen, performed by a block-and-tackle band from a bleak industrial ruin in the Black Country. Halfway through his second bottle of Bordeaux red, blue lights began revolving outside the window. Drink had never done that before. Closing his eyes and opening them didn't get rid of the notion that someone had come for him from Mars, or even Jupiter. They had travelled all that way especially for him, an experience he could well do without.

The hall also was lit by flashing space stations. Or were they navigation aids? The doorbell was so loud it almost killed the music. Back for reassurance in the kitchen, he pulled up the lid of the Aga to check that it was hot, but the signalling continued, as if someone had wedged a matchstick in the bell and run away.

He remembered that every December he went into the local cop shop and put a tenner in the orphans' box. Perhaps they had figured who he was through the two-way mirror, and noted the plate of his car as he drove away, and had come to say thank you. Or maybe a burglar was outlined on the roof and they wanted to save his collection of incunabula. Having unloaded a multiple-barrelled battering ram from the car, they now set to work on the main door.

'Yes?'

'It'd be best if we came in, sir.'

Unmannerly to make them stand in the drizzle, though the porch was dryish. On the other hand there were no neighbours to hear what they would take him away in irons for. He'd at least had the sense to get drunk enough not to worry about something like that.

What a fullsized wicked thing to do, though. Was there no end to her vengeance? She had called at Reading and phoned a rent-a-cop firm, giving her credit card number (no, his, to rub in the salt) and told these two costumed berks to put him through this pathetic practical joke. They must have served their time at RADA because they were so good at it.

He recalled a colleague at work being sent a policewoman. She had gone into his office with a clipboard as if to reprimand him for all the parking fines he'd flipped into the gutter, then started to get her kit off, a lovely full breasted young woman, who kissed him on the mouth and wished him a happy birthday, to Force Nine laughter from friends outside.

'Quarrelled, did you?' was the first question registered out of the confusion.

Neither would sit, and Tom stood so as to be on the same level. Say as little as possible when the cops start talking to you. 'We always do, there's nothing unusual in that.'

'Did you note the time when she left?'

'I'll need to call my lawyer.'

'I'm sorry to say it's nothing like that.'

She had sprung something big on him here, by forcing him to tell the whole sorry yarn, the deadliest mantrap on the shelf, except it seemed she had driven into it herself. Or so they said. 'I'm sorry to have to tell you this.'

Killed by an old age pensioner. Well, he was sixty-five, the ancient fart. He was driving the wrong way down the M4, in a hurry to meet his Maker, and not too worried who he took with him, except that: 'Oh, he's not dead. Not a scratch. Got out and walked away. Ran down a bank when our car got close. God knows where he thought he was going.'

The other laughed himself purple. 'He walked away from two write-offs! Would you believe it?'

'You'll have to come and identify her, sir.'

He didn't want them to see his legs shaking, and sat down. 'I can't believe this. I'm not alive.'

They performed this social service all day and every day, probably their only duty, with so many sudden calamities. A smile like maggots under the skin was close to their professional concern, which led him to wonder again whether they were dropouts from RADA, or old lags who'd been to acting classes given in jail by a superannuated thespian. Why hadn't she sent him a busty young policewoman instead? Well, she wouldn't have done that, would she? The ginger-bearded copper gave him a poor sod look. 'Do you think you're going to want some counselling?'

It had to be your birthday to get a policewoman. 'Counselling? Certainly not.'

Tom liked the edge of contempt in his voice at such a need. 'Just thought I'd ask.'

'Most do, these days,' the other said sadly. 'But I would keep off the bottle, sir. There's lots to do.'

A hangover had never gone so quickly, though the full drill of his willpower was called on to stop the shakes. Poor old Bakewell had missed this, just. He rubbed his face, but the picture of metal and gore remained, a way out he had never wanted or thought about. All his malice had been in the mind, and he had never considered this as a possible end to any of his marriages.

The sun at the funeral was weak but welcome. People stood in groups, and you had to know which you belonged to in case you got nudged in with the coffin. Diana's parents, who had always regarded him as wicked and unfeeling, stayed well clear. Only Jo Hesborn came to him. 'Of all the people from the past, I loved her the most.'

Bakewell would have struck that line out, but Tom felt like Blondin going on his high wire over Niagara Falls, and held Jo's hot dry hand in his to steady himself. 'I could say the same.'

Her handkerchief was wet, tears falling through onto her leather three-quarter length coat. 'She was marvellous. We had such good times together.'

'I'm sure.'

'I'll never forget her. It's too bad.'

'How do you suppose I feel?'

'I can imagine, believe you me.'

He couldn't think why he experienced such a rich fondness for this near forty-year-old lesbian by his side. No wine glass close for her to hurl at him, he would kiss her even if only to enrage the others. His lips at hers, staying too long for seemliness, but to which hers with suddenly more shape in them responded, sent a wave of the purest erotic feeling through him. He felt momentarily shamed and threatened, as if Diana had entered sufficiently for him to act in this way, but the emotion was erased by happiness when Jo held his hand again on their way to the car.

After the wake, when everyone had gone but Jo, their farewell kisses turned into an embrace, passion increasing as mutual tears wetted both shirts. Words were ripped from him. 'I love you, darling, I love you.' Then he thought: but I don't, I don't. Then: I do, I do, so what the hell? Could be I'm doing something right for a change.

What burned in him came, he was sure by now, from the familiarities with Diana that flowed in them both. For Jo it was a weird log-blazing fire she had never known with a woman. Well, it was different, anyway, telling her amazed self that such fervour couldn't possibly mean anything with someone like Tom, and a man, too, though she cried out, smiling with head back and eyes full of tears: 'You're lovely, it's wonderful!'

Comforting one another in their agony of grief, unable to separate because of it, they kissed their way upstairs to the spare bedroom, neither having much say in the matter, awed but happy at the responsibility they hardly recognised.

Jo also wondered whether it would have been the same if they hadn't both been intimate with Diana. She hoped not, though in another way didn't. She tried to make out what Diana would think, if she was anywhere where she could think at all. It really didn't bear consideration, since the attraction between her and Tom was too mysterious to fathom. Questions would come later, she told herself during her first days at the house, but foreseeing they might be too hard to answer, thought she would ignore them when they did.

She must have got pregnant on the night of the funeral. Lust was insidious and sly, though she supposed that if you put a philanderer like Tom in bed with a hamster there'd be a lot of little ones scampering around in the morning. Laughing and crying at the same time, she felt like a fourteen-year-old schoolgirl who knew knock-all, the Pill something she'd never had to think about.

'We'll order in ten minutes,' Tom said to the waiter, stroking Jo's hand across the table and filling their glasses with the other. Angela's pregnancy had ended in disaster, and Debbie, thank God, had taken precautions because she hadn't trusted him to behave like a sensible grown-up, while Diana had been so long on the Pill before they met that she was afraid to come off it in case of side effects, and didn't want to have a kid because it would rob her of time painting her marvellous pictures.

'You can always have a DNA test after it's born,' Jo laughed, in case his joyful astonishment was a show of mistrust. 'Can't be anybody else's, though, let me tell you. I was a virgin.'

His jump rattled knives and forks. 'A what?'

'I've been a lesbian since before I started my periods.'

Had he been waiting all his life for this? No, it was too kooky. 'I'm absolutely delighted.'

'Yes, I can see you are.' She took off her tie, leaned across the table and kissed him on the lips, to the arch look of a passing plate-girl who took them, he supposed, for father and daughter. 'You look really chuffed.'

'Well,' he said, 'I am.'

'Me, too.'

He never thought he would live long enough to see Jo Hesborn blush. 'Let's drink to it, then.'

She was slenderly pregnant, with an elegant belly, and didn't leave her job till six months gone. One Saturday afternoon she drove her battery of modems and Internet technology in a hired truck from the flat in St John's Wood to Tom's place.

She jumped from the cab. 'I can do most of my work in the top room,' then unlatched the doors to get things out.

He set his coffee mug on the garden table. 'Don't! Let me do it.'

She had heard it said that every country got the ruler it deserved (or some such thing) and surmised that every man ended up with the woman he deserved, sooner or later, the same obviously for a woman. So she surrendered to the extent of taking the wires and plugs, and then laughed at him heaving the heavy stuff upstairs into her new office like any removal man.

After supper she lay on the couch scanning the latest issue of *Net User* magazine. 'We should have got together years ago.'

'I know, darling.' Maybe they hadn't because of her hurling that glass at Norman, while she wondered if it hadn't been his fault for taking Diana away from her at Charlotte's party. 'I can only suppose,' he said, 'that there's a time for everything.'

Three-month-old Diana frothed and gurgled as if fully supporting the idea of her parents being married. 'We're spoiling her rotten by doing this,' Jo said.

Tom stood portly and upright in suit and tie, and had only half a smile on his lined face. The small gold ring in his left ear glittered, and a short ponytail was neatly tied. He had lived ten years in one, and what was previously thought of as love hadn't been close to this by a million light years, since it had never included the potent ingredient of understanding. As unregenerate as ever, he even so liked to foresee a treaty by which he and Jo could live in mutual tolerance, she to take over the girlfriends he discarded, and he to comfort the rejects from her. What firmer union could there be than that?

Jo acceded to all the creepy notions of the marriage book, and so did Tom, but then he would, wouldn't he? During the ceremony she held up her left foot and moved it in a circle. She turned her head from side to side half a dozen times. She swayed backwards and forwards with a goitrous smile. The registrar broke off to ask if she was feeling all right.

'Just,' she said. Tom hoped she'd stop larking around, but she jigged a little more to make her point, only wanting to get the farce over with. Such fatuous platitudes about love and obedience were meaningless, since she and Tom would stay together because of Diana, and that was that.

Tom was so besotted with his newborn daughter that even if his fantasy of an exchange deal with lovers never came about he would be satisfied with this one area of happiness. He and Jo seemed so mated that getting married for the last time for him and the first time for her had been the obvious step.

His drinking and driving days were finished, and after the wedding he went with Charlotte and Henry by taxi to the Park Lane Hotel. Jo followed with Emmy Brites the novelist, and Barbara Whissendine her agent. The six made up a table for lunch, Tom at one end and Jo at the other.

Henry, looking up from his brandy, ineptly quoted the remark of Doctor Johnson's that, 'A gentleman who had been very unhappy in marriage, and married immediately after his wife died, showed a triumph of hope over expectation.'

Tom reflected during the watery silence that he couldn't recall Henry ever having talked before, and if he had it had only been to ask Charlotte if he could, and she'd said no, unless he'd asked for the salt, which he got grudgingly because she'd read it was bad for the heart. Henry muttered something about being sorry, the soft brown glow of rebellion in his eyes dimming as he reached for his milky coffee.

Nothing could trample Tom's jubilant mood; he had always known that silence meant unhappiness. 'It might do you some good, Henry, if you started to live, by having another crack at wedlock, for instance.'

Charlotte smoothed her Mao-blue gymslip. 'That was uncalled for.'

'I know,' Tom smiled, 'but a little working-class fecklessness now and again can't be bad.'

'Pack it in.' Jo knew that for a marriage feast to end in a fusillade of bottles wasn't unusual, so wanted the gathering to be friendly. 'Johnson's sexist quip was like something that windbag Norman Bakewell used to belch up out of his sour stomach.'

Emmy Brites also spoke little, but her cornflower blue eyes and pink shell-like ears recorded every nuance and comment of the occasion. Tom's notable coup had been to get her into his Augean stable, on the assumption that she would become more popular – and perhaps more deadly – than Norman Bakewell. Her pretty lips had taken in nothing but fizzy water to drink during the meal. 'He wasn't a bad novelist,' she said.

Tom watched his cigar smoke drift across the table as after the last cannon shot at Waterloo. It was as well that Norman had popped his clogs, and wasn't here to witness the conclusion of a story which he had followed with the pertinacity of an entomologist. To come in at such a time would have fused his whole being. The notion of any situation having a conventional end, especially among those who were so far under his creative thumb as to be regarded as his friends, would have brought out all his cantankerous self-indulgence, and reduced their wedding feast to a shambles. Tom wondered what publisher would have been able to afford the advance of the novel he made out of that. Instead, having done them the favour of dying, he had pulled the plug from the waters of the alligator playground, leaving them high, dry, and blinking their eyelids at the prospect of living on dry land.

Drinking a toast to him was the least they could do, Tom thought, standing to raise his glass.

A Respectable Woman

TRAVELLING SOUTH, Paul enjoyed the slow melting of cloud after passing the watershed, *les partages des eaux*: white lines waving on a brown board prominently displayed by the motorway, but the pleasure often had to be paid for with worsening weather on the homeward trip from the Mediterranean. That was life. What you didn't expect, you didn't appreciate. An electric dark blue sky between downpours turned into a threatening decline of the day.

Somewhere beyond Rheims, heading for Calais, white headlights made little impression on swathes of water at the windscreen, wipers sluggish on the fastest rate. He seemed to be driving under the sea, and marvelled at the occasional car overtaking confidently into the slush.

Life was too short to be maimed in such a way, or even killed, so he argued with himself about parting from the motorway at the nearest exit. Eight o'clock meant he would be lucky to get a room in Cambrai, but a sizzle of lightning settled him to try.

He trawled the streets, deserted under heaven's free wash, calling at three places that were full. Coming again out of the main square, onto a road he didn't know, he pulled in at the Hotel de la Paix, and took a room large enough for a family, no option but to pay up and bless his good fortune.

The way had been long from the house in Tuscany. After leaving Wendy at Pisa airport, with their two sons who could not be late for school, he drifted up the motorway through mountains he had always wanted to walk in. Wendy didn't like the car trip, but he enjoyed doing it alone, whether or not he was late slotting back into managing his electronics firm. A long drive was good for mulling on problems he might find on getting there.

He backed into the last vacancy of the courtyard. All other cars faced inwards, but a quick getaway, though rarely a necessity, was always neat to think about. He took his overnight case to the room, washed and changed into a suit, and went downstairs before the restaurant closed. The tourist season lagged on, and he stood between the bar and reception counter waiting for a table, rain at the glass locking his gaze as firmly as had the tarmac sweeping all day under the car.

A dark blue Renault stopped at the door, and he assumed the GB plate because of the side the driver stepped from. She ran in like a goddess coming from the ocean to be born – he couldn't help telling himself – and when she asked at the counter for a room he felt some satisfaction in knowing the answer.

'Damn!' she responded, 'nothing at all?'

The clerk told her.

She had been all over the town – and so have I, Paul thought. 'Isn't there another hotel you can recommend?'

It was no feat to pick up her responses: 'I can't go on in this atrocious weather. What the hell am I to do?' His feeling of guilt was overridden by exultation at having got there before her.

'They'll all be full,' the clerk said. 'I telephoned around for some-one a few minutes ago.'

Paul, no reason to be concerned at her plight – though he was – sensed her annoyance at whoever might be responsible, and he for one wished he knew who it could be. A day on the road sleeved by the rich landscapes of France acted on him like a drug, opening his mind to spaces that made him ready for anything, especially after the relief of finding such an opulent billet. He couldn't think why he said it: 'I might have a solution to your problem.'

She stood in the doorway, a tall woman, in her late thirties perhaps, with short reddish hair and gold-framed spectacles, an opened raincoat showing a pale cream blouse, a loose purple skirt, and short black boots that zipped up the front. 'Well, it's *my* problem. I'll just have to drive on.'

'I took the last room, I'm afraid.'

'I suppose someone had to.' A trace of vinegar indicated that she was too proud to let him assume he might have done her an ill turn.

'I had to take a room far too big for me. It seems a shame for you to go out in that, and me with a large double bed going to waste.'

He told her his name, and held out a hand, French style, which she barely touched, though looked at the card which he took from his wallet and laid on the bar, wondering what he thought he was up to. Of medium height and slender, with thinning dark hair combed dryly back above a pale relaxed face, he seemed too well dressed for a holiday bird of passage. Maybe he tried this stunt every night, staying all day in the hotel and waiting to pounce on such as her. She forced a smile as if to show she was embarrassed by such a proposition. 'What do you mean?'

'I've driven up from Italy today, and I'm absolutely done for.'

'You don't look it.'

'I'd be at death's door if I did. But after dinner I'll drop onto one of the beds and won't wake for nine hours. All *you* have to do is fall onto the other and do the same.' He regretted having spoken, since she thought he wanted to make love to her, which he had no intention of doing. 'Have a drink while you're waiting. By the time you've decided against my practical suggestion the rain might have eased off.'

Very smooth, yet she was tempted. After much experience she had evolved the notion that you should think everything but let no one suspect your thoughts. She sometimes wondered why it came so easy, but in that way, common sense – or an instinct for self preservation – decided your actions. No harm therefore in taking up his offer. 'I could do with a Martini.'

On trips to and from her house in the Haute-Loire she whiled away the miles with a fantasy of such a meeting, and now that something like it was happening she would drink her drink and get back into the weather. Fantasy was one thing, and reality another game altogether.

He eyed his pastis as if to make sure every swallow was worthy of the honour. His idea of paradise, he told her, was the smell of pine trees in the hottest sun, subtly mixed with odours of rosemary and olive, preferably while sitting on the terrace with his wife at midday over a bottle of wine and a platter of dark bread and salami. Such an injection of relaxed living, at least once a year, was the best way he knew of keeping sane. In the afternoon – though he didn't go this far – he would dispatch the boys into the hills with map and compass, and a haversack of things to eat, so that he and Wendy could go to bed as in the days of their honeymoon. He hoped that talking about himself would make her feel at ease, and not be so suspicious at what ought to seem his generosity in offering to share his room. 'I'm a practical person, basically. I have to be, in my job, so it seems only logical to put the spare bed at your disposal.'

She smiled at this good sense, good for him, anyway, and as if to confirm it even more, rain drummed louder at the windows. She asked herself, during the second Martini, what her thoughts would have been on passing him in the street, and decided she might have found him interesting enough to want to know more. She could even, in a certain mood, have 'fancied' him. Such a judgement had no bearing, but the warmth within reddened her face.

He would have the advantage of a good story, if only to tell against himself, about how he had rescued this very personable woman in distress, and been correct in not trying to seduce her.

'If you don't accept my suggestion you leave me no alternative but to push on. I'll stop in the first layby, and sleep soundly at the wheel, more than happy in knowing you're well taken care of. Here's my key. I'll have a word with the clerk.'

Occasional dips into the bread-and-sausage bag along the way had left her famished, and the two Martinis, quickly drunk, were having an effect. Though his plan ought to be rejected in no uncertain manner, she heard herself say: 'All right, I'll take it.'

Such an adventure to look back on couldn't be bad: 'This *very* kind chap actually gave up his room for me. Would you believe it? No, he wasn't *that* sort. He was such a gentleman that on thinking about it I rather wish he hadn't been.'

He put his glass down. 'There's just one condition.'

Oh Lord, her grey eyes said, now I've dropped into it. Why are men always so sly? He probably plays chess. If he'd come straight out with it I'd at least know where I was.

'I can see what you're thinking.'

There was too much triumph in his tone for her liking, but he probably knew that, too. She was ready to leave. 'Am I so transparent?'

'Oh no, nothing like that. I only want you to have dinner with me, before I ask the clerk to transfer the room. I always hate eating on my own in a strange place. I hope you won't take too long to decide, though, because here's the waiter coming to say our table's ready.'

What am I doing? – he refilled her glass from the bottle of Côtes du Rhône – me, a supposedly respectable woman getting into a situation like this? 'My name's Margaret,' she told him. He reasonably wanted to know about her, so what could she do but say she was a teacher at a girls' school. She couldn't think why such plain truth seemed so out of place: 'An aunt died and left me enough money to buy a small house near Le Puy. A cottage, really, but I don't imagine you can use such a word in France, can you? There was enough left over to buy a car, so I go when I can.'

On leaving, and putting the key under the earthen flowerpot outside the back door, she drove down the winding cobbled track with bushes scraping the car. On the main road she already thought of her flat in Ealing, and the cat her neighbour was looking after, though she was too much a lover of France not to enjoy the scenery before reaching the more rolling country of the north. 'What delicious onion soup. I'm feeling better already. I was done for when I arrived.'

'So I noticed.' He wanted to touch her wrist, and say how sensible she had been in agreeing to stay, but held back in case she changed her mind. A man and his soignée wife of forty-odd sat at the next table, and she saw him look at their slim daughter who had a rather mousy helmet of hair but an exquisite bust. He was merely noting how each had a plate of open baked potato with grated cheese on top, the whole in a bed of curly lettuce. 'They believe in a healthy diet,' he said, seeing the waiter with his steak tartare and her platter of cutlets, 'which seems such a pity in France.'

He leaned against the rail and levelled his binoculars, but it was hard to see the assembly lines of cars coming onto the boat, so he moved to the loading end, knowing he would curse himself for the rest of his life at not having stayed for breakfast. Hurry was in his bone marrow, and it was impossible they would meet again. Unable to stop thinking of that warm and womanly figure under her clothes, he had passed half an hour in a layby hoping to see her tuppenny sardine tin trundling along.

Five minutes to sailing, the ship loaded with trucks, buses, cara-vans and cars, he supposed it was too late now for her to make it. Maybe he would have a cup of coffee at Dover, and wait to see if she was on the next boat.

There were moments on the hundred motorway miles to Calais

when she forgot who she was, whereabouts she was, even what she was doing. Everything went, the brain went, the car went from around her. All protection went, but she came back to safety – thinking herself lucky – and ran once more through her adventure of the night.

The smell of wine on their combined breaths filling the shuttered and curtained room had not stopped them falling asleep almost immediately on their separate beds. In the middle of the night she was awakened by him going to the bathroom, flushing whatever it was, and washing his hands. Drifting back into sleep, and wishing it could happen without embarrassment, she felt him beside her, and they moved against each other to find an even greater comfort than oblivion.

When she awoke, more raddled than after an insomniac few hours at the flat or cottage, he had gone, and his lack of politeness in not saying goodbye so that she could at least thank him properly left a sense of injury which didn't dissipate on finding another of his cards with 'Thank you for everything' scrawled on the back. At breakfast she felt as if half of herself was missing, the only advantage in being so shamefully maudlin was that maybe he was in the same state.

She made a stupid blunder in asking whether the bill had been paid, as if a man she had picked up had left her to do it. A bit more know-how would have saved her a funny look from the clerk. Carrying her overnight bag to the car, she wondered how far or if at all a respectable woman could be called sophisticated. She had always had so many and such strident opinions as to how 'men' ought to behave that she did not know to within any shade of accuracy what exactly 'men' finally were. Well, now she did, a little more anyway. They were all different, and he was the most different one she had known.

The motorway was visible for miles ahead under high-flowing clouds, landscape hillier than she had previously noted. Every turn of the wheels brought the sea closer. A man who would use an offer to give up his room so as to get into her bed must be given top marks for ingenuity – and skill.

A postcard, in an envelope, to his business address, could do no harm – with her own locations firmly scripted in. When he next came up from Italy he might want to stay at her place overnight, an offer almost as good as his. And the detour shouldn't faze him.

Beggarland

BEST NOT TO ASK how old she was. Her letter had said eighteen, but she could be anywhere between twenty and thirty. Her reference had sounded all right, so Jane thought she would give her a try.

She wore a red Fair Isle jersey, tartan skirt and lace-up boots, a woollen coat over all with a slim fur collar. Maybe that was how they dressed up North. Yellowish hair straggled both sides of her face below a flowerpot hat of many colours.

'You'd better come in.' The last au pair had shot off at no notice to do a tour of Europe with a boyfriend, so Jane wrote to Greta whom she had previously turned down. Beggars can't be choosers, she said to Tim, so here she was coming up the steps, thin lips tightening as she lugged a suitcase fastened with a trouser belt.

Jane led her into the kitchen, moving the Sunday papers for her to sit down while coffee was made. 'Are you hungry? There's bread and cheese. We don't eat till two.'

Greta's eyelids were almost closed, as if she hadn't had enough sleep on the way down. 'I am 'ungry.' She looked around, perhaps hoping for a bed to lie on. 'Where's the kids?'

'In Holland Park, with my husband. They'll be glad to see you when they get back, I know.'

'I 'ope so.'

Jane put a full spoon of Instant in the mug. 'The reason you're here is to keep them amused while I do my work. That's the main thing. I'm working to a deadline on a book, and can't have them scratching at my door all summer wanting to be let in.'

Greta cupped her coffee and stared at the steam. 'My sister's got three, so I'm used to kids. Where's that bread and cheese, though?'

'Oh yes, I'd forgotten.' Too late to say she might not want her. 'Then I'll show you your room.'

In the lounge after dinner Tim said: 'Where did you find that funny little thing?'

They had been married seven years, and such questions always implied that she had made a mistake. 'Why?'

'Doesn't look up to much. Not like the last one.'

'She ran out on us, remember? And I have to work, remember?' He had been redundant for three months, though was to begin a new job on Monday – funnily enough for a bigger salary.

'Touché,' he said.

If she put back half a bottle of wine on her own she felt cheerful, and if he did the same while alone he turned benign, but a bottle between them always brought on a skirmish. 'Anyway, listen to them laughing and screaming upstairs. They've never taken to anyone so quickly.'

'Now then, kids, we're going to play a game called "Washing Up", and the one who don't break any pots can come to the sink and squirt in the detergent.' Greta had lost her sleepy aspect. Her bustling body and shining eyes showed that she liked the game as well.

Jane looked in from her work. Sturdy blond Ben had the dreamy and cunning eyes of his father, while malleable and well-behaved Angela could suddenly break into hellerdom, like herself at that age. By the end of the game the kitchen was brilliant. If they were all like that from the North she couldn't have enough of them.

'Oh, mummy, thanks a lot,' Ben said, when she gave Greta ten pounds to take them out. 'You're wonderful.'

'Where to?' Greta fitted them into their coats.

'Anywhere you like.' As long as you get them off my hands. 'Just pop into the kitchen and make them something to eat. You needn't come back for lunch. Then I'll give you a map of the Underground.'

Greta made Ben leave his plastic gun. 'Yer don't want that.' He would normally have argued, but put it by without a murmur. 'We aren't going to rob a bank!'

Funny how she could get twice as much done when the house was empty. At this rate the deadline would be easy. Then the resident neighbourhood pneumatic drill started up, and the first car alarm went off. Still, you couldn't have everything, and double glazing cut most of the noise.

'Mummy! Mummy!' Ben screamed when they came in at six, a little late but better that than too early. 'We went on the Circle Line, round and round, and played counting the stations. We passed Notting Hill Gate *three times.*' He showed a pencil scrawled Tube map. 'I went up and down the *exerlators,* and Angie got caught in a door.'

Greta took them upstairs for a bath, then asked would it be all right if they ate in her room? It certainly would. Jane had noted how snappy Tim was at such family meals, especially since Greta was as far from a so-called sex object as it was possible to get.

'We're playing "Restaurants".' Ben scooped up knives and forks. 'We're in a caff on the M1, and Greta's serving us.'

'Isn't she wonderful?' Jane and Tim sat down to a quiet supper. 'What a rich fantasy life they're having.'

'They'll probably turn into writers.'

'Don't be so contemptuous.' The arrangement was so good he was hoping to spoil it, but at least he was laughing.

Next day Ben ran to her. 'Mummy, can we have those big boxes the stereos came in? Me and Angie want to play "Cardboard City" in the garden.'

She frowned. 'How do you know about that?'

He squeezed her hand, as always when wanting something badly. 'Greta took us doing hide-and-seek at the South Bank, and I saw 'em. All those beggars in cardboard boxes! Me and Angie want to

---

play beggars, don't we, Angie? You can come by and give us five pee now and again.'

'You certainly can't play "Cardboard City".' Jane talked about the unfortunate people who had to live there, mostly through no fault of their own. 'And don't say "Me and Angie". It's "Angie and I", as you know.'

Ben's tears dropped on the sleeve of his blazer. 'We still want to play it, though. It's only a *game*.'

'All right, but don't make a noise.' She looked for her purse: no use moaning about what the world was coming to when it had come to it already.

Obsessive Ben found Tim's hiking gear and lay in a sleeping bag by the nettles, while Angela, wearing a filthy old jacket, stooped at the unlit camping gas as if cooking his stew. Greta walked by and threw them a coin. They couldn't wait to get in the garden after breakfast, but their passion for the game came to an end, and Jane had to squash the cardboard flat and jam it in the dustbin a few days later.

'And what are you going to do today?'

'I'll take 'em to Battersea Park.' Greta was adept at finding places on the map – considering she hadn't got to within shouting distance of O Levels.

'Take this, then, for ice creams and whatnot.'

She felt guilty, but work was getting done. She'd never seen them so happy and excited, on coming home from wherever Greta took them. Sometimes you would have thought they had been down a coalmine, but she soon had them naked and laughing in the bath. 'They got over the railings and into the flowerbeds before I could pull 'em back,' she explained, though with no apology.

Jane soon stopped imagining there were any mysteries about her, as she had with all the au pairs till she got used to them. She was happy enough to sit in her room, sure now of meeting the deadline of her own long story. Needing more background one morning she had to go to the London Library. It was a bother, but she liked to be accurate in social and scientific details.

Traffic was piling up at the roadworks as she went into the Tube. Students from language schools mingled with countless tourists, and she had to stand all the way. A pathetic old tramp held out a hand so she gave him a pound, her vagrant tax for the day.

She could have walked the quarter mile instead of changing lines, but pushing along pavements would have been even more tiresome than the confusion of corridors and escalators. The crowds carried her along on the outside flank, by a woman with two kids at the bottom of the steps before turning left to the platform. Some good souls were clattering money into their tins, so Jane was glad not to bother because a train was ready to go.

She stood by the open door, hearing but not seeing the poor headscarfed beggar and her children calling out for money even though there was little chance from people hurrying to get in before the train left. Their voices startled her, and on bending down to look she caught a two second photo-flash before the doors closed. When she tried to see more the way was blocked by people on the steps.

Those around her must have thought she was another poor mad woman wandering the Underground looking for an unoccupied platform to leap from. She banged the door to get out, then turned her glassy eyes at the communication cord. Her grimace caused a man to lift his newspaper, either to hide behind or keep her off his territory.

Sturdy Ben, hand holding the tin, had the starvo hard-done-by pitiable face of Tiny Tim. Angela was sitting on Greta's knee, chalk-faced and hungry, as if she hadn't long for this world. As for Greta, Grim Greta, she dared people to go by and not drop something into a tin.

Jane thought she would faint. I'll kill her. Her impulse was to go back from the first stop and throw her under a train. But the carriage was squeaking on its way, and as during her panic the day after marrying Tim, she told herself it would be better to have a cup of coffee somewhere and think about it calmly.

Hard to decide, she was paralysed. Minutes went by, before walking along Piccadilly and down to St James's Square, imagining that everyone passing had seen the woman and her beggar kids in the Underground. She didn't feel fully sane till searching for her books in Science and Miscellaneous. On her way back they had gone, probably to a scene of better pickings.

Words shied from being corralled into sentences. Luckily she was close to the end so could rehearse the grand telling off to Greta the second she came in. Sentences formed for that all right, so many that she hardly knew which to let out first.

She was making a tisane when the door was kicked open and Ben fell in. 'Mummy! Mummy! We're been playing beggars again!' He wrapped himself around her legs. 'Oh, it's such good fun. We love playing beggars, don't we, Angie?'

Greta came smiling up the steps clutching Angela's hand. 'It was all I could do to keep 'em quiet. They saw a woman and two kids the other day on the Embankment, and gave me no peace.'

Jane's vitriolic phrases melted. Whose fault had it been, after all? 'Well, you aren't to play that game again.'

Ben was ready to cry.

'Never, you understand. Never.'

'How long has it been going on?' Greta was packing her case after supper. Where would she go at this time of night? Apart from that, who told her she had to leave? 'We'll send them to RADA,' Tim had said, taking nothing seriously.

'Only a few times.'

She was curious. 'And what about the money you collected?'

'We was saving it, to go to Southend.'

Inventive and stalwart were the words that came. It was impossible not to laugh. 'Only to Southend?'

'Well, I couldn't take 'em to New Zealand, could I?'

She laughed again. What else could you do? 'All right, but you don't have to leave.'

'Don't I?'

Was she happy to hear it, or wasn't she?

'I just don't like black looks, that's all.'

Jane took her arm. 'Nobody does. So just stop your packing, and go up to see that the children are all right.'

Ron Delph and His
Fight with King Arthur

'WELL, CHILDREN,' the plummy voiced teacher said, 'this morning I'm going to tell you a story about King Arthur and his Knights.'

Ron Delph was five at the time – or was it six? – and looking back he supposed it must in any case have been very early on. What nights? he wondered, leering from his favourite place on the back row.

'His knights,' she said, and it felt as if her voice was right inside Ron's head. Nights were dark, even in summer, and he would rather hear about King Arthur's days, because in daytime everybody could see what they were doing, so their antics were bound to be more interesting.

'King Arthur had twenty-four knights.' The teacher walked to the blackboard and wrote the number in blue chalk. 'Twenty-four stalwart knights.'

Twenty-four nights wasn't long, just over three weeks, even less than a month, and if each night was stalwart it must have been darker than an ordinary night. In any case what was a king doing, even if his name was Arthur, going round at night? A king should be in his castle at night talking to his queen or courtiers about boiling the oil for when another king attacked the castle. If she wasn't going to tell us about King Arthur's days, Ron Delph thought, I'd rather hear the story of Robin Hood and Maid Marian.

'King Arthur,' she said, 'ruled England in the olden days.'

He wanted to groan: not them fucking olden days again. We're allus getting them rammed down our chops. But he didn't groan, because teachers with plummy voices could have very sharp knuckles. He didn't need to have been in school more than a few months to sense that. He was only five or six. He wasn't born yesterday.

'And in those days' – they were almost listening – 'everybody was happy, because King Arthur was a good king.' She screamed at somebody. 'If you fall off your seat again I'll send you out. Yes, you. You! It's *you* I mean, you!'

He realised with a shock that the 'you' was him, the most important connection he'd made in his life up to then, though it had become his safeguard ever since to know that you and me were the same person, especially when a policeman decides that's how it is. If only he had known how quick he was learning he could have kept it and become a millionaire instead of a poet.

'King Arthur was a just ruler.' If he was just a ruler why not say straight out he wasn't bent? Nobody expected a king to be bent. Only old men and old women were bent. They were bent when they walked, so they could never be rulers. That was why the king wasn't old. He had to be straight to be a ruler.

'His people loved him. The Romans had left, and the Saxons had not yet arrived, so for a hundred years there was peace and prosperity everywhere.'

He didn't believe her. If you had a king he lived in a castle, and in a castle the oil was always on the boil to stop people capturing it. You had battles, with lots of killing.

'He pulled a sword called Excalibur out of a stone.'

There was a picture in the book, and she passed it around for them to look at so that they would believe her. The sword was long, like a cross, and there was this bloke with a helmet on and a skirt round his waist heaving the sword out of a slab of rock. The next picture showed that he'd done it, but how can you pull a piece of steel out of a stone? You can't. First of all, how can you push it in? You can't. And if you can't push it in, then you can't get it out. So Ron learned something else, that you can't believe anything you see in a book, even if it is a picture.

He didn't go back to that school after the second day because he stared too long at the sword and rock when the teacher pushed the picture under his nose. He was unable to stop looking, his fixed eyes trying their best to see how such a thing could be done as pulling a sword out when it was stuck fast in a rock. Staring and staring, his eyes got so hard that he didn't feel they belonged to him anymore. They became stones. The colours of the picture glistened and swam, and his mouth locked and his legs shook, and he fell to the ground, ripping the book to pieces. The teacher was very clever to notice that he was having a fit, and to send for his mother.

'It's nerves,' the doctor said, 'that's all,' but he screamed it was that bleeding picture the teacher had tried to melt into his brain. She had opened his skull with a sword and poured the book inside and stitched him up again, and the headache made him fall into a fit, because how could a man even though he was a king pull a sword no matter how strong he was out of a piece of rock almost as big as a cliff? They'd told him a lie and he didn't like it. King Arthur was a tricky bastard just like the rest, though maybe he had never pulled a sword out of a rock at all and people only said he had. People said all sorts of barmy things to kids.

His mother believed him, yet he could tell she didn't, and only said she did till he was better. Then she found another school for him to go to, so that he would have preferred it if she hadn't believed him in the first place.

But everybody had to go to school. He learned arithmetic, which wasn't lies. He learned to read and write as well, and liked it. It was a special school for kids who weren't quite proper in the head, but he didn't mind. He opened a book and saw a camel. In history he saw a horse and chariot. Every morning there was free milk and then dinner, and in the afternoon they slept. There was more play than learning, but whenever he turned a page he felt his heart bump and his lips twitch and his legs quake in case he suddenly saw that rock and sword and King Arthur heaving for all his guts were worth to get it out. At that school he never did, because they were all a bit mental already and the teachers knew better than to do anything what would send them outright crackers. King Arthur was for kids who believed every word about it.

The closest to reminding him of that picture was one day when a boy at the chair in front lifted his finger for Ron to look at. The finger had a rusty nail through the middle, which was worse than seeing a sword in a rock. Dirty blood seeped through a bit of hanky, and Ron couldn't understand why he had only a sombre look on his face and not a squint of agony.

Poor sod, Ron thought, look what's happened to him. He must have said summat while having his porridge that morning that his father didn't like, so his father had tried to nail him to the ground, but he had pulled his finger clear and escaped to school, wrapping a bit of old rag round it before getting here.

It was the most horrible thing he'd seen in his life, and what made him do what he did he didn't know, but he gripped the kid's wrist and with the other hand took the end of the nail and pulled as hard as dotty Arthur must have tugged to get that sword out of the rock. What had started as a joke, a trick nail hooked around the finger to look like real, became a bitter tug o' war with Ron pulling one way and his pal (a pal no longer) almost dragged along the floor, howling with rage, and pain from a sprained finger.

No wonder they thought he was insane from a very early age, but he was merely gullible and easy-going, wanting to believe the world was nothing but good, which it was far from and so no laughing matter. The teacher saw his error but was frightened at his intensity. He had only wanted to get the nail out of his mate's finger and suck the wound better so that he wouldn't go on suffering.

He stayed six more months at that school, but every morning

they expected him to run amok or go berserk, and kept such an eye on him, talking to him only as if he was a baby and giving him everything he asked for (within reason), that he felt himself turning into an eternal puppy dog.

When his parents left to live in another house they couldn't be bothered to get up early and put him on the bus anymore, so he went to a normal school near where they lived, by which time he was convinced he had left that rock and sword world forever.

Life was normal, and he lived like any other kid and loved it. One Christmas his sister Molly got a present from Aunt Dolly, and when she opened the book there it was as large as life, a story about King Arthur and a whole-page picture of him pulling that shining sword from the green rock. They were sitting on the bed, and he jerked back so quick from the shock he rolled over his brand new fire engine and bent the ladder.

When he tried to snatch the book Molly laughed and said she would make his nose bleed if he didn't pipe down and leave her alone. 'It's my book, but when I've read it twenty-seven times I'll let you have a look,' she said. 'Till then you've got your own toys, so you'd better not nick any of mine.'

What could he do? That book haunted him for days. He'd never thought to see one in the *house*. Molly knew he felt something special about it, so read it aloud to torment him, and though he pressed his fingers to his ears he couldn't help but hear the words she spoke. His mother told Molly to stop tormenting him but she took no notice. Father laughed and egged her on: 'Now we know what to do when we want to get some life out of him. He looks half-dead most of the time.'

The anguish wore off, fingers at his ears relaxing till, little by little, he got the whole story of King Arthur and his loony knights. Even at school the tale came up too often for him to ignore, or think for a minute he would ever stop hearing it. The trouble was that the others in the class lapped the yarn up. They loved every word. They wanted the story over and over again, and the teacher – a man now – would open the book for the last period on Friday afternoon, and begin to read where he had left off the previous Friday, with such pleasure on his face and tremors in his voice as if he was an actor on the telly that the whole world adored, one adventure rolling into another. And when King Arthur was mortally wounded (he relished that word *mortally*) and when his sword was slung into the lake, and his body was carried away in a boat, you would have thought the whole class was about to burst into tears the room went so quiet.

But I ask you – chuck a sword into the water, and a hand comes up and makes a grab! It's as far-fetched as a man pulling it in the first place out of a slab of rock. I reckon a swimmer underwater just happened to be there at that moment and had the gumption to lift his hand up when he knew the sword was going to be thrown in. He caught the handle a treat, yanked the whole fucking lot under, swam to a quiet part of the reeds, and made off with it hidden in his cloak to a town market where he got a good price and was blind drunk on the proceeds for weeks afterwards. What other explanation can there be?

When the teacher got to that place in the book Ron laughed out loud. You'd have thought a firecracker on Guy Fawkes night had burst among them. Everyone jerked their necks and looked around. Teacher stopped reading, and stared.

'Come out, Delph,' he shouted.

Well, of course he would say that, wouldn't he? Ron thought. You can't have your mam write a note to the teacher telling him I wasn't to hear anything about King Arthur or I would go off my head. His hands twitched as he stood up.

'Come out when I tell you,' the teacher screamed, glasses joggling up and down on his winkle picker nose, as if his long hair was going to fall off. Ron was fixed to the spot, and it would have been as hard to pull himself free as to get that tinpot sword out of the rock. Then the notion came to him, at the worst possible moment, that the rock hadn't been rock but cardboard, and tricky King Arthur had only made a show of pulling his guts out to get it free. This made him laugh again, a screeching hee-haw as if from a horse whose head was trapped in a door.

The teacher smashed his fist on the desk, because the others were starting to laugh. 'Come here when I tell you, donkey, oaf, nincompoop, fool,' or words like that, only worse. All Ron's troubles sprang from that sword and rock of batty King Arthur, otherwise he would have had a blameless life. He had stopped the teacher dead from reading his favourite story, which was bad, he knew, since that was his only way of keeping them quiet. But Ron didn't go. He couldn't move. His feet went right through the floor to the middle of the earth. The teacher came to him, pushed him back into his seat, rattled him over the head, and went back to his desk holding his hand for pain.

From then on Ron stopped hating King Arthur and his Knights, because he thought they were just funny. There was nothing else to do but laugh, and make up his own daft bits to wile away the boring time when the book was being read to them, knowing or at least hoping that on going to another school after he was eleven all that stuff would be a thing of the past.

On opening his book again after making Ron's head ring the teacher couldn't get the same shaky tone to his voice that he'd had before. His reading went dull when it wasn't shaky, which served him right, Ron thought, for feeding us too much of that old King Arthur rammel.

The trouble was that though he considered it funny in his waking time, Ron dreamed about King Arthur and his Knights, and didn't think that was good for him at all. When Arthur pulled the sword out it was human flesh instead of rock, and when the sword was thrown into the lake a snake's mouth caught it, the long coiling body locked around Ron who was held in the slime below the surface. Evil Merlin the witch doctor led him in chains through crimson blood-dripping caverns to chop him up and cook him in a cauldron for the Knights' supper. An eagle pecked his eyes out, and when he wanted to wake up he couldn't even open the holes that were left.

He was still dreaming when he thought he was awake and blind, and saw the words – even though by now he had no eyes – written in fire in the sky which said: 'You are having a *knightmare*.' His mother and father were shaking with fright when he woke up screaming instead of laughing. The dreams went on for weeks, and his sister had to live with Aunt Dolly till he didn't have them anymore, and she could stand to be in the same house again without having bad dreams herself even during the day.

Ron soon learned that you can never get away from King Arthur. Everybody in this country thinks he was the greatest king of the olden days, he told himself, when everybody ate apples and honey and drank mead, and the sun shone except when rain poured down to water the crops, and the men had a bit of excitement now and again when they went off singing to have a shindig with the Saxons. In other words, a marvellous time was had by everyone, especially if you were a knight.

He liked his next school, knowing he was no longer an infant, and thinking he had left that King Arthur shit behind. A few weeks into the term the teacher got up in class one day and said: 'We're going to put on a play, and I'll need quite a few actors for the parts.'

'What play is it, sir?' a bumcrawler called.

He straightened his Mao jacket. 'Wait and see.'

Why not? They didn't mind. All the time it was game or gamble, wait and get a shock or a nice surprise. It made life exciting, especially since they had nothing else to do but learn.

'I want to know, first, how many budding actors we have in the class.'

His sister Molly had been given a cut-out theatre and they had put on plays, at first making them up as they went along, but then talking it over before starting, which way made the play last longer. They would take turns acting 'God of the World', and talk about making things happen that worried the other most. If he being God wanted all the toys in England to come into his room she would act a group of parents telling him it wasn't right to rob children of their toys. Then she would play a boy or girl who would tell him what they thought of him. Or she would play the owner of a toy factory, saying he didn't like – and neither did his workmen and women – that all the toys should go only to a greedy little bastard like him even if he was God.

You could imagine how they would go on for hours, but soon they got bored at every new idea even before they had put it on, and for more excitement acted at Punches and Judies till they made each other's noses bleed. They even got fed up with that, and then their mother caught them one Saturday afternoon up to what she called 'dirty tricks under the stairs', saying that was enough of that.

Ron shot his hand up when the teacher asked for actors. Only a couple more did, so half a dozen had to be cajoled into putting their names down. Ron fancied himself on the assembly hall stage dressed as a clown or a sailor, tramp, prophet or pilot. He couldn't think of what the theme would be but knew it must be something interesting.

'Now I'll tell you the text,' the teacher said. 'You'll all be pleased to know – at least I hope so – that it's one I've written myself. It isn't Shakespeare, or Sheridan, or Shaw or Brecht – so you needn't groan, Delph – but something based on a time when this island of ours was a happier and more interesting place than it is today. It all happened a long time ago, when men were free and respected and full of dignity . . .'

He knew already. He wanted to cross his heart and die. He should have known. It was that King Arthur and his Knights turning up again. His veins were bumping, and all he wanted to do was jeer, though didn't dare, having a good idea where it would lead.

The teacher looked at him while his batty talk went on because he'd been the first to volunteer, so thought he was dead keen to get on that stage. Thank God I'm not tall enough to be King Arthur, who would have to yank a sword out of a stone, because he knew he would never do it. He would push it further and further in or, if he did get it out, would slay the first fucking Knight that clapped him on the back, and called him King of Camelot for doing so. He couldn't believe he'd been so daft as to get trapped in his own deepest pit.

'This is the list of characters.' The teacher read them out and told Ron who he would be. 'It's late now, so we'll go through the play next week.' They groaned at being left on tenterhooks, but the teacher smiled and said the tale was so good it could easily wait. 'There are two months to go before the performance, so there'll be plenty of time for rehearsals to get you into shape.' He tapped his pack of papers. 'I'll have some photocopies made, and give out one between the two of you.'

King Arthur, he kept on saying to himself on the way home, King Arthur again, and when his mother said he was looking glum at teatime he said it was because he was going to be in a play at school. 'Well,' she laughed, 'that's not so bad. You'll enjoy it, if I know you.'

Tea slopped in his saucer when the biscuit he was soaking broke and dropped three quarters into the cup. 'It's about King Arthur and his Knights.'

'So what?' she said. 'You won't be him, will you?'

It turned out that he was to be Mordred, his son. So More Dread he was. 'I hope they'll invite me and your father to see it,' his mother said when he told her.

He held his shaking hand: they were bound to.

Merlin the magician brought More Dread up, he learned, and his job was to kill King Arthur. This news cheered him no end, because he'd always wanted to put a stop to that sword waving know-all of the round table. Unfortunately the cast only had wooden swords, and even the biggest stab he could give wouldn't go in the King's guts. In any case, Arthur was played by a pal of his, and he had no intention of hurting him.

'You've got to look furtive and sly,' the teacher shouted at him during a rehearsal, 'and not have that silly smirk all over your face. You're King Arthur's son, and you're going to kill him, so act as if you might, but not so that he would guess.'

It was hard to do both, but he tried. In fact he tried too well, because he became so furtive and sly that the teacher didn't know what he had in store. 'You've got to be two people,' the teacher said, and two people he made up his mind to be because as far as he was concerned one person had never been enough. Two was obviously better than one. Two was double, which meant that you could do twice as much. In fact if you were two people and people only thought you were one you might even get to doing four times as much, which was better still, except that four might be a lot to look after.

Never mind, he said, listening one night in bed to the speech he was to give near the end of the play, a part the teacher liked because when he remembered all the lines and spoke them even he clapped at the end.

He told Ron not to strut as he walked across the stage, but that was what the speech called for, and he couldn't help himself. 'Walk,' the teacher told him. 'And remember, you don't mean what you say. It's not really how you feel. You're trying to hide the real you who will kill him when the time comes.'

But the other part of him took control, though when the teacher shouted advice he said it as close as he could to the way he wanted:

'My father King Arthur and his valiant Knights
Were victors in a hundred fights.
They rode into battle, rank on rank,
And took the Saxons in the flank.
At night they sat around the table
Wassailing over yarn and fable.'

Ron strutted like a cockerel, and the teacher clapped when he made the words as clear as if he believed in them. In his sleep the black-red dreams came back, and the only way he could fight them off was by making up his own speeches to replace those the teacher had sweated blood to write, thinking they were the best poetry in the world. Because he only wanted to save himself Ron couldn't help himself, and he altered the speech as easy as pie. He'd never known he could do his own stuff so well, though it only came a few lines at a time, but in the morning he remembered them and wrote them down until the next two came. His dreams were H for Horror films, but with writing they didn't even get started while working out what he was going to say.

With so much mist in the streets it was a wonder anybody turned up, but the hall was three-quarters full, and their teacher was happy as, behind the stage, he ran from one to another of his actors with his hands full of paper making sure they remembered their lines. Ron knew his, right enough. He could hear people laughing and talking out front through the big curtains, which made some of the lads pale and nervous. He felt as calm and brave as if he really was one of King Arthur's screwy Knights.

The play seemed to go on forever, and in between walking on and off and remembering his lines Ron told himself that never again in his life was he going to have anything to do with King Arthur and his Crazies. He was only waiting to mouth his speech

122

at the start of the last act, surprised all through at how the people were loving their performance, and in some way sorry he wasn't one of them who could see the play from the seats they were in, though he knew he would have hated it and maybe even gone into a fit if he had been.

All his life he had been persecuted by King Arthur and, now that the curtain was opening for the last time he was going to have his chance. He puffed out his chest and lifted his sword as if it weighed a ton, and strode to the row of lightbulbs at the front of the stage to chant his lines, not able to see anybody but knowing they could see him. He had been told not to shout, 'but rather to recite,' yet called out at the fiercest register of his voice, as if he wanted to be heard all over the city and even the world:

'King Arthur and his screwy Knights
Got into many stupid fights;
They rode to battle dressed in tins
And there committed wicked sins;
They fought like dogs and fought like rats
Hitting each other with cricket bats,
Then got blind drunk around the table
And fell asleep in the castle stable
With Alice and Janet and Marlene and Mabel.'

People clapped and laughed, and somebody called out: 'Good old More Dread,' and when the commotion had died down Merlin came up to him, looking a bit pale through his beard, Ron thought, and the play went on it its awful end. When the curtain calls came he was sure people clapped him louder than anybody else, but at the back of the stage the teacher looked as if he was going to run him through with the big sword that had been snatched out of the rock. His face was close up to Ron's, who could tell he'd had more than a couple of big whiskies. 'What did you think you were doing, eh?' He would have throttled him if his parents hadn't been out in front waiting to take their little *Lawrence Oliver* home – as his father mockingly called him for a few months.

'I remembered my lines, sir, didn't I?' was all Ron could say to the teacher's flushed and rabid face.

The teacher turned, and stalked off, and Ron knew he wouldn't get much change out of him anymore, that in fact the school wasn't big enough for the two of them. The teacher must have realised the same, because he went to some other school not long afterwards.

On the way home Ron's mother said: 'I enjoyed that little performance. Everybody did. You were smashing in your part.'

Never again did he put up with anything concerning King Arthur, because if someone began to yak about him he just switched off, or let them know in no uncertain terms that he wasn't interested in such fairy-tale stuff.

Maybe that was what turned him into a poet, Ron Delph often thought. Or it was the start, anyway, because if you can see how much of a boring sham all that Camelot crap is you're bound to learn the secrets of the universe, or at least make a start on it. Apart from which he had always known that asking questions about things people think they have the answers to never got you anywhere.

Ivy

'IF YOU WERE EVER in love with a man, and that man died while you still loved him, you could only have one love in your life. You'd always remember.' Ivy knew what she was talking about, because it had happened to her. She meant it to her dying day, yet wondered at the time whether it was herself speaking when she said it.

Ernest Guyler had worked at the same tobacco firm but was forced to stop because he had caught TB. It wasn't a good place to be when you started to cough. On saying, with a bleak smile of reality that was new to him, that he would most likely never get over it, everybody laughed and told him he would live forever. He knew he wouldn't, and Ivy saw that he couldn't, though she joined with the rest of them in saying that he would, because if you loved somebody what else could you say?

'We never live for life with those we fall in love with,' one of the women at work told her afterwards, when she was hard enough to comfort.

'No,' Ivy answered, 'but we remember them,' though she hoped, from the way she felt, that she would not have to go on remembering much longer. The grey-stone parapet of the railway bridge, with a colliery humming and clattering behind, and steel lines multiplying towards Radford station in front, took her so far from grief that she felt frightened of casting herself down into the emptiness after a line of coal trucks shook the world on its way by. Grief came back in the vision of Ernest's face and, knowing he'd tell her not to be such a fool, she walked down the footway into the field and on towards home.

She couldn't forget the Sunday afternoons when he had walked up the lane from the railway bridge, after taking the trolleybus from where he lived in Town. Her mother and father were upstairs in bed, and Ivy leaned on the rickety planking of the fence to wait, only her head and two arms showing. There was a reddish tint to her golden hair, tied with a band so that it spread over the shoulders to her full-sleeved dark blue frock. She was the more serious of the blacksmith's grey-eyed daughters, with an occasional knowing laugh that the others were wary of, for there was a determination behind it that even her father saw as having come more from him than her mother, and so was something to be reckoned with.

A light overcoat would be folded over Ernest's arm, and she knew there was a white scarf in one pocket in case it turned chilly, and a cap in the other should it rain. On a summer afternoon – the only ones worth recalling – there was a smell of fresh sawdust from the yard, where her father and Dick had worked that morning to make the week's logs, and a sour odour of bran mash and muck from the stye where the pigs ceaselessly grumbled, as well they might, considering that one of them was to be killed in the autumn.

Ernest was tall and thin, and wore a brown suit, with a collar and tie, and there were three small triangles of white handkerchief showing from the line of his lapel pocket. Dark hair was combed more back than to the side, but was neatly parted. Ivy's heart bumped when she saw him walking up the lane, eyes in front as if he hadn't seen her. But she knew he had. They played a game as to who would see who first, and laughed when they decided that neither could ever win.

She ran to meet him for a kiss, uncaring as to who might see, though aware that few would be able to on the sunken lane half obscured by overreaching elderberry bushes, not expecting him to run in his condition, though he did increase his pace.

They walked hand in hand by the house, and then across the field and into Serpent Wood, and she would never forget what took place there, though he always did something so that she wouldn't have a baby. They were old enough to know better than that, in any case, because it was the nineteen-thirties, and both had been born with the century. On the way back she walked him to the bus stop, the nattily folded handkerchief gone in a good cause from lapel to trouser pocket, their moist hands clasped tightly.

Even her father had little to say against him, which was something of a marvel, because he had snubbed the occasional other she'd had. Perhaps her father didn't dislike Ernest because he had the same first name as himself; or, as was more likely, he sensed he wouldn't live long enough to marry her. She could just imagine that. But though her father seemed friendly enough when he met Ernest in the yard, she knew he didn't like him coming to the door, which was why she leaned over the fence to spot him walking up the lane, and then hurried down to meet him.

Ivy was my aunt, and I recollect everything vividly from those days, some of which was not of course properly understood, since I was only seven or eight at the time. Yet in my heart I feel I know almost as much about her as she did herself, thinking back and putting all the evidence together. She was an aunt who is the ideal mother, no leaden hearts to join, nor even strings attached. The humorous connection of love and trust on both sides was even less complicated because she didn't have a husband to be wary of, or children of her own.

A great event that she always harped on in after times was that of her giving me, as she said, my first bath. I must have been dipped when newly born, but wouldn't have remembered that anyway, which therefore couldn't be proved. One summer's afternoon, when I was sent to stay because my mother was having another baby, she and her sister Emily chased me around the tree in the yard they said, 'like a little pink pig that wouldn't come in to have its throat cut!'

They caught me by the chicken coop, dragged me back kicking, and protesting with all the bad language already picked up (which was a lot, because even then I had a love for words) and plunged me into a large tin bath on the cobbles outside the door. I must have had an occasional soak with my brothers and sisters in front of the fire at home, but this seemed to be my first because the circumstances were so unusual. Not only was the bath for me alone, it was in the open air, fresh air, too, a breeze smelling of leaves and heather, odours soon to be overwhelmed by the smell of the same White Windsor soap that my grandmother used for the weekly wash. By the time my aunts had finished scrubbing me it looked as if they'd also had a bath.

That would have been on a Saturday afternoon, because next day Ivy was standing by the fence looking for Ernest Guyler. Being by her side – there was a log to stand on – I saw him too, and she held my hand on our way down the lane. 'Come and meet my young man,' she said, and I could sense her excitement, and also that of Ernest when he put a hand on my shoulder and said how big I was for my age but all the time looking into Ivy's eyes.

He took out a packet of Players and gave me the cigarette card. Because he'd bought them from a machine there was a ha'penny as change in the shilling packet. He held the coin between his fingers. 'Heads or tails?'

'Neither,' I told him.

'It's yourn, then.' He gave it to me, and laughed, though his brown eyes didn't.

He offered Ivy a fag and, ill though he looked, smoked one himself as they walked towards the field. Ivy called that I should go back into the house, where Emily would look after me, but I stood on a stone looking at the three pigs, now and again aiming a bit of coal to hear them grunt, until the stench made my eyes run, when I went into the house to annoy the cat.

*

The loss of Ernie Guyler wasn't the end of Ivy's life. She did go out with a few men during the War, once with an American soldier, who gave me some chewing gum when I met them on the street, but none of them were considered up to much, or they went abroad and were never heard from again, so she stayed on at the small house in Town where her parents had moved, with her sister Emily who hadn't married either.

When she was sixty, and her parents had been dead ten years, I heard her laughingly tell my mother that she felt only half her age, and in many ways she looked it. That was when she met Albert Jones, a small thin man of sixty-five who had just retired after a lifetime's work on the railway. If he reads this story I hope he will recognise himself, though it's unlikely he's alive. I don't think he's capable of reading anyway, but if he is soldiering on I'm sure he's still puffing at his foul tobacco and putting back his daily quart, the only habit which could keep him going.

Ivy met him in the Boulevard Hotel, a glorified pub really, not far from the house, on what must have been the worst day of her life, though she wasn't to know that for some time. She had called at the bar with her sister, and Albert happened to be standing there. It was a Friday, some time in the late fifties, and he wore his suit. Wavy grey hair, thinning compared to what it had once been, gave him a staid aspect, only belied by the light in his eyes which Ivy mistook, fatally, for a sense of mischief and fun.

He told them his wife had died only a year ago. 'I buried her, and if you'll marry me, duck, I'll bet a quid I'll bury you, as well!'

'I suppose you say that to everybody, you cheeky devil.'

'To every nice lass, I do.'

'Anyway, you don't look strong enough to lift a spade,' Ivy said, 'never mind bury anybody. You'd sprain your wrist.'

'Not bad enough to pick this up, though,' he said, lifting his newly drawn pint. He knew himself for a bit of a card, and was so full of conviction he could see her thinking so as well.

He made sure always to be there when Ivy went in for her weekend drink, and after a month of falsely charming banter asked her to marry him, making sure the light went out of his eyes so that she would see he was serious.

Nobody had asked her since Ernie Guyler, who had died before she could. She had never wanted to marry after that. Going out with a man now and again was one thing, but to live with one after a lifetime being bossed by her father, no thank you. She had her job, a house, and her sister to look after. So why did she say yes?

My mother told her she ought to have more sense, but three months later they were married at the registry office. 'Aren't you being a bit of a fool, Ivy?' she heard a voice say during the ceremony.

'It's all right for you, Ernie, but you're dead, and I've got to go on living.'

Albert was about to put the ring on her finger. 'Who was you talking to?'

'Nobody. My lips must have moved.'

'I thought it was pigeons warbling.'

'Come on, let's get on with it.'

She found out later that Albert had been living with his sister, and had tormented her so much she told him to pack his trankle-ments and go, into lodgings for all she cared, because she wouldn't put up with his selfish ways anymore. Her name was Hilda and she came to the wedding, but hardly spoke to Ivy, kept a tight lip as if, should she say much, a quarrel might ensue and Albert would go home with her.

He must have thought he would have the time of his life with two women to wait on him, but Emily liked the new arrangement less and less. She never said so, but Albert knew it, and begin to mock her slow ways. Emily had always been the backward girl of the family, and her mother before dying made Ivy vow to look after her. Ivy would never have thought that getting married would make it such a hard promise to keep.

'You get on my nerves,' Albert would begin.

'And you get on mine,' Emily snapped back.

'Why don't you go out for a walk?'

'I don't want to. Why don't you?'

He mimicked her in baby talk. *'Why don't you?'*

'This is as much my house as yours.'

We'll see about that, his grin seemed to say.

'Leave her alone,' Ivy said.

Instead of two women waiting on him hand and foot, they combined to turn against him, he thought, and such venomous resentment he hadn't bargained for. Ivy was appalled at the infantile way he carried on, which brought out more childishness in Emily and, God knows, Ivy thought, she had enough as it was. Even she didn't always like it, but Albert made it worse. When she told him this he either asked her not to interfere, or acted as if he didn't know what she was talking about, which made Ivy doubt her own grown-up judgement, though never for long.

Instead of having one old age pension to play around with, he soon had three. The house cost only twelve shillings a week, and he took charge of the rent book. Payments were often in arrears; they didn't need to be, but he did it to keep Ivy in a state of worry. He often went out to the pub and came back drunk, though most nights he sat by the fire watching television. Ivy and Emily liked to smoke a cigarette now and again, but Albert's continual puffing of his vile brand of tobacco made them complain of the stink.

I was in Nottingham for a few days, and knew my aunts would be glad to see me for half an hour. It was some time in the sixties, when I was always glad to get out of London and back in the steadier, certainly less frenetic life, of my birth-town. Knocking at the back door, I walked in without waiting for an answer, being one of the family. In the big pocket of my overcoat was a half bottle of whisky for my aunts – I knew they liked a drink – and a tin of the better sort of tobacco for Albert.

They didn't seem happy but then, would they be able to show it even if they were? Happy wasn't much of a word in their dictionary, nor in mine, for that matter, and though I didn't particularly like Albert, if I had known how he behaved to my aunts, and how they detested him for it, I would have liked him even less. I knew something wasn't right between them, but hoped the tobacco would put him in a better mood.

It was obvious though that Ivy had got herself into a lobster pot of a marriage, and I thought maybe it would cheer her up to talk of old times and the people we had known. Her hands shook as if she had some kind of palsy. She wasn't well, and it was only too plain that Albert didn't care, that he even resented it. When she asked if I wanted a cup of tea I told her I'd just had a bucketful at home. It amused her to hear me go from London talk back to my rough childhood voice.

'I met Ernie Guyler yesterday, up Radford Woodhouse.' The words were impulsively out. 'Do you remember him?'

Her grey eyes looked straight at me, hands seeming to shake less. 'Oh yes, I do.'

'I liked him, because when I was a kid he used to give me cigarette cards, and the ha'penny from the packet of Players fags.'

She sat down, a hand quickly over her cheek. Albert turned to the fire because he could make nothing of our talk. I looked around the room to see all the objects of my grandparents, remembered from when they had lived at the cottage: the pot dogs with such benign almost human faces on the shelf which I supposed were valuable antiques by now, my grandfather's showcase of the last half dozen horseshoes, the stacked tea services of my grandmother in the glass-fronted cupboard, and many other tasteful gew-gaws hardly seen anymore, each a solid memory for me, but an eternal veil of protection for Ivy and Emily who had known them from birth.

'Ernest Guyler used to take me rabbiting,' I went on. 'I'll always remember him. He's still thin, and coughs a bit.'

'He'll never alter,' Ivy said with a smile. 'I know he won't, not Ernie.'

'He was walking under that railway bridge towards Old Engine Cottages where grandad and grandma lived.'

She was hardly able to speak. 'Was he?'

Albert turned. 'He sounds nowt but a bleddy owd poacher to me.'

'What do yo' know about it?' My tone was so hard that the light of unassailable malice went from his eyes, because he knew that as old as he was I would have thumped him if he'd said much more. Yet I knew enough as not to anger him in case he took it out on Ivy after I'd gone, even though I'd kept the tobacco in reserve so that he would feel jollier when I had.

Ivy winked at me, and smiled again, and when I said I had to be going gave me two passionate kisses, a good one for myself and loving one for Ernest Guyler, or so I wanted to think.

The next time I called she was obviously ill. So was I, not in my body, of course, but from some bleak misery or other, locked up in a life she could know nothing about, and which I shouldn't have been in at all but was, and which she would certainly have laughed at as being of no consequence.

She should have been in bed, but wasn't, coming from a family where bed was something you got to exhausted in order to sleep until getting up next morning to work – or to die. Her hands shook as she lit a cigarette. For me to help would have been an insult. 'I've just come out of hospital,' she said, adding it was the first time she had been in such a place. 'But I'll be all right now.'

Albert took his tin of tobacco, his claw reaching out, and gave no thanks, because he knew that to do so would be a compliment to Ivy for having such a generous nephew. I'd got his number all right, but to throttle him would only make it worse for Ivy, and Emily.

In spite of her affliction she made me a cup of tea, and while Albert was down in the cellar filling a bucket of coal for the dying fire she looked at me with her grey eyes shimmering with tears and said: 'Alan, take me away with you. I can't stand him or this anymore.'

Then she smiled, as if to inform me that she knew it could only be a joke, giving me the opening I both wanted and had to have, and smile in turn as if to agree that I knew she didn't mean it, that the notion of me going back to London with an ailing seventy-year-old woman was out of the question – knowing that she knew but that having said it was all she had wanted to do, to see what I replied, and knowing that at least I thought of the right answer and was troubled by saying what I did which proved enough that I loved her. Because of course she couldn't uproot herself and come with me to my uncertain life, even if I'd pleaded that she should.

But I wish I'd spontaneously said yes, please come, I'll look after you, thus giving her the chance to turn me down. It was one more betrayal in my life, one more solid trail of anguish fading into the rear horizon that will dog me to the end, but another zenith of self interest because guilt and anguish of that sort are necessary motors to keep me going.

'No,' Emily said, 'he can't,' as if to add, though it wasn't necessary either to Ivy or to me, 'What will happen to *me* if you go?'

Albert came up with the coal and put a lump onto the fire, and I said I must be going. She died a couple of years later, and I didn't go to the funeral because I was away in some foreign country or other. I tried to imagine Emily stuck in that house with Albert when I heard the news, and can only think it must have been the worst cat-and-dog situation. However it was, conveniently for him, she had a heart attack on coming out of church one evening, while crossing the road and making for the pub on the opposite corner.

I called on Albert some time later, and he hadn't changed. He barely mentioned Ivy, though I talked about her. I thought such lack of interest meant he was going ga-ga – he certainly wasn't grief-stricken – but at eighty he was still healthy, well able to look after himself, and smoking his pipe all the time.

The house was condemned by the council, the mangonels of synthetic modernisation on the march, and Albert had to leave. It was still a good house, solid enough in structure, but thousands were being demolished when they only needed a bathroom above the scullery for them to last another seventy years. High rise hen-coops were deemed to be the order of the day by those who would never have to live in them but had decided that that was how the 'working classes' ought to want to live.

Albert had talked his way into living again with his sister Hilda, in a village thirty miles away, and when she threw him out for the second time, as no doubt she would, he'd become the Hitler of the old folks' home and live comfortably to the end.

Before the house was knocked down I went to have one last look. There were boards at the windows, but I went up the yard to the back door and kicked it in. The place was empty, yet clean and neat still, as if only waiting for the next tenants to move in with their furniture.

I stood for a moment in the front bedroom, in which both my grandparents had died, and Ivy also, the same paper on the walls, then stepped across the narrow landing to the other bedroom, also empty. I wondered what Albert had done with the furniture, and all of my aunts' possessions. He couldn't have taken it to his sister's, or to an old folks' home. He had obviously sold it, and pocketed the bit of money the junk man had thought to give him. What about the tea service, and my grandfather's horseshoes? He'd had his own way, but there was no one to blame but myself.

Traffic streamed inconsequentially by along the road and, turning from the window, I noticed a piece of screwed up paper on the floor, the only sign of untidiness. I picked it up, and slowly unfolded it from the tight ball.

If he had been in the house just then I would have bludgeoned that smile from his face, killed him no less, or threatened him to death. The paper was the marriage certificate of himself and Ivy and, before departure, his last act had been to throw it away, and leave it behind like a piece of rubbish.

I couldn't imagine where he had got such spite, what he'd had in him to hate her, why he was so rotten as not to put up with the best qualities a woman ever had. He must have known that he had none by comparison, but you might have thought, after she was dead, he would realise that people living together have much to put up with from each other, and that forgiveness is all.

I walked out with the certificate carefully folded in my pocket, wondering about the one big mistake in Ivy's life and, on the train back to London, speculating on the fact that so many people make at least one.

Holiday

DANIEL HAD WORKED through Christmas to New Year so as to wangle a fortnight's holiday in January with Jean to Egypt. On the all-night run down to London the A1 was awash with rain, and the Dartford Tunnel no picnic, but they made Gatwick car park with an hour to spare at half-past six.

The booking halls were calm and they were soon through passports and security. Daniel bought whisky, vodka, and four cartons of fags at the duty-free before taking that funny little internal train to the final departure room. Jean bagged a seat and read the *Sun*, looking after his big tranny radio which he couldn't be without because he wanted music and football results at all hours and wherever he was. He even carried a coil of aerial wire to get stations loud and clear. She smiled at him striding around the shaver and watch showcases like a security guard trying to pass himself off as an ordinary passenger.

Rain beaded the windows as the Boeing built up revs and began its run. 'I hope it don't skid' – at which he could only laugh. The packed plane lifted straight into grey-belly cloud, juddering a few moments before breaking through and leaving the miserable weather below. She had noticed no dawn in the lounges but now the sun was brilliant in an upturned basin of blue.

'God's kitchens must be up here,' she said. Such a picture didn't help the jitters, which she didn't mention in case Daniel got rattled. He was never nervous, because every year before they were married he'd flown to Benidorm with his mates. Safety belts unclicked, she released his hand. 'I hope the kids'll be all right.'

'They will, don't worry.' He passed a cigarette, and held the lighted match. 'Your mother's good with 'em.' She talked as if there were ten, instead of only two as yet. 'She'll keep the house warm as well.'

'How long before we get there?'

'Five bloody hours.' He pulled out the airline magazine to see where they were going. 'They'll give us summat to eat soon. A bucket to drink as well, I hope.'

The yellow-orange sunball just above the tops of the palms was sinking while they looked at it. 'I never thought I'd see this.'

'It's marvellous.' She held his arm. The first room they had been shown to had a double bed, but they wanted twins because otherwise why would you come to such a posh hotel? Then the twin-bedded room looked out over a lot of sheds so Daniel went downstairs and gave 'em what-for at the desk. An hour later they were able to change to one with a view over the river.

'I've always wanted to come to Egypt.' He looked towards the far bank wooded with palm trees, a slender minaret pointing like a biro about to write on the pale slate of the sky above a dimming line of hills.

'It's the Nile,' she said. A solitary mop-headed palm above the rest looked as if it would rub out any message it didn't agree with.

'If we go down to them bulrushes we might find little Baby Moses!'

A sandbank seemed to get bigger and greener in the dusk, as if waiting for someone to scatter seeds and grow something good before the flood came. Tucked by the side of the hotel the blue patch of swimming pool was deserted. Pennants on moored boats waved in the breeze. 'Must be cool as well outside,' she said.

An hour before supper she went into the bathroom, and came out in underwear bought specially for the trip. She was thirty, her skin clear, eyes open and blue, hair so buffoned up she looked about twenty. 'Hotels always mek me feel sexy.'

She went up to him, and he needed no second telling.

They walked hand in hand along the avenue of recumbent rams at Luxor temple. Some had heads missing, paws gone, horns and tails snapped off as if, he thought, a football coach had stopped and the lads had got to work, though they'd had to give up and leave most unscathed because the stone was too tough, even for Randall's Vandals – as the gang used to call themselves. 'How old did that book say it was?'

'About three thousand years.'

'Looks it.' He hadn't fancied the salad at last night's buffet, so the grub had stodged his guts. You couldn't even clean you teeth in the tap water in case you got the screaming ab-dabs.

The temple was a place for hide-and-seek, with so many columns and back ways. 'It's a bomb site, really,' he laughed. 'Lovely to see, but just like a bomb site.' Among the ruins, as if to encourage his opinion, an aerial photo was displayed behind the glass of a notice board, which indeed looked like a picture of Dresden after it had cooled down.

He was bored with aimless circuiting, and they wanted some coffee. 'They're trying to tell us that people lived four thousand years ago. I could 'ave told 'em that. I don't think I'd have lived very well in them days. I'd have been a slave, I expect, building these bloody temples for people like us to come and gawp at.' He was sweating under his straw hat. 'The sun's getting hot.'

'Even for January,' she said. They walked down the riverbank road and into the Old Palace Hotel. He led her to the cool arcade by the swimming pool. 'There's no music here,' she said. 'I hate it when it's too noisy.'

They sat in the silence till midday, when the ululations of the male faithful sounded like a nation of sheep going to the slaughter. 'Just listen to 'em.'

'It's their way,' she said.

'They can have it.' He ordered another coffee. 'Karnak they call it,' he said, 'and I'm kar-knackered already!'

'It's only the first day.'

'Don't worry, love, we'll have a good holiday. I'm enjoying it, anyway.'

'So am I.'

'We'll go into that tourist office after we've had some dinner. Maybe they'll give us a pamphlet and a map.'

The drivers of taxis and horse-drawn carriages called at them to get in and ride, but they preferred walking the streets. A fly crawled up a beggar's nose as if to get its elevenses, he quipped. The Mar-haba Restaurant was only half full but it took twenty minutes to get served.

'It's a go-slow,' she said.

At least there was pitta bread and two beers on the table already. 'Like being at home, at Akbar's Snack Bar. I wonder how the lads are managing without me. It gets hotter in that boiler-room though than it does out here.'

'Somebody at the hotel was saying it's like an oven in summer.' They had asked for kebabs but got koffta – whatever that was – but it sounded all right. 'I wanted kebab,' Daniel said to the waiter.

The waiter shrugged. 'No more kebabs.'

Ten minutes later kebabs were taken to the next table. Daniel stood when the waiter came. 'What's that?'

'Kebabs,' the waiter said.

'You told me you'd got none left.'

'New ones come in.'

Daniel sat. 'I should throw him to the fucking crocodiles.'

'Eat your dinner, duck.'

'The croc would choke. Let's have some more of this delicious beer.' He stirred at his plate, rice instead of chips. 'I like the Egyptians, but I wouldn't like to be one.'

'Well, you're not used to it.'

'I never would be, I'll tell you that.'

She finished her food. 'That was delicious. I wouldn't like to wear one o' them veils, though.'

'If you did I might fancy you even more!' He gave the waiter a twenty note to meet the bill, and waited for the change. 'He's forgotten,' she said. 'We've still got to finish our smoke and coffee, so don't fret.'

'I won't,' but when the waiter passed he called: 'What about my change?'

'Two minutes.'

Daniel read the bill: several kinds of service already deducted, it seemed. The small denomination bank notes were so worn he thought the whole population played a game of passing them around before they fell to pieces. He left some for a tip. 'It's more than he deserves.'

'They've got to live,' she said.

'Let's go, then.'

The man in the tourist information office stood as they came in. Daniel asked if he had any gen on the area. They wanted to cross the river but didn't know what was what on the other side, though what they could see looked beautiful. He was dressed in a fawn suit with waistcoat, a young man who, Jean thought, was very handsome, especially since he seemed to be giving her the eye all the time they were there. But I suppose he'd even do the same for a woman of sixty. He produced a booklet, and a rough kind of map, pointing to the places with the tip of a real pen.

Jean spread out her best smile. 'Can we have these?'

'All yours,' he smiled back. 'But before you go, I would like to invite you to have tea with me.'

Daniel wasn't much interested in a friend for life. 'We'll be stuck for an hour.'

'I'd be honoured if you'd accept.' The man still looked at Jean, she was sure, as if he wanted to strip her there and then. 'Just a glass of tea,' he said.

He was serious, but Daniel didn't want to give in, or insult him, since he was pleasant and friendly enough. 'Thanks very much, but we've got to go to the bank. We'll come back tomorrow.'

He wasn't put out by the refusal, and offered his little blue and scented card, which Jean took. 'Have a nice time over the river.'

'He was a lovely chap,' Jean said. They walked along the river side of the road on their way to the ferry, the pavement bumpy and sand showing underneath. She could have fallen in love with him, and that was a fact. He was something to dream about, but there'd be no reason to see him again and that, she told herself, was a pity.

'We could have gone on that conducted tour from the hotel,' Daniel said, 'but it'll be a lot better doing it on our own.'

They went down the wide flight of crumbling steps to the river, stopping for a ticket on the way. Among so many people he kept a fist over the money in his trouser pocket, and walked half-left behind Jean, watching her handbag and camera. He would have done the same anywhere. 'Let's get on the top deck, and see the view.'

A large square of seats faced inwards, young men in long garb and white pillbox hats sitting or standing to talk. A bootblack and a couple of peanut vendors touted for a bit of trade. 'I didn't like the looks some of 'em gave me as I walked up the stairs,' she said.

'Don't worry. They won't say owt.'

'What would you do if they did?'

'Tell 'em to fuck off.'

She laughed. 'There's not one woman up here.'

'They're stowed in the lower deck. I saw 'em as we came up. Don't you want to go down and sit with 'em?'

'If you come with me.'

'I'd definitely get a knife in my back,' he laughed.

A sailing boat left a wake in the water shaped like a scimitar. Milky blue turned the sun pale. A rusty barge with impeccable white superstructure headed south. 'Put your hat on, duck. It's hot.'

He looked around. 'Where is it, though?'

They'd bought it in Nottingham for fifteen quid, a real straw Panama. 'You must have left it somewhere.'

'In that restaurant, I expect.'

'You had it on there. It must have been in that tourist information office. We can call for it tomorrow. I'm sure that nice young man will put it by for you.'

The crossing was short, water eddying inshore towards jungly banks, a narrow beach either side of the quay. Low cliff, palms and fields beyond, went the whole length of the river. He drew fingers through thick fair hair. 'The sun won't penetrate this bit o' thatch.'

'Still, you need your hat.'

From the gangway it looked impossible to get through the ranks of taxis to the road beyond. 'Just follow me,' he said, 'and stick close.' He felt sorry for them, all desperate to earn a bob or two in a country where there were so many people that life was a struggle from crib to coffin. He wanted to stroll with Jean, however, to another ferryhead half-a-mile upriver, as shown on the map. Weaving between bonnets and wing mirrors, he ignored shouts to get them to the Tombs and back – for nothing if they liked.

A few hundred yards, and they were out of chaos. 'This is heaven' – she aimed her camera across a meadow against a background of sugar cane. Goats chewed head down at the herbage, a gaggle of dazzle-skirted bright faced girls minding them. Behind the dense palm groves rose a line of purple hills.

'Better than a picture,' he said.

She kissed him, quickly, adoring his enthusiasm. The girls came towards them in a colourful line halloa-ing and hands waving for baksheesh. 'We'd better go. I got two or three snaps and I'm sure they'll come out. They're lovely kids, though.'

On the trip back there were hardly any passengers, and an amiable old ruffian came around asking for a tip for the captain. 'The captain?' Daniel laughed. 'Piss off!'

'Let's have some more of this Coptic plonk.' He read the wine list at dinner. 'It's dry and red, good enough for me. Maybe it'll melt some of this oily grub.'

'It's delicious.' At the buffet they heaped chicken, rice, string beans and peas onto their plates. New groups had arrived, German tables easy to pick out because they were crowded with bottles of beer. The French tables had wine, and the Egyptians mostly water, while the British had scatterings of everything. He shovelled the food in. 'I'll burn my gutache out with the whisky later.'

'Take it easy, love.'

'I feel hungry, seeing this marvellous spread.'

White sun melted into the haze, still some way above the horizon. They strolled by the swimming pool, by day surrounded with what he saw as cooking flesh, a pleasure he didn't want to sample. Dark came quickly, monochrome grey over rippling water, the far bank vivid green. Then everything suddenly dark. He wasn't feeling well. 'Let's go up.'

'You must have a cold.'

He switched the air conditioning full on. 'The noise meks it sound like it's time to fasten our safety belts,' she said.

'I'm kay-lied. Or pole-axed. I can't tell which. Wake me when the plane's ready to go.'

She came up from breakfast with a boiled egg, a roll and a bottle of water. He finished it off. 'What's the difference between a cold and the flu?'

'I don't know,' she said.

'I've got one or the other, and can't decide. I've never been in bed as long as this in my life.'

It must be a cold or the flu, because he wasn't poisoned, and that was a fact. As long as he could belch he wouldn't throw up; and as long as he could cough he wouldn't choke; and as long as he could fart he wouldn't shit himself. All he could do was lounge around and take it easy. Funnily enough he wanted Jean to come to bed, but knew he wouldn't be able to get it up even if he swallowed a cup of starch.

'You'll feel better tomorrow,' she said. 'I'm going into town now, to get your hat. You must have a touch of the sun.'

The woman at the counter didn't know anything about it. 'A man served us yesterday.' Jean was about to describe him but thought she had better not: dark and handsome, and I fancied him no end.

The woman came back from the rear office. She was good-looking as well: dark haired and olive skinned, with a rich figure. Daniel would have fancied her. 'No hat has been left here. I'm sorry.'

Daniel felt awful nearly all day. Whenever he thought he might be getting better, the gripes came back. Even so, he had an appetite and enjoyed his cigarettes, so maybe it was only a cold. With the flu he'd never been able to eat or even look at a fag. The dentist had given him a bottle of antibiotics last year for an abscessed tooth, so he went into the bathroom and swallowed a dozen pills with a tumbler of half toothwater, and the rest whisky. His head zinged a bit, but he felt better straightaway.

He tuned in the radio hoping for news or sports talk, but the aerial didn't work because the room was fairly well sealed. Attaching the coil of wire to the short-wave screw with his Swiss army knife he threw it out of the window, bringing in London loud and clear.

Jean called at the restaurant but nobody had seen the hat. He would have to get another. Sweating so much, she got into a horse-drawn carriage following along the kerb, and told the man to drive her to the hotel. Sitting on the high seat, a breeze coming from somewhere, she saw white knife-pointed sails on the river, and felt like a queen, dreaming she had the handsome man of the tourist office by her side as the scrawny old nag trotted along the road.

Daniel in the bar had two bottles of beer on his table. He was looking at the map in the brochure. 'I feel better. Let's go over the river this afternoon and see the Temples. It says here there's lots of paintings in the Tombs.'

Across at the quay they got into a taxi, and the driver said his name was Mahmoud, a youngish man with a piratical look, but they liked him. 'Tombs first,' he said, 'then Temples. OK Johnny?'

Daniel set his new khaki cap at the proper angle. 'Drive on, Macduff!'

'You look just like a swaddie in that hat,' she laughed, the tattoo of snake and sword showing below the short sleeves of his shirt.

'I know good guide,' Mahmoud told them.

'He means his brother,' Daniel said. 'Don't need one,' he shouted. 'We walk on our own.' He waved the pamphlet. 'This'll tell us all about it.'

Tombs? More like foxholes and cellars among the ashpits of the scorching plain. Some had regular entrances, a guardian at each, hand high for baksheesh, which was never enough. When they came into daylight the way was pointed to the next guardian. 'It's a game of "Pass the Tourist",' Jean said. 'I liked them paintings, though the ceiling was a bit bumpy.'

'Beautiful.' Daniel noted some Tombs closed off as being restored. 'They're doing the paintings up in them. I suppose they get a new coat every few months. We'll have to send a postcard to your mother.'

Next on the list was the Temple of Seth the First, by a crumbling village of mud houses. They thought they had seen everything, but Mahmoud said that if they came tomorrow he would take them to other Temples. 'I'll be waiting with my taxi,' he said at the pier, and didn't grumble at the tip.

Jean couldn't stand. 'Feels like it's my turn now. I wonder what it is?'

'Same as what I'd got, I expect.' What he still had, in fact, but two couldn't be badly at the same time. They'd look a bit daft, both in bed with aches and pains. He felt guilty because she hadn't wanted to have dinner last night and he'd persuaded her. He had ordered a bottle of Omar Khayyam red to go with the mutton when they should have stuck to bread and sherbet. I'll never learn, he thought. They'd finished off the whisky upstairs beforehand, which had maybe softened his brain, though he sometimes knew it was soft enough already.

He sat at the desk and wrote a postcard of the bomb site at Karnak to his mate Harry. 'We're at this health resort on the River Nile. Sick as a dog, weak as a kitten, but everything going well. See you soon, I hope. Dan.'

Jean stayed in bed, sweating and feverish. She enjoyed being languid, in and out of dozing, mollified by stark dreams she couldn't remember the second they'd gone. A drum and tambourine played softly outside, a real holiday, no cares at all.

So as not to disturb her Daniel sat in the lounge watching the talent, a few interested looks from the occasional passing woman. The tea was like piss, so he read about the Temples over and over till the pamphlet was like a rag and he put it in a waste bin. He went up every hour to see that Jean hadn't died.

'It's only malaria, love, so don't worry. If you'd been for a swim in the river it could be worse. It'd be Bill-something or other. I've often wondered what would happen if the river flooded and came into the hotel. You'd have crocodiles swimming up the corridors snapping people up in their jaws. Can you imagine the headlines in the *Sun*?'

He picked fussily at the buffet for lunch, then phoned for a roll, butter, jam, and a bottle of cold water from room service, which Jean enjoyed. 'The best cure for a gutache is to eat – something, anyway – to give it a bit of nourishment to chew on.'

He should have added on the postcard that he was bored to death, but only when he didn't know what to do with himself. He stood the tranny upright thinking to have a listen but there wasn't much beyond mush. He kissed Jean on the forehead to be sure she was asleep, then opened the window and slung out the length of aerial. The people in the room below would think a gremlin was on the end coming in to burgle them.

The connecting screw must have been loose, because the pale coated wire free-floated onto a terrace two floors below. He hoped his effing and blinding hadn't wakened her, but that was that, he wouldn't hear a peep out of London now. The wire melted into the paving so that he couldn't even see where it lay, though maybe he needed a drink to clear his eyes.

Both felt wobbly walking through the museum, and there were no seats to sit on. They'd had to queue to get in, and found the cafeteria closed. Peering through the crowds, they saw as much as they could, then sat outside on a low wall in the sun, hungry because they'd eaten nothing but a few biscuits at breakfast. An American woman was telling her daughter how Betty had had a wonderful time in wherever it was – swimming, sunbathing, eating everything, all with no effect whatever. Two days after she got home she felt funny. The doctor told her not to worry, just rest. But she got worse and was rushed into hospital. Polio. A week later she was dead. 'So you have to be careful, no matter how good you feel.'

'That cheered me up no end,' Daniel said. 'If we go sick when we get back maybe the doctor will send us South to recover.'

'On the NHS.' She took his hand. 'Let's go and have a snack somewhere.'

It was strange to be so up and down, but the next day both said they had never felt healthier. Mahmoud picked them out as they came off the ferry at Thebes. 'I've got very good Temples for you,' he called, as if they might want to buy one.

'Come on, then, Mahmoud. Let's have a look.' The car swayed in the middle of the road, and they waved at two cyclists who had Union Jacks and GB signs on their back mudguards.

By the fallen colossal statue at Rhamesseum Jean pulled him close, to listen to a dark haired woman with glasses reading a poem called Ozy-something or other. Everyone clapped after it, and one old man in a Panama hat had tears in his eyes. 'I think I heard that poem at school,' she said.

'I remember it, as well.'

At the Medinat Habu, a building in fairly good nick, he thought, an Egyptologist was giving a scholarly rundown on its history. 'I love to listen,' Jean said. He was tall, dark and thin; she found the men very good-looking in Egypt.

Daniel's mind drifted off after a while, but he was brought back on hearing the man say: 'The hereafter is a cul-de-sac.' Couldn't have been, if you think of all them mummies, but that's what it sounded like, unless my ears are melting in the heat.

They sat on the steps to eat cheese rolls and bananas from Daniel's haversack. After the great breakfast – first an English one, and then a continental – he couldn't face much more. He passed the bottle of water. 'I expect Mahmoud's eating his grub in a tomb.'

'He'll have a siesta as well. It's cooler there.'

'That's what we want,' giving her a look she knew well.

She kissed him on the lips. 'Any time.'

A man of about sixty stood lower down the steps with a vacant and exhausted look. Must be English, because he's studying a map as well. Wispy grey hair straggled at the neck, though his receding chin was well shaven. He looked as if he'd had a comfortable life, so it didn't matter that his chin gave him a weak look. He put his pale straw hat on and lifted a little pair of binoculars from around his neck to look at the view.

'I think I've seen him somewhere before.'

'Probably on telly.' Daniel put the banana skins in a plastic bag. 'We'll have one more turn around the temple, then whistle up Mahmoud to take us to the boat.'

Opening the curtains at half-past seven, he felt rid of all his ills and miseries. The large island sandbank in the middle of the river seemed to get bigger and greener every day. 'You wouldn't guess it was only a few miles wide if you didn't know.'

A haze above the palm trees and fields lining the opposite bank suggested that the cultivable area went on into infinity. She yawned. 'I suppose we'd better get our breakfast. Hey, though, I enjoyed that vodka last night.'

'Me as well. Booze is allus good medicine. We'll get some more on the way back.' Maybe the light was different from a few days ago, but the length of his aerial wire lay clearly on the terrace where it had fallen. Unless he had some grappling irons, to scale up from outside, the only way onto the place was through one of the rooms on the first floor, but if he went down to a door, knocked on it and said: 'Do you mind if I go through your room and get over the balcony onto that terrace so that I can fetch my aerial wire back?' they would either think he was loony and tell him to fuck off, or call the security guards, in which case he would end up working in a quarry for ten years. 'Let's walk around the bomb site again. I liked it there.'

A white bird swam on water eddying inshore. 'I want to go over the river,' she said. 'I love being on that boat.'

'All right. Tombs today, bomb site tomorrow.'

But in the morning she was down again. Whatever it was came

back full strength. The trouble was, he thought, that when you're with somebody who's badly it's easy to feel the same way yourself. He fought it off, and fed her the antibiotics she had refused at the last bout. He came up from lunch with choice pieces in a serviette, but at the sight of them she turned to the wall. She took a glass of water dashed with vodka and went to sleep. He laid a hand on her forehead, but there was no fever.

The area between the hotel and town was squalid and crumbly, in no way like neat rows of houses at home, so he turned back when halfway there. You need someone with you when walking in a foreign place. A tubby little tanker lorry laid black smoke along the road before turning into a petrol depot. Even when only two hundred yards from the hotel a horse-drawn carriage slowed in the hope of a fare. He wanted to throw a tip without taking a ride, but that would be insulting. Back in the busy lobby he went to the counter and changed another fifty pounds. While signing for them he remembered the aerial of his radio.

Dozens of doors lined either side of the corridor but he knew roughly which one the terrace was level with, and as luck would have it a door near enough was wide open. Wearing plimsolls, he went noiselessly in. The bed was made up, a suitcase by the table as if somebody was about to leave or had just come. No other sign, He stepped quickly across and lifted the handle of the window-door. So far, all clear. In seconds he was over the balcony and down six feet onto the terrace. The sun made liver-red streaks over the palm trees across the river.

Now that he was down he couldn't see the aerial. Eyes in every room must be riveted on what I'm doing, bent double and staring at the concrete. Let 'em stare. He wanted to be in contact with the world, and nobody was going to stop him. He grabbed an end of the thin wire, wrapped it around his fist, and joyously put the neat ball into his pocket.

Four small sailing boats were moored within the left-hook of the hotel harbour. Feeling triumphant, he looked around and waved at the great facade of windows. All he had to do now was get back into the corridor, but on reaching the balcony he didn't know, to half a dozen windows, which one he had come through.

Sweat made patches on his shirt, ran into his eyes as he went back and forth like, he thought, a panther trying to get back into its cage. One room he looked in showed as near as damn it a man and woman having it off on the bed – at least that's what he would tell Jean, a blow-by-blow tale to get her randy.

The next room was empty, as untidy as if thieves had rifled it. A lock kept him out, but just as he told himself he would be here forever, or get caught as a prowling Tom, he found a window on the catch. Edging a finger inside, he pushed and stepped in. Somebody was there but, with banging heart, he had to get back upstairs and see how Jean was.

A young woman writing a letter at the desk looked a bit shocked, he had to admit. 'Maintenance,' he said.

'Maintenance?'

His wire uncoiled, touched the floor. 'A wireless aerial fell on your terrace, and I was told to come through and get it back.'

Her accent was American, and she was thirty if she was a day, dark haired, and slightly sallow as if she'd had the odd bilious bout since her arrival. 'They should have informed me from the desk.'

'I thought they had. They're very forgetful.'

She was cool, and gave a half smile. 'You're really a guest, aren't you?'

He nodded. 'I can't get the BBC without the wire, and it fell out of my window.' He told her the rest of his difficulties, which set her laughing: 'I sure won't forget that.'

The little plump bosom behind her red top moved when she stood, her smile showing the white and even teeth of a well cared for woman. He didn't want to go. 'Are you staying long in Egypt?'

'Only a week. My husband's ordered a boat to take us to Aswan. Then we'll go back down the river to Cairo.'

The little red guidebook to Egypt on her table was so thick it must tell you everything. 'Sounds good. We're having a fortnight.'

She sat down again, enjoying their chat, and turned her chair to face this tall brush-haired thinnish man with his tattooed arm more squarely. 'Are you a mercenary?'

'Mercenary?'

'A hired soldier.'

He would be, if he could, and thought he'd say yes. 'When I can get the work. I'm running a boiler-room at the moment, where I come from, in a factory.'

'You must have a few good stories.'

'I have. I'd like to tell you 'em sometime' – if I could get you where you'd like to listen. All women were different, but she was another world, though not so far out that after a while they couldn't get used to each other. 'I must go, though. My wife's not well. It's been nice meeting you.'

She came to show him the door, and shake hands. He was sure the pressure he put on was mutual. 'I hope you get your radio to work,' she said.

'Sure to. I know all about 'em.' He waved as he went down the corridor.

'Have a nice day!' she called.

'What do *you* think?' he told Jean. 'In two minutes she was on her back naked with legs wide open and I was kneeling, bare as well, with the biggest hard on in my life. In three minutes she came, and in four I did. In five minutes her husband barged in, and we had a fight, so in six minutes I knocked him over the balcony, and in seven I grabbed my things and ran. I got dressed in the lift between two floors.'

Her laughter meant she was on the mend. Bogger the radio, he thought, at the look in her eye when she asked him to tell it again, only slower and longer, before saying come on, get into bed with me.

He fixed the wire, and reception was still uncertain. No powerlight came on, but new batteries made it as clear as a bell with the built-in aerial alone.

Next day on the West Bank he was carrying the book seen on the woman's desk, bought for fifteen quid. He'd read all that was said about the area, opening it at every tomb and temple, and now there was little more to be seen. Mahmoud asked them to visit his house on the way to the ferry and have a glass of tea. Jean said yes, hoping for one more memory to take back.

'He doesn't mean it. It's only their way, to offer.' Daniel didn't much want to, but the invitation was repeated, almost insisted on: 'You meet my wives, and we say goodbye.'

'He likes us,' Jean said.

Mahmoud drove beyond the village, turned sharp right and took them into a courtyard surrounded by a wall of mud bricks.

'I don't like forceputs,' Daniel said.

'Let's do it.'

'Ah, all right, duck. I'm not a hard man!'

The mint tea was delicious, and sweet cakes went down a treat. Mahmoud's six kids stood in line, fascinated at Jean and Daniel seated on wooden boxes covered with cloths. Daniel thought the two rickety storeys would fall down if you blew hard enough. 'Lovely kids,' he said. 'And you've got a nice house.'

Three aunts and an old mother surrounded Jean, touching her all over, and Daniel saw how she enjoyed it. An hour passed quickly in talking, and smoking fag after fag. Mahmoud liked English brands. Jean stood up to go. 'We ought to give him a present. I'll bet it's the custom.'

'What, though?' He looked through his haversack, not wanting to let the side down, and picked out his prized Swiss army knife, almost brand new. 'Why not this?'

'Yes, we can get you another.'

He opened all sections, which stopped the talk from dying away. 'Yours, now. From us to you. I hope he's pleased.'

'I'm sure he is,' Jean said.

Mahmoud smiled. 'Very happy!' He admired an unbroached box of English matches seen in the haversack, and Daniel gave him that as well. They shook hands, Mahmoud saying they were friends for life, and accepting another cigarette.

'Come back and stay with us for a long time,' he called from the top of the steps at the ferry, a grand and solitary figure in his robe, saluting as the boat pulled away.

'He's had a good week,' Daniel said.

'He needs it, with all them kids. Fancy having two wives!' She looked down the broad sleeve of green towards the south, wondering where the river went. 'They're nice people here, though.'

'The guidebook says it goes right to the middle of Africa,' he told her, 'and it's four thousand miles long. About twice the distance from here to London.'

'Don't you know a lot?' she mocked.

She noticed a haze-ring around the moon. 'Do you think it's going to rain?'

'I hope so – after we've left.'

'What a nice holiday it's been.'

He poured the last of the vodka into two glasses. 'In a couple of years we'll go to Turkey, or Israel.' That American woman might be walking along a street. He would spot her, and they would get talking. She would be on holiday without her husband, and remember him finding his length of aerial wire.

The men might be dishier there, Jean thought, even more than Mahmoud, or the man explaining all about the tombs, or the dandy at the tourist information bureau whose card she took out and looked at when Daniel wasn't close. 'I wonder what happened to your hat?'

'I expect that soft young man will be wearing it after we've gone.'
She liked to imagine that.

'It'll be funny, getting home,' he said. 'Back in overalls and lagging them crumbling pipes. Still, at least I've got a good job, and I'm never bored at it.'

She looked at the line of palm trees and distant cliffs, and moon rays laid on the glass-like stream. 'It's been a dream here.'

He finished his drink. Where would we be without 'em? 'You can never have too many dreams,' he said.

A Matter of Teeth

DENIS'S GIRLFRIEND lived a few hundred yards from his dentist, so any onset of dental decay – which seemed to be necessary now that he was in his forties, and call for a long sequence of restorative bridgework – was not unmixed with a feeling of masochistic anticipation that he saw no reason to question. With such a perfect alibi, who cared about the muddy whirlpool of the psyche?

He said to his wife that the dentist's only disadvantage was in being slow, but a man who took time over such work was none the worse for that. Deception was a murky trade, as he well knew, because hadn't the British excelled at it in the Second World War?

For the sake of his mouth he sometimes wished Sylvia lived elsewhere but, being English and with the sort of teeth that went with it, he came to accept the situation, if not with complacency, then in the knowledge that there was something to be said for heredity after all. The managing director of a biscuit factory, he was as far from looking the part as possible, so casual in dress it was a wonder, his wife often thought, that the business hadn't gone bump years ago. But his lackadaisical stance was deceptive, for he got things done, and at the same time swore it had never been his idea to work more than necessary. 'Things trundle along. We sell. We make a profit. The biscuits are even good. As long as we keep the bank manager at bay – and we're doing that, believe me.'

Such an attitude, Glenda thought, was the bane of the country, but who was she to complain? Bringing up three children kept her busier than his work seemed to keep him. Complaining was whining, and too many people did that – another thing wrong with the country.

His meeting with Sylvia had been a boon to be taken immediate advantage of. He went alone to the party because Glenda wasn't feeling well. Hadn't she known that parties posed the kind of risk that he was in no mood to shirk?

Sylvia had been leaning against a bookcase as he went up the stairs, tall coffee table volumes on the lower shelf exaggerating the shape of her legs. Her face was no less interesting – thin (as was her body) but he noted the lively way she looked at him as he went by, and she thinking that he hadn't taken in her glance. But he had: she would have to be sharper than that. She was: 'I knew exactly what was on your mind.'

So his remark about 'the well-heeled liberals of Hampstead' drove the other man away. 'That won't get you anywhere,' she said, 'with so many dishy men around. I've never seen so many dishy men at one party.'

The fact that he was disliked on sight may have been what drew her towards him, for he always went to such places dressed in the opposite kind of garb to which he wore at work: a man of small stature, with dark hair, wearing a formal suit but casually knotted silk tie. Even so, he considered himself broad-minded and liberal, though a fatal ability to say the right thing made it difficult to put his views in that coherent braying voice usual at such places. If he succeeded and someone argued against him he reacted with such vehemence that they regarded him as an extremist of the opposite camp. 'I think socialism's a wonderful idea, but not when it's used as a device by the middle classes to keep the workers in their place.'

Such outdated quips sent a shock through Sylvia that was not entirely of dismay. Neither knew what it was about the party that made him decide she was the most fascinating woman there, and her to agree that he was the nth dishy man. He heard her telling someone, as he was meant to, that her husband was at a scientific congress in the States. Maybe there was a full moon, though he couldn't be bothered to check the almanack.

In the next few days he recalled her to mind many times. The coloured Polaroid shot stamped the fact that she had red hair, wore a grey skirt, and had black stockings. Or would he find they were tights? Her thinnish face was somewhat plain, except for the slight bow of vulnerable curiosity which shaped her lips. A week after the party he telephoned her, and she wondered why he'd waited so long.

When he fixed an appointment at the dentist's he didn't know whether to arrange it late in the day so that he could visit her first, or make an appointment early in order to receive some consolation afterwards for any discomfort undergone. Whatever he chose, she made him a mug of coffee, the ritual drink before the run upstairs.

He couldn't recall such keen pleasure during his other affairs, and wondered if he wasn't getting randier in his old age, or whether the prospect of the dentist's drill didn't act as an aphrodisiac. But maybe it had more to do with her, because she began undressing immediately – the ethnic sack over her head, revealing no bra (she hardly needed one) and the briefest of pants on the bedrail before he reached the third button of his shirt.

Decisions were complicated by her husband, but they managed it well, both agreeing that they did not want to cause pain either to him or to Denis's wife. 'What it really means is that we don't want any pain for ourselves,' he said.

She stared. 'I wouldn't like to be married to you.'

He didn't care to inform her that the feeling was mutual, left hand planing across her breasts. She only pulled the counterpane back, so that they made love on the blanket, and when afterwards he laid his head beside hers, unable any longer to support his own weight above her, the wool hair texture irritated his recently worked on, or about to be messed about with, tooth. While dressing, he took out a cigarette.

'Not in the bedroom.' It was all right downstairs, but even there she didn't approve, though her husband smoked those vile cigars now and again. She descended first, and he heard the abacus slide of the curtains, not sure what any sharp-eyed neighbour might think. 'Coffee?'

He sometimes wondered whether or not he was in love with her, but really in love, apart from just loving her. The longer the affair went on the less he seemed to know her, which was strange after having thought, at first sight, that he had taken in everything.

Her abrasive, almost nonchalant manner enthralled him, and he sometimes found it hard to decide what else did. She was cool enough while making love, even when she came. 'Please,' he said.

'Sugar?'

'Do you love me?' he couldn't help asking.

A lithe grey cat jumped on the table to get closer to the caged bird. She put it gently down, sprayed coffee powder in his mug. 'Of course.'

'Put in two, then. And more coffee.'

The liquid blackened. 'When's your next appointment?'

'I'll phone you later.' The cat tried again to get at the birdcage, dug its razor-points into his thigh and, he thought, fetched blood. He threw it off. 'When does hubbie come back?'

'Tomorrow, but only for a few days. And next week he goes to Japan.'

He closed the garden gate, thinking she ought to put some oil on the hinges, and walked down the street, far too old a campaigner to have left the car close to the house. A man, bearing the heavy duty briefcase that doubled for luggage and saved endless waits at airport carousels, passed him, and Denis recognised the click of the latch. He was a large bear-like man, going home after a week's work, to the comforts he had no doubt dreamed about from the moment of leaving.

He sweated so much at the assumption that her husband had

seen him coming out that the thumping toothache was forgotten even as far as the dentist's chair.

When he phoned to inform her about his next appointment a man answered, and Denis made the elementary mistake of placing the handset down instead of asking for someone he knew couldn't live there. The gaffe bothered him, but the following day Sylvia came on as usual. Even so, he was unnerved by a situation in which the husband returned a day before he said he would.

Glenda and Denis had often joked about having affairs, but she had been too busy, too tired all the time, too proud perhaps. She couldn't be bothered, had never got the hots to the extent of action, and in any case had the sort of luck that any handsome man who stopped on the motorway to help her change a wheel after a puncture would die of a heart attack from the effort. And Denis said he had the kind of luck that if he helped a beautiful woman by the roadside he would die from a massive cardiac arrest at forgetting to ask for her telephone number.

Their sixteen-year-old son Jonathan came in from school, for some reason even scruffier than usual. 'Glenda, I saw Dad this afternoon sitting in a car with a woman. I waved, but he didn't see me. I was on the bus.'

'It's not surprising, then, is it?' She felt the sort of palpitations as on discovering when she and Denis first met that they had birthdays in the same month.

'Who do you think it was?'

'Something to do with work, I suppose.'

Denis was home later than normal. 'I saw you in the car this afternoon,' she said, 'with a woman.'

He laughed. 'I wish you had,' and opened his briefcase to show his appointments book. 'I was in St Albans, looking at that new site. The traffic was atrocious. But I had to do it today because I must get my teeth seen to tomorrow.'

He wanted to ask what she had been doing in Swiss Cottage, but couldn't, poor man. She'd got him there. But if he really had been in St Albans, and she wouldn't put it past Jonathan to try mixing them up, since he'd been in a very bolshie mood this last six months, then she had as much as admitted to being where she didn't normally go. And she refused to make up a reason, in spite of that little boy pleading act which Denis put on.

Everything comes to those who don't make accusations, if they live long enough. So she hoped, arranging things into their relevant racks in the kitchen, just back from buying bagels and black bread, vegetables and fish, hopelessly overstocking in the last few weeks.

She opened and closed the refrigerator, always finding other items on the table. Yesterday his dentist telephoned to say that his next appointment had to be put off, which enraged him because he had kept a whole morning clear for it. He was more distracted than ever, a state which seemed to be catching. Perhaps the biscuit trade was going downhill. 'Not likely,' he said, with what she could only think of as a sly smile. 'If it was we'd put in more sugar, jack the price up a penny, and snuff ten grammes off the weight. If you can't shift biscuits in England, where can you?'

Coming back from a visit to her mother's she saw him in the call box on the corner. Funny place to be, with a functioning, telephone at home. 'I tried,' he said when she mentioned it, 'but the dialling tone seemed dead.'

She held the flimsy bit of plastic to her ear. 'It's all right now.'

When the engineer came he could find nothing wrong, and looked at her as if she was ready for the funny farm. Lying in bed that night – Denis wasn't snoring for a change – it was as if she could actually hear the full white moon, rustling, perhaps moving, trying to talk to her.

*

Denis had taken the green Volvo from the drive, as was his right. Her dented Mini at the kerb was ten years old, but except for a little rust around the left headlamp it was the best runabout she'd ever had, always refusing to let him buy her a Golf or a Peugeot.

She waited nearly a minute to get onto the main road, didn't know what she was doing, impelled by something over which she had no control but which in no way upset her. Curious as to where the mood would lead, she knew it was to do with Denis, but whether she wanted to meet him by accident, or trap him by design – well, she didn't know that, either.

Traffic was more fluid beyond Hampstead, ponds at the hilltop shimmering against the sky. In one way, to be blind was to be lucky, but today was different, as she parked between the trees a couple of hundred yards before the dentist's.

It takes all sorts to make a fool. She mulled on his lies, knowing him the worst kind of all, because he was finally a coward. Unable to believe his words, you could only rely on your eyes, which she regarded as unjust.

When he came out he walked, nonchalant and unaware, up the avenue, and took the first turning right. She was proud of her skill in following without being seen, as if excelling at a new kind of sport. His overconfidence was a great help, as was the fact that they had the same sign of the zodiac. Being finally alerted, more clues fell into place than she could ignore.

The house was on a curve, easily recognisable as the one he had gone into, though having to lag behind she couldn't see who had opened the door. Not that there was any need.

Jinking back onto the main road, a lorry screamed its horn, its enormous fender missing her by inches. The sign of the zodiac now gave her the decisiveness that only he had so far made use of – if you believed in that sort of thing. Inconvenient to be killed at such a time, but a miss was as good as a mile. The Town Hall wasn't far, a matter of minutes to get the names of the people who lived in the house. Easy enough then to find the telephone number.

'How was the traffic today?'

'Exhausting.'

'You poor darling. I think you need a holiday. You're working too hard.' She knew everything, but said nothing, not out of mercy or fear, or even inanition, but because she sensed things would end worse for him if she let it go on. Merely to say something would be no guarantee that he would stop the affair. 'Go to the dentist today?'

'Just to have them cleaned.'

'Isn't that the end of it?'

'Two more sessions. There'll be one next week, and another the week after.'

No need to make *her* call from the public box. Bound to be out of order should she try. If a woman answered she could press the trap down, but at a man's voice she would say what she had rehearsed a dozen times. What, however, was that? Easy to forget, but no doubt instinct would push her through. She felt a sense of purpose and excitement, though Denis couldn't notice how good she was getting at the game, which diminished it somewhat. When he emptied his briefcase she looked into the diary for his next dental appointment.

'Good morning. You don't know me, but your wife is very familiar with my husband, has been for some time. I think he'll be calling next Tuesday, at either nine or half-past ten. No, I can't say, I'm afraid. But you might see him.'

It was the only way to end it without Denis knowing that *she* had done so, by accident, as it were, the husband putting a stop to it if he was half a man, or to his wife if he wasn't.

The moment she put the telephone down she imagined the man so enraged at catching them 'at it' that he punched Denis's face and so ruined his bridgework that he needed another twelve months in the chair. In which case – she fell back laughing – he might be forced to change his dentist. Jonathan, scared by her hilarity, looked up from his homework. Well, it was too late now. All she had to do was wait for him to walk in holding his jaw together. She ran upstairs crying, shouting through her tears to Jonathan that he could get his own bloody tea.

'Menopause,' he scoffed, moving across the kitchen.

Nothing happened. She couldn't understand it. Denis went on being his own smiling self, even had the gall to say he needed a few extra appointments at the dentist's. There was nothing left but to sling the whole weighty emotional dossier into his face when he walked in the door. Break his bridgework on that. Impossible to love him, though she felt a vibrant liveliness in the last few days, so that last night it had been better in bed than for years, as if both sensed something about each other that they were discovering for the first time, which alone should have made him wary.

The doorbell sounded, someone selling things perhaps, a shape visible through the glass. Well, she could always scream, but opened the door. It wasn't raining, so she needn't ask him in.

'You don't know me, but we've spoken on the phone. Or you did, anyway.'

Tall and well-built, he almost obscured the lilac bush, wore a light overcoat, forty or fifty, she couldn't say, sparse fair hair and rather large features, lips indicating an attractive sense of humour, pale blue eyes spreading curiosity all through her. 'Come in, then.'

He carried a large briefcase, as if going on a trip, or returning from one. 'Do you mind if I take my coat off?'

She didn't.

'I wanted to see what kind of a person you were.'

Weakness wasn't from shock. She moved into the kitchen, and he followed, so she could only say: 'Coffee?'

His fundamental insolence seemed based on justifiable self-esteem. 'Any brandy? I've just come off the plane.' He lit a thin cigar. 'I followed your husband after he left my house last week, and found where you lived.'

She sat facing, hands over the coffee steam, glad that he had. 'A couple of schemers, aren't we?'

'Better the evil you know than the one you don't.'

He looked the ideal family man, and she asked; 'Aren't you afraid of going off the rails?'

'Oh no,' he said, 'I never go off the rails. I only change lines! I thought it would be more interesting to make your acquaintance than to spoil theirs. Everything has its price.'

'Really?' She blushed, which meant more than she liked to own, was more pleasant than it ought to be, but she thought she would get used to it, as he put a hand on hers.

'Your wife will wonder where you are, though.'

'The plane was delayed. It often is. Or she's too busy to wonder, don't you think? Ever since you called I've been thinking about you. It was your voice. So unhurried in what you were telling me. You must have known it was dynamite.'

'I suppose I did.' She actually laughed – carefree. She hadn't thought anything about him when they talked on the phone, but maybe that had done it. It was all for herself, for the first time in her life, and such single-mindedness had obviously drawn him.

'I could tell you were beautiful and attractive – and wonderfully intelligent.' He was like a blanket, but a warm blanket whose warp and weft knew everything about her when he put his arms over her shoulders and she went close.

Battlefields

A TANGLE OF MOTORWAYS around Mulhouse gave way to a winding and narrow ascent. Passing the foresters' house into a zone of alpine restfulness Hilda recalled that Victor had always gone home further south, through Belfort. He quoted each time from military history to the effect that *'le trou de Belfort'* was a natural invasion highway into France, and therefore the easiest way for a motorist to go, as if as soon as they were through the *'trou'* he could smell the Channel.

Victor had died two years ago, however, and these days she found a different way back from their cottage in the Ticino. To keep so rigorously to the habit of one route had proved he was growing old, which she supposed he was at seventy. She was that age now but felt twenty years younger, and plotting alternative routes on the map was a pleasure rather than a problem. With Victor as the driver she'd had little to say in the matter, nor felt the need to.

On looking at the boxy dark green estate car a month after the funeral, she couldn't imagine driving such distances in Europe, but there were two good reasons why she had to become confident at the wheel. The car had been so much an extension of Victor that it was a way of keeping him close, and the challenge of moving it around London had to be taken up since he was no longer here to insist on driving her. Cold needletips of rain had beat against her glasses as she looked at the large vehicle, door and ignition keys pressed so hard into her palm that she was sure a mark would be left there on loosening her hand. Which would be something else to remember him by, though the hurt soon went.

A green expanse of mountain pastures opened out at the summit of the Ballon d'Alsace, a great statue of Joan of Arc looking across folds of wooded land. The twenty kilometre ascent had been well worth it. Victor used to laugh at her navigation when she got them lost, but these days she almost never went wrong, stopping if in doubt and finding her way with confidence.

A cup of coffee at the hotel, and another ten kilometres of hairpin road, put her on the main track again. She coasted freely till held up by traffic in Épinal. Such congestion tired her, so she stopped in a layby a few miles beyond to eat a lunch of Swiss cheese, bread and an orange.

She decided to bypass a junction of seven roads in the middle of Neufchâteau, going more carefully for fear of missing the fork. Even so, she overshot to a village beyond, and opened the atlas to fix her position. Backing into a lane to turn seemed no problem, but maybe she was more tired than she thought, though it was only three o'clock. Or perhaps she became absent-minded in the hurry to reverse.

A crunch and tinkle of glass from the back of the long car told her that something had gone wrong. Getting out to look, a short post with a bulb on top had been obscured by tall grass, and she had knocked it halfway down, as well as denting the tailgate.

Vile words came, but what the hell? She got into the car and drove away to find the detour. Victor would never have done such a thing, and if he had would have waited an hour to give a full report to the local policeman.

Back at the correct byroad she felt young and irresponsible, heading across country from the scene of her misdemeanour and hoping no one in the village had noted her number. She disliked having any blemish on the car, but the insurance should take care of that. The notion of being a renegade on the run through France excited her. Maybe a gendarme would ask for her passport at a roadblock, or she would be caught at Calais and put into prison. What an extra bonus to her trip!

Following the green banks of the sluggish Meuse brought her to Verdun. The Hotel Bellvue outside the ramparts looked a good old fashioned house, so she carefully parked the car in a space beyond the pavement and went in to ask for a room.

Nine times out of ten, Victor had said more than once, people fall very quickly when they start to go down in life, lose their footing more disastrously than on going up. He also said that youth is but a short time of ten years, whereas age lasts at least thirty, if you were lucky. She recalled how they used to laugh at 'The Thoughts of Chairman Victor'.

His wisdom was true enough, she told herself, viewing the battlefields and monuments around Verdun next morning. At the sight of so much white stippling on the landscape – hectare after hectare of an unparalleled hecatomb – she felt weary and had to sit down. Gravel underfoot between reafforested trees, she walked to the remains of a concrete fortification, appalled by a unique visitation of death that could not be fought off.

The site had to be seen, but she didn't know what had drawn her to such a small area in which hundreds of thousands of men had been killed and maimed. Sculpture to the glory of a great nation was the theme, but the butchery of husbands and sons and fathers seemed futile and meaningless so long after the event. Yet she felt closer to France and the French, just as when Victor had taken her to the Somme's innumerable cemeteries she had been drawn closer to her own country.

The battle had taken place before she was born, but the tombs and sarcophagi made it seem as if it had happened only yesterday. She was saddened to think that all the little agonies of ordinary life were as nothing compared to this awful internecine slaughter. In spite of it, she ate her bread-and-ham lunch with more appetite than usual, and the coffee from her flask tasted so good that she lit a cigarette, mesmerised by the endlessly wooded view that tried to cover so much of the past.

Naked and exhausted, she got into bed, only waking in time for a bath before dinner. The freedom to stop two nights had been granted by the death of Victor, a thought she didn't like but had to face and, having digested it, saw no reason not to approve. The only time she felt a whiff of loneliness was when sitting in a hotel dining room and having no one to talk to, but a guidebook to glance at soon brought her back to being a woman traveller who had no problems – except that the picture of her scarred motorcar nagged from time to time.

Two French couples were talking quietly, which again convinced her what a pleasure it was to eat on her own. She loved the food and cleanliness at French hotels, choosing always the cheapest 'menu', which was usually sufficient. If there were dishes she hadn't eaten before, so much the better.

While pouring her first glass of red from the carafe she noticed a couple sitting in the far corner, and thought they might be German or Dutch, till the man said: 'Spread the napkin properly over your knees, then you won't make such a terrible mess.'

His tone was acerbic and startling, not brutal to begin with but loud enough to carry. She could only see his back, but his elderly wife placed in her direction had a leathery rather dead face, and straggly grey hair as if she hadn't been able to comb it properly. A white blouse did not help her pallor when she grimaced and tried to do as her husband commanded.

Steam from the tureen as soup was ladled into her plate made her salivate, hungry after her light lunch. She broke a roll and set it on the cloth. 'Hold your knife and fork properly, can't you?' the man called. 'Or do you want me to do it for you?'

A squeak of response merged with a placating smile at such hard sarcasm. Hilda thought she would throw her scalding soup over any man who talked to her like that. She supposed them to be forty years married, and he had got into the way of such behaviour through impatience and contempt. The woman smiled again, but as if suffering under his regime. No business of mine, Hilda told herself, trying not to eat more of the bread than she should, though the man's uncouthness disturbed her. All through the meal his talk was painful to hear, even the French couples glancing in their direction from time to time.

No marriage, she supposed, was free of memories for couples to punish each other with. Victor used to say, when she had caught him out, that she should ignore it, and come to bed each night as if for the first time. He would do the same with her, then there need be no upset about infidelity from either of them.

The man reached over to his wife so aggressively that Hilda imagined he was going to hit her. If he does I'll tell him to behave, in no uncertain terms. 'Keep your plate close,' he ranted, 'then you won't spill so much. And get on with it. You're eating too slowly.'

She shuddered while reading about that sanitised battlefield again in her guidebook. For months the town of Verdun had been bombarded, and she wondered what it was like to have an artillery shell burst in your apartment. All your precious living space of books, pictures, pottery and sentimental gew-gaws would be devastated. The most telling vision was of a bunch of flowers spattered over shredded curtains.

'*Can't* you do *anything* right?' he demanded when the woman dropped her fork. On telling the waitress to bring another he spoke in a quiet and polite tone obviously never used with his wife.

Listening to such a boor ruined Hilda's meal. Men like him turned good wine sour. Who did he think he was, making her ashamed of being English? He didn't, she laughed, though there was no let up to his high-pitched nag. The disturbance made her eat more slowly so as to avoid indigestion, which meant they left first – but not without a finale from him.

'Now you've dropped your napkin.' He bullied her into picking it up, making her even more beaten and pathetic on going out.

I must get up at the crack of dawn, Hilda decided, so that I don't have to listen to that again. Her day touring the battlefields had been so interesting, and now this! The meal had been good, after all, and she would complete it by going to the bar for a Cointreau. Victor had hated sitting at bars, but she liked their air of glamour, and what remarks might come from the barman. In any case Cointreau hadn't agreed with Victor's dyspepsia.

A cigarette helped to make the sweet and peppery liqueur delicious. The barman had nothing to say, and then was busy elsewhere, so she sat in peace and silence. She and Victor as a couple had grown to treat each other as if each was a different country bound together by viable diplomacy, who might even quarrel over the most basic issues but never declare war. As such they had survived together.

Her finger end burned on putting the cigarette stub in the ashtray when she saw the man come in who had mercilessly harangued his wife throughout dinner. The counter wasn't much more than a couple of metres long so of course he had to take the stool next to hers, then asked for a double brandy and began to fill a large curved pipe from a tin of English tobacco.

She wanted to lambast him but first needed to get a better look at him. He was in his late sixties, she supposed, seeing heavy lines of worry on his brow. His face was broad, and a moustache bristled when he brought the glass to his lips with slightly shaking hands. The odour of his pipe reminded her of Victor, which she found to her surprise made her think even less of the man.

He wore old fashioned clothes, a pale green shirt and camel coloured waistcoat, a cravat, hacking jacket, brown twill trousers and highly polished brogues, as if when he was twenty someone had left him in their will half a dozen of long-wearing everything on the assumption that his weight and character would never change. Since it hadn't, he must have been a man of habit from early on.

She had the dreadful feeling that he wanted to talk. Her Cointreau was only half sipped, but she wouldn't be driven away. 'Thank God she got herself into bed,' he said. 'Now I can have a quiet smoke and a drink.'

'She certainly has a great deal to put up with.'.

'And well you might say so,' he responded grimly.

She wanted to keep quiet but couldn't help herself. 'I would have left you years ago.'

'Would you?'

She wasn't deceived by the puzzled tone he put on, certainly not enough to damp her rage at having strayed into conversation. 'I've never heard such dreadful bullying.'

He smiled, seeming almost human, even more so when it was followed by an expression close to pain. 'I love her, you see . . .'

'Well, if you call that love.'

'I don't expect you to understand, but I'm trying to get her back into shape.'

Hilda turned away with contempt, yet not liking herself for letting it control her. 'That's certainly what it sounded like.' Such people were unregenerate, so there was no use getting upset. At least he stopped talking, though she feared he was only making up his mind what to say next.

'You think I'm a villain, and maybe I shouldn't tell you, but she had a stroke three months ago, and this is the only way to do it. She's actually improved enormously over the past week. I suppose it does sound dreadfully callous, though.'

Tears on his cheeks seemed as if they had come out of the skin itself. He took a neatly folded handkerchief from his lapel pocket to wipe them. 'She loved France, and asked me to bring her. She's done much better on our first week of touring. I'm taking her around the battlefields tomorrow. She used to teach history.'

Hilda's face burned with contrition. His pain passed to her, and she touched his hand. 'I'm sorry. I thought . . .'

'Yes, I know.' He stopped, then: 'We've been happy all our lives. Still are, and she knows what's going on. I'm determined to get her as near back to normal as I can. I don't want to lose her, you see.'

Since it was obvious he wanted to go on talking she asked for another Cointreau. 'I'm sure you don't.'

The see-saw of euphoria and misery joined them for a few moments. Hope keeps tragedy and loss at bay, she thought, and he was well-qualified to fight. His nightly brandy calmed him. 'We're battling every inch of the way.'

By eight o'clock she was paying her bill. The man upstairs had been drilling his wife into her clothes when she passed their door. An impulse to knock and wish them well was quashed, whether from kindness or cowardice she couldn't decide, thinking them best left alone in their struggle.

She had planned to walk around the town of Verdun but went onto the motorway for Paris. Le Havre was the place to make for, to take a boat from there. Navigation would be simple, no reversing necessary. She would also avoid those other battlefields seen with Victor, memories unwelcome in her sombre mood.

The landscape of France dispelled such feelings, and she pondered on the joys of freedom as the car ran smoothly along the highway, thinking to spend a couple of days in Normandy before taking the boat home.

Call Me Sailor

'CALL ME SAILOR,' he said, as if there had been a saint of the kind way back in history and it was the proper first name for a man like him. Such a moniker must fit somewhere, and time would tell, though women collecting their kids from school saw what a suitable name it was as he stood by the pillar, enjoying a short pipe of tobacco such as no shop ever sold, and looking at white clouds above the slate roofs of the estate as if to foresee the malice of any weather on its way.

The tall leathery-faced man replaced by Sailor had given no hint of his departure, such birds of passage being soon forgotten, until one morning Sailor stood by the gate in dark blue dungarees as if it had been his post for years.

Short white hair came to a line at the back of his neck, and his face was of such pinkness from being scrubbed every morning that the features had little time to settle into place until the afternoon. Prominent lips didn't go much towards handsome, they all agreed, and there was little definite shape to his nose, but the lit up blue of his eyes suggested absolute ease with himself, and confidence in getting unlimited trust from others.

Such eyes shone as if he would like to own any woman who looked at him, though most saw him as no more than an amenity for which they were grateful. Some regarded his smile as too facile, a turn of unhappiness to the underlip noted by those whose lives hadn't been of the calmest.

Kids took to him because his authority gave them a frisson of fear, which brought obedience. The previous caretaker, with his permanently worried face, saw them as grains of sand slipping

185

through his fingers into danger before he could get them safely across the pavement, but Sailor let them know he was their shepherd, his smouldering briar indicating the lollipop woman at the roadside: 'They're all yours, Madame! Take 'em away!' Out of his orbit, they spread alone or with whoever met them into the various drives and crescents of the estate.

Ann noticed him on her way to get fags and a paper from the little Pakistani supermarket on the main road, even before she had agreed to look after Teddy Jones while his mam and dad went on a ten-day bargain holiday to Turkey. The job wasn't as easy as she'd thought. Six-year-old Teddy was a cheeky little swine, and she had only to go into the garden to shake crumbs for the birds to come back and find him opening cupboards and pulling doilies all over the floor.

If you wanted the house to stay neat you couldn't let him out of sight for a second. While she was vacuuming the bedrooms he hauled her dictionary off the shelf and scrawled its pages with a biro, for which he got a slap across the face. He could tell Bill and Edna what he liked, because after they had gone she heard that other neighbours had turned them down flat when asked to take charge of him.

On the second afternoon Teddy ran from the school gate like a limb of Satan and headed straight for the road. Mrs Grant the lollipop woman, about to step out and halt the traffic, was touching her glasses into their proper focus when a black low-slung hatchback came at such a rate that, everyone agreed, if kids had been on the crossing the school would have commemorated a day of tragedy for ever and ever.

Teddy was blank of mind, and nobody could guess the paradise he was running to. Nor had they time to think of him as a goner, because like everything that happened too quick it had already happened.

Nor could anyone swear they saw Sailor move. For someone close to sixty he made lightning look slow. If Teddy survived to be an adult he would probably never recall the not ungentle arm holding him inches from speeding bumper. Maybe he thought it was a game, even when Sailor, once they were clear, put the biggest fist he had seen to his face and said: 'Run like that again, lad, and you'll get this for your dinner. And not with custard on it, either!'

Something must have got through, because Teddy's smile didn't reach full growth, though he squirmed free to strut by the lollipop woman, who was still too shocked to give him the guidance he obviously needed to keep him in the land of the living.

Ann saw it all, and got hold of his arm for the sort of shaking that would send him into the middle of next week and back again without him knowing where he had been, but it turned short and feeble because there didn't seem much in his young head to rattle. 'You stupid little thing. Didn't you see that car?'

'What car?'

'I got his number.' Mrs Grant, as good as her word, wrote it on a pad. 'There was four young lads inside, so you can bet it was nicked.'

Sailor tapped his pipe against the wall and put a boot on the dottle. 'They'll get away with it, though. Nobody cares enough to put 'em inside for five years.' He went back to his stand at the gate. 'I'd hang the buggers. I'd let 'em know life's a battlefield.'

Teddy gripped her hand for comfort, called her auntie on the way home, and wanted to know what was for tea. She blamed herself, thinking that if she had been at the gate two minutes earlier he would have run to her instead of going like a newborn bull across the pavement. Bill and Edna would have screamed blue murder with grief if he had been killed or injured, so it was thanks to God he hadn't. Only on opening the front gate did she realise the caretaker hadn't been properly thanked.

She tucked Teddy into bed and told him a story about a family who lived in a copse on the edge of the estate, of how the favourite came running out of school and got killed by a car. When he began to cry she read nursery rhymes till his head fell sideways, then eased him snugly into the sheets.

In the living room she switched on the telly. 'You'd do better reading a book. Or why don't you knit me a scarf? Better still, come out with me for a walk.' Sidney had wanted her to talk. He always said she didn't talk enough, and now he was three years dead she regretted the time wasted on silence.

He had been chief clerk in government offices downtown, and when he laid his head on the desk, one afternoon, its weight was such as to stay there till he was put lifeless onto a stretcher. The placid black tom called Midnight brushed her ankles, and for months after Sidney's death had roamed the house looking for him. Still not one for talking to people, she conversed in silence with herself, as if it were her only means of thought. The cat slept on the hearth, the black hump suggesting it hoped to see Sidney on waking up, which was more than she could say for herself. All the same, she imagined the smell of Sidney's tobacco, and recalled two unopened tins she hadn't had the heart to take from the cupboard upstairs.

'That was good, what you did yesterday.'

She had come early so as to thank him properly. In mid-April it was impossible to tell whether the wind was blowing blossoms or it was about to snow. 'I never saw anything so quick.'

He stood away from the pillar, as if her compliment came from an officer of the watch. 'He was lucky.' He boomed at Teddy: 'Weren't you? Nearly had to carry you home in a plastic bag, didn't we? People would have thought you was a goldfish pulled out of a pile-up on the motorway!'

He squirmed from Sailor's grip, and Ann fastened his coat,

sending him along the asphalt path towards the school door. 'You saved his life, and that's a fact.'

'They teach you to look sharp in the Navy.' His blue eyes burned her, and she turned away, yet didn't want to leave. Other women would soon be at the gate with their children. 'I was in from a boy, and ended up master artificer. If you weren't quick you were dead. It was a harder school than this one.'

Half a bottle of whisky, or maybe rum, would have made a fair present, but it only occurred to her now. 'Do you like being a caretaker?'

He plaited his fingers and pressed so that every knuckle cracked, signalling embarrassment at her interest. 'It's a doddle, but don't tell anybody, or they'll kick me out and hire a robot. I was made for it. I have a cold sluice at six, and start at seven to fix the heating. Then I make sure everything's shipshape before the kids swarm in. I knock off at eleven, and don't go on again till they come out. There's a bit more to do when they've gone home, but it suits me.'

Any ounce of trouble in his life must have been taken very easily. He liked to talk, and she to listen, but she let him get on with his work, and went to buy something for Teddy's tea, apart from his favourite sausages or hamburger steaks.

On Teddy's final afternoon she got to the school even before Mrs Grant at her lollipop station. Sailor was filling his pipe from a leather pouch as he sway-walked between the trees of the playground. She had put on lipstick, changed into a white blouse buttoning at the neck, and switched into a skirt instead of everyday slacks. The mirror had shown her skin as smoother since Sidney's death, though it could be the light, or wishful thinking that said dark skin kept its texture more than fair. At forty there was only a fleck of grey in her tied back ponytail.

She took the two tins of Gold Block from her plastic bag. 'I thought I would give you these. My husband bought them three years ago, so it might have gone off. I don't like things going to waste.'

Whorls of smoke drifted by her eyes, distorting what she tried to see. 'Gave up the weed, did he?'

'He had a heart attack.'

A woman teacher popped kids out of the door like beads from the end of a string. 'It's just the sort of tobacco I like. A lovely gift, for an old matelot.'

'Have it, then.'

Thinking he would take her hand, she drew it away and hoped he hadn't noticed, but his eyes saw everything. The lollipop woman stopped a bus and two cars, letting the first group across. Ann looked over his shoulder for Teddy. 'I'm glad you can use it.'

Eyes lost their glitter as the head came close with its odour of aftershave and tobacco, and mint on his breath. A neat cut from the razor embellished his cheek like a small decoration. 'I pack it in at seven.' He must have known she willed him to go on, even if only to get it over with. 'After half an hour's spruce up I light off to The Black's Head for a noggin or two. Why don't you come and sit with me?'

For all he knew she might have married again. She hadn't, but the longer you grieved the more you got used to living alone, and didn't fancy getting bogged into anyone else's life. On the other hand what harm was there in going for a drink? She felt warm and flattered to be asked but said, as if sixteen and knowing it never did to say yes the first time: 'I have something on tonight.'

He was too much a man of the world to let it bother him. 'Another occasion, then.' The light came back in his eyes as he turned to watch the children, sorting out Teddy as if he was special, and bringing him towards her.

*

Teddy sensed the subtle borders of aggravation while playing with the cat, and never drew out its briar-like claws. She was pleased he was learning, and well enough behaved by the end of his stay that when Edna called over the fence to say they were home she felt as sorry to see him go as he, for a few seconds anyway, was reluctant. They came round to give her the twenty pound note promised for Teddy's keep, and a metal teapot covered in funny writing as a present from Istanbul.

The house was emptier so she talked to the cat. When it didn't seem to listen she muttered to herself. She couldn't be going scranny, she told her face in the mirror, because she knew she was doing it.

The hands of the carriage clock were afraid to move, though the precision of its time-keeping fingers and metal case kept her in mind of Sidney. He had handed her the receipt for safety, which showed the clock had cost two hundred pounds: 'It's better these days to have a pedigree object in the house than money in the bank.'

Such a prized item kept its value by giving satisfaction to look at, and pleasure to turn in the hand, more loyal as a clock than Sidney had been as a husband. If there had been any twinges in his unreliable heart he would have firebacked all that was in the shoebox at the bottom of his wardrobe.

The first letter leafed out let her know what he had been up to with a girl in the office. Rage blended with grief to keep the shock going. His constant gallantry of calling her the perfect wife damaged her forever. The perfect wife should be good enough for any man unless, being so perfect, she was too much for him to tolerate. No one could be the perfect wife, and he had only said she was so as to blunt any suspicion of his pathetic gallivanting. The real torment was that she had never thought to wonder.

Her chance of an affair with someone where she worked as a receptionist had been turned down with more contempt than necessary. She regretted it, having fancied him enough, though deceiving Sidney wouldn't have been easy. He was too well aware of all the dodges, and such behaviour was easier for a man. When she lost her job he talked her into working part time at the local library, but last year they too had cut down on staff. At least he had left her with a pension.

After he died she had the telephone ripped out, and sometimes wished she hadn't, though who would call her these days? Because Sidney had used it to talk to his girlfriend when she was out shopping, she couldn't stand the sight of it and thought good riddance.

The sun in a glow of turquoise and yellow over the opposite roofs dimmed the living room, and she didn't relish pushing in the telly button to look at pictures so far removed from her feelings. A drink at The Black's Head would be nice, but if she met Sailor what would she have to say?

She went up to the bedroom to see if anybody was there, then came down to check the kitchen and clothes' cupboards. Nobody was. A rattle of the curtains shut off the first star of the evening, and a man beyond the hedge cycling home from work. Being shut into her domain after dark was a relief, but her legs wouldn't let her sit down. She put on her coat to go out and meet the chip and burger van trawling the estate for trade. A mutton chop in the fridge could wait, and veg in tight plastic would still be fresh tomorrow.

Clouds moved in and it looked like rain, but the smell of an unusual supper made hunger her first real sensation of the day. A police siren, warbling like someone fleeing the pains of hell, joined a chorus of ambulance and fire engines clearing the road to save souls who had not yet been there. She tightened the belt of her coat and hurried on in case the van pulled down its shutters and went elsewhere.

Half a dozen people talked while they queued. She stood on the pavement, her brain not latching into their words. A car slowed to take the corner, and there was still enough light to spot the peculiar sway-walk of Sailor crossing the road as if they had a date. He had on ordinary trousers and an open bomber jacket over a white shirt, which she smiled at the idea of him ironing. She noted a tie fastened in place by a gold pin, and shoes instead of the boots he worked in.

He sensed her amusement and said: 'I haven't seen you collecting your boy from school lately.' Foistering young Teddy onto her must be his flattering way with women. Another was not to give time for comment: 'The old chip van's useful for supper a couple of times a week. Not that I mind cooking, though never a meal as takes more than half an hour. Life's too short to stand long at a stove.'

Any woman could have told him that. 'What do you cook?'

He put a hand on her back when the queue moved and, as if to excuse the liberty said: 'Sausages, If I can find good 'uns. Sometimes steak, or chops, but always soup first. Or I might make a stew that lasts a day or two. Then a tinned currant pudding with treacle or custard on top. Or a bit of fruit: I must have dessert, and it's nice to ring the changes.'

'Don't you ever cook fish?'

His face turned into a gargoyle of distaste. 'Fish eat people. They love drowned sailors.' When the couple in front were served he took another opportunity to put a hand on her shoulder, which she accepted as friendly. 'Here you are, duck, it's your turn now.'

She got her bundle and wished him good night. He held out a hand to be shaken, a mauler so big it covered hers. They now knew where to find each other, but he might have a wife in every port.

After emptying Midnight's supper into his dish a week later she went to the chip van but Sailor didn't turn up. Perhaps the drizzle put him off. Ten minutes went by, and she wondered why she was getting her feet wet and letting the fish and chips lose their warmth in her hands.

*

He said when they had been served, not caring that the chip man and two bikers would hear, and using the van's light to make sure she saw his earnest blue eyes: 'Why don't we go back to my abode and eat our stuff there?'

On the way she was unable to see what was in it for either of them, and stayed silent, holding his burger and chips bundle while he stooped to fit the key in the lock. In the entrance hall a line of footwear from wellingtons to bedroom slippers shone ready for pulling on. Luckily his irony was obvious when he told her in the small kitchen not to look too closely at the dust. She'd never been in a neater place. He switched on a big old fashioned radio she hadn't seen since being a kid in the fifties. The green eye glowed and news seemed to come from every wall at once. 'Haven't you got a television?'

'I can see all the pictures I want in my head, without even having to switch on. There are plenty I don't like, as well.' She didn't ask what they were. Scoured pans rested on a white formica top, the empty sink polished, plates and dishes wiped and stacked on a shelf. He put their coats on hangers and took them to a hook in the hall. 'I had ants when I moved in, but they didn't last long.'

It wasn't cold, but he popped the gas fire into light, the spent match going into a glass dish special for the purpose. 'The walls are nice and clean,' she said.

He carried plates, knives and forks from the serving hatch, as well as bread and butter, and a huge green enamel pot of tea. 'I can't abide paper, so I stripped it off as soon as I got here, and painted the walls.' He set the meal on a card table because the large one was covered with an unmade jigsaw puzzle. 'It's got a thousand pieces, so I don't suppose I'll ever finish it.'

A few edges and three corners were fitted together, and her fingers itched to work on it. 'What's it of?'

He swallowed some food. ' "The Battle of Trafalgar". I've had it for years. I did some at my last place – I worked in a factory then

– but I had to put it back in my ditty bag for the move. One day I hope to see poor old Nelson being shot!'

She appraised the room. 'You certainly know how to take care of yourself.' Sidney had been waited on hand and foot, but he had been out at work all day. So had she, some of the time, but that didn't seem to matter.

He shook the breadboard over his plate, mopping up crumbs and fat by pushing a crust around with his fork. 'I wouldn't be much of a man if I didn't. I can't stand untidiness. There was a bloke I was stationed with in Trincomalee . . .'

Taking no further note of time, he talked about India, China and Japan, of Temples and places she would never see, beaches of white sand running for tens of miles with no one there but himself, palm trees you had to be careful when walking under otherwise a coconut would fall on your napper, of Oriental cities so crowded you fought your way from point to point.

She listened till the tin clock on the shelf said a quarter to ten, though felt no inclination to leave, liked him in fact for talking so much, recalling how Sidney often said of her long silences: 'I can never tell what goes on in that mind of yours. I'd give more than a penny for your thoughts.' Maybe he was fishing to know whether she suspected his carryings on, but even if she had she wouldn't have talked, because it was no use wasting your breath till certainty struck you dumb. As for blurting out her thoughts, such as they were, you always had to have something that was yours and nobody else's. Tell a stranger what was in your head and it didn't matter, but if you blabbed everything to your husband you would soon have no self to call your own. More often than not she considered her thoughts either too vague to grasp or too daft to mention.

'The only thing I lack here,' Sailor was saying, 'is a garden. I used to dream of having one when I was at sea, though there was little time for dreaming. I'd fancy the spade going into English soil, mixing it with wood ash from a fire, and planting rose bushes. I've applied for an allotment, but they're like gold these days.'

He looked beyond her and she wondered where to, what palm tree shoreline, or wet cornfield in summer. 'I used to smell woodsmoke when I was sweating to death up and down the China coast. English woodsmoke, not smoke from dung fires the Indians make. Once as a lad I made a fire at the edge of a field and sat trying to keep it burning, because most of the wood was still alive. After it got going, a bloke came out of his allotment and asked if he could have some of my ash for his garden. I wanted to say no. "I'll only take a little," he said. "It won't affect the fire. It'll be marvellous for my soil." So he scooped up the ash with his trowel and bucket, and left me a nice clean fire but no ash at all. In five minutes it'd gone out, and wouldn't start again. Talk about barefaced robbery! Never trust anybody, I thought, as I walked home.'

'You've had a very full life,' she said, getting in a few words of her own. 'And you don't seem to have many regrets, either.'

He shook his head. 'I did get married when I was young. We had a daughter, but after cat-and-dogging it for a few years I threw in the towel and went back to the Navy.' By his tone she sensed a tale he wouldn't like going into. 'Vain regrets never did anybody any good,' he said.

Her marriage had passed as if in ten minutes, with nothing worth half as much telling as the least of Sailor's yarns. Even if there had been she was too much at ease in his cosy den to bring them up. A man who went out of his way to talk to a woman was unusual whether or not it was because he needed to. She repaid him by listening, and in any case enjoyed it. Maybe he was only talking to be polite, but nothing mattered as long as they felt at ease.

The tot of whisky he splashed out for the road caused a joyous giddiness on the way home, and before going to bed she took the framed photographs of Sidney off the shelves and put them in a box under the stairs.

She saw what a precise and careful driver he was in his banger of an Austin Countryman when he took her to his favourite pub in Radford. They sat at a corner table. 'I used to come here in my younger days,' he said, 'and that's a long time ago. What I would like to know, though,' and he leaned close to ask, 'is whether or not you'll marry me.'

'It's a bit sudden, Sailor.' It wasn't. She had imagined it already. He was no longer young, a person who knew his age as well as his mind.

His pint sank to the halfway mark in one long swallow: 'Everything always is.'

Sidney often said you never knew your mind till you had made a mistake, and who would know better, though she didn't like thinking of him at the moment. 'Still, if you let such a notion put you off, you'd never do anything,' he said with that possessive smile. 'Human beings aren't rats in traps.'

She felt comfortable with Sailor, who had grown used to her silences and never tried to disturb them, but it was difficult to say a straight yes when she so much wanted to. 'I'll need a few days.'

'I wouldn't respect you if you didn't.'

It was hard for both, and she wanted to dissolve the tension by getting the matter done with. She might not be clear in her mind even if a whole year went by. She liked his proposal because to marry him would mean there'd be no more big decisions to make. 'Now you've asked me, don't you want a day or two to think about it?'

He seemed surprised. She was questioning his sincerity. 'Once something gets into my head and I say it, my mind's made up.' Two people suited for each other would sound foolish uttering romantic words, but he must have read her thoughts when he went on: 'I fell in love with all I didn't know about you, as well as with what I plainly saw. I can't say fairer than that. I can guarantee though that the rest will take care of itself. I might not be much of a catch, but I'll look after you, you can be sure.'

Sidney had never spoken such heartfelt and reassuring words, and it suddenly struck her that you always had to wonder what someone was hiding when they accused you of never talking. Sailor's warm hand came onto her wrist, and she met the full blue of his candid eyes as if for the first time. 'I do love you, Sailor.'

'Well, I hoped to hear that, and I can't tell you how happy it makes me. Another thing though is that there's more than one way of answering my question, so take your time over it. When we've had another drink we can go to my place for a cup of coffee. Then I'll escort you home.'

She let on about her plans with Sailor while talking to Edna by the front gate.

'Sounds all right,' Edna said, 'but you've got to be careful, duck. If he is a sailor he might have women all over the place.'

'How can anybody know about anybody?' Ann wondered, convinced she knew all she wanted to know of him.

'I've seen him a few times at the school,' Edna went on, 'and he looks a nice enough chap.' You couldn't put anybody off what they were dead set on doing, and who was she in any case to prophesy how things would work out? All you could say was good luck to people, and let them get on with it.

On signing the book Ann saw that Sailor's first name was Paul, which was so far out of kilter with how she regarded him that Sailor it would be forever. Bill and Edna, with Teddy, had come into town as witnesses, and Teddy cried because they hadn't brought Midnight, tears slopping onto his best suit, till Sailor picked him up and promised he would see the lucky cat soon enough.

A few packs of confetti were scattered over the couple as they came out of the registry office, a photographer semaphoring from behind his tripod. Ann in her smart costume smiled arm in arm with Sailor, thinking everything was good today, though she wanted it to be over since the best was yet to come.

As if just back from six months at sea, Sailor took her in his arms for their first public kiss. He stared into the lens towards an oblivion he alone could see, facing his chemical reproduction in a dark three-piece suit, and tie whose small knot showed off the impeccably ironed shirt. Getting spliced, said his stance, was a serious matter, and it wouldn't do to lose your soul over it by not looking tiptop.

Frank Orston came with a walnut-cased wall clock as a present from the school, and they listened to its chimes in the living room to a round of double whiskies. Sailor leaned against the mantel-piece, his glass at arm's length towards Ann. 'Here's to the deed that's going to last all my life. And to commemorate the occasion in proper style I'll take the lid off the champagne.'

He aimed the cork at the ceiling like a master gunner, all eyes upturned to the as yet invisible mark he might leave there. The explosion sent Teddy running for cover behind the settee.

After the bubbly it was wine, or whatever choice of liquor from bottles ranged along the sideboard. Bill, a lean long-jawed man with coal black hair, forked up ham and salad. 'A penny bun costs tuppence now – or so my father used to say.' He held back a ribald addition because he wasn't sure how Sailor would take it.

Ann and Edna sat on the settee, a bottle of Cyprus sherry on the small round table between them. Midnight leapt onto the tele-vision, and Ann was glad Sailor stroked him into a purr. She lost count how many times he asked if she was all right, loved him for wanting to make her happy, and knew their marriage was forever. The romantic uncertainty of the night to come made her feel as she had when leaving the office in her teens to meet a boyfriend for a stroll beyond the bus terminal, ending by all but going the whole way in the darkest part of the wood.

Tired of playing with Midnight, Teddy clamoured for whisky, and Sailor let a couple of canary drops into a glass of water. 'This'll make you drunk in no time,' which sent him tottering around the room and slurring his words.

Mrs Grant straightened him up when he fell. 'You are a silly lad.'

'Life's not worth living,' Sailor said, 'unless you treat it as one long holiday, whether or not you have to work. So now we'll cut the cake.'

With so much food and drink the party went on till after dusk, Teddy asleep on his father's shoulder when Edna said it was time to leave. After they had gone every plate and cup in the house needed washing, and Sailor filled the sink with suddy water to get them clean. Ann's energy came back in putting the food away, the fridge packed with dishes covered in Cellophane.

Sailor kissed her as she went by, looking at the clock so that he could, she thought, decently surmise the hour for going to bed. 'I suppose there are certain things I should tell you now that we're married, my love.'

Matched with what she ought to say would cancel both sides out, though she was pleased by his offer. No ripple should pass through their perfect day. 'It doesn't matter. Nothing matters now except us, Sailor.' She kissed his worried face till the boyish smile came back, and when he led her upstairs the flush of eagerness was on both their faces. Drifting to sleep against his naked back, she knew him to be a man who could make a woman happy.

Ann offered to read the map but Sailor said he had given it a good looking over before she got out of bed. 'All I do is set course southwest and keep my hands at the tiller. Towns are like islands, and I'll stay clear of them when I can. It's the same as going across the ocean to me.'

In the afternoon he steered his black Austin Countryman up the gravel drive of The Tummler Hotel, and a naval-looking man with a thick beard took their cases in. After approving the room with its four-poster bed they came down to a set tea in the lounge. A solid black-boxed body of a dog, with a jutting black box of a mouth, waddled lamely from under the next table for a piece of Sailor's scone. 'It's funny getting a whiff of the sea again. Did you smell it, when I opened the window upstairs?'

'Let's go for a walk when we've finished. You can have a paddle if you like!'

'No fear. I swam in it once, and not for fun.' She was glad he was fuelling himself against the memory, eating to live. 'We'll take a look at it, though.'

Pale stones clashed underfoot. 'I wouldn't like to walk ten miles on this.'

She kissed his cheek. 'Nor me.'

Cold gusts struck when they descended the hogsback from which to view the water. She watched the subtle guidance of wings on gulls riding the thermals. Sailor didn't like the muffler-ring around the white button of the sun. 'Stand behind me, love, if the wind starts chilling you.'

An isolated white cloud on the horizon rose like an iceberg out of the nondescript. 'I shan't see anything, then.'

'Let's walk down the bank. It'll shield us both.' He took her hand, finding dry patches along the muddy path. Stopping by a gate, they looked inland up a hillside of sheep. He breathed heavily, as if the walk had worn him out. Or maybe the sight of the sea had put on a year or two. She took his arm. 'You're tired, sweetheart, after driving all that way.'

A white-topped wave, neat as a quarter mile straight-edge, crumbled on cue at a line of pale cliffs, making way for another behind. She was surprised to see what little distance they were from the hotel, smoke at the cold end of September coiling out of its chimney. 'Maybe you're right,' he said.

He stretched full length in an armchair by the lounge fire, while she read an old Georgette Heyer from the shelf, dozing towards sleep. Sailor touched her arm. 'Come on, my love, let's have a drink before dinner.'

Two double whiskies were followed by pints of lager with his platter of roast beef, Yorkshire pudding, boiled and roast potatoes, cabbage, carrots and peas. For her he ordered a half bottle of iced champagne, which she relished to the final fizz with the Dover sole and sorbet that followed.

He finished as if he hadn't had a hot dinner for months, though for a big man it wasn't so much. 'You were hungry,' she said.

'Must be the sea air.'

Tramping the humps and hollows of Maiden Castle they looked both ways, at land and sea. Sailor's energy was renewed, and when she lagged over the thick damp grass he put out a hand for her to catch up. 'I don't like the sea anymore.'

'Why is that?'

'I've seen too many people drown in it. Hundreds, though you had to expect that. I've taken against it in my old age.'

You wouldn't think so, the way he talked with Ben the manager, who had been on a destroyer in the Falklands. They were locked into each other's tales, alternating up to midnight with pots of beer and measures of whisky. Ann, content with her book, was happy to recall Edna's doubt that Sailor had been a sailor. The only other guests were a couple who stayed most of the time in their room.

A week at Scarborough with Sidney had been as nothing compared to her days at The Tummler Hotel. Sailor was a man hard to know, but love was more enduring with someone you couldn't entirely fathom. He let nothing worry him, though he was far from simple, suggesting that he had been through hard times after all. From thinking all men were more or less like Sidney she now knew there were different sorts in the world and that Sailor was one of them.

He was relaxing to be with, and as long as she went on being curious she would never stop loving him.

The first thing Sailor brought from his flat at the school was a coat of arms of his last ship served on. Then came his precious life's papers, and a Japanese tea service which he set on the living-room sideboard. 'That's been round the world a time or two, but it's found a home at last.'

A paper-thin cup held to the light showed a Geisha girl with a parasol. 'Isn't it lovely?' She polished the front-room table and laid out his thousand piece jigsaw puzzle.

'We'll do it between us,' Sailor said, 'in our idle moments.'

She wondered when they might be, because like all true mariners he cherished his drink. Most nights they went to the pub in Radford, sat among smoke and beer fumes at a small round table in the saloon bar. She was happy to be with Sailor because he was so obviously glad to be with her. She drank her half pint of Midland ale, while he bandied with his friends, or held her hand and told stories of his travels, pints going like magic. He ordered a whisky for them both before the towels went on.

'Will you be all right driving?'

He steered away from the kerb. 'With you in the car we're as safe as houses. We'll be back to our bread and cheese, and a nice pot of tea, in no time.'

When she stayed at home one night with the cat and watched television Sailor came back with flowers. 'Where did you get them, so late?'

'There's always somebody selling 'em.'

She loved it when he brought her little gifts, and told him so.

'You're worth it, my love.' He filled a vase with water in the kitchen, then drew her onto his knees. 'First, I think of you as would like to have them. Second, I think of the poor old drudge as comes round trying to sell 'em. Third, I get selfish and think of me who'd like to do a good turn to the seller, and an even better turn to the woman I love and who I know would appreciate it. That way I get credit for everything. You can call it selfishness, if you like, but more things fit mortise and tenon in this life than you might think.'

'You're my young man, and I love you, Sailor.' He was sixty, but could be any age, always sure of himself in knowing what he wanted while rarely admitting he needed anything. He was also a man of habit and regularity which, he said, made life easier for all concerned, and she liked that.

He laid the table for supper, and lit the gas for the kettle, though she told him after more kisses to fill it before putting it on the flame. 'You must have had a drop more than usual.'

The screw top of the pickled onions was no match for his big hands. He stabbed in his fork. 'I'll tell you what, though . . .'

She laughed. 'You've been thinking.' He sometimes was, behind those blue eyes. 'What about, Sailor?'

'I'm beginning to feel I've done enough work in my life. I'll be glad when I've finished at school.' He put a sliver of cheese into her mouth. 'Would you mind if I started taking my ease a bit?'

'I thought you'd still got two years to do.'

'So I have, but there are times when I wonder if it's worth waiting for.' The shade of uncertainty was a welcome confession of intimacy. 'I never do anything in a hurry,' he said in his usual voice, 'though even if I don't wait there should be enough money coming to us.'

On their wedding day his account had shown five hundred pounds, and how much remained was his business. He never enquired about her savings, which had been more than a thousand at the last statement. It wasn't much these days, but as long as there was something in both books they felt secure enough.

Sailor fell into sleep soon after kissing her goodnight, and Ann knew nothing till morning when the still warm space told her he had gone to work.

At the school party she served tea and cakes, a cloth folded around the handle of the large metal pot. Sailor, togged up in beard and scarlet, shed gifts from a sack sewn up out of sheets, and said a few gruff words to make each child laugh.

When they got home he needed a glass of whisky, Ann topping up hers with water. 'You should have been an actor, the way you charmed those kids.'

'I should have been a lot of things,' he said, as if he easily could have. 'I know who I am while I'm acting, though, so you can be sure I'll always be myself when I'm with you.'

'I know that.'

'I want us to have as easy a life as possible, something I've only thought about in the last year or two.'

She didn't say life was already good enough for her, in case it disturbed him. Nor could she ask why he didn't think it was, because she knew he respected her for not bothering to probe. Love depended on such unspoken treaties. 'Do what you think best, Sailor.'

He put on the finest smile, and spread his arms. 'Welcome aboard!'

Such a covering embrace heated her sufficiently to say: 'You are a devil!'

'Now you're flattering me.' He spoke passionately in her ear. 'If I am, though, let's finish our supper, and get to bed, which is where I like you most.'

Every bottle lining the sideboard on Christmas Day displayed a badge of Sailor's popularity with parents at school. He sniffed the odour of roasting pork permeating the house, and twisted the cork from a bottle of sherry. 'We'll have a look at the jigsaw puzzle after our dinner. It's time we set to on it.'

A glass of wine, followed by brandy, made her sleepy, but she looked at the painting on the box while Sailor had a go at sorting sky and bits of rigging. Dark blue to the left faded into grey at the right, slivered by the tips of masts. Between billows of white and orange she followed the trunk of HMS *Victory* with her fingers, solid in its girth and strength, as if cut from one great oak, down to the main deck where red-coated marines with white crossbelts held muskets ready. Men stood back from fire and shot, a fallen sail waiting to become a shroud.

The job would be a long one, though a few pieces latched in every evening would one day get it done. 'It'll take us quite a while, Sailor.'

He fitted up a corner, but she supposed he had got that far before. 'We'll do it, my love, never you fear.' He worked along the top line till it was almost done. 'The sooner the better, though.'

The jumble of ships brewing slaughter touched anxiety in her. 'You think so?'

Flattening every piece face up till none were hidden, he turned away as if he also was disturbed. 'We've made a start, but let's go up for a kip now. We can have another go after tea.'

She expected to see more of him after he retired from work, but he often went out alone and came back half seas over at well gone closing time. Pubs would put the towels on, then lock the doors, with favoured customers still inside. When he stood in for the new caretaker and went straight from school she had no idea where he ate, if he did, because he didn't care for supper. Persuading him into a few mouthfuls, she guided him upstairs, to get his shirt and trousers off before he fell on the bed.

Some evenings she sipped a glass of whisky to ease her mind, soothing the tremor that something would happen to stop her seeing him again. Every possible mishap pictured itself, especially as he drove the car so blithely. She looked at the clock, and when such notions rushed back with their worry, she had another drink of whatever was on the sideboard.

'Never be afraid of things like that, my own dear love. After the perils I've been through in life nothing can happen to me.' He closed the door, taking a video, and a bottle bought at the pub, from the pocket of his naval jacket.

'Where have you been, though?'

He sat with a hand on each thigh. 'I was at The Black's Head,' he said in a gentle tone. 'Ask anybody, and they'll tell you. I got talking to Arthur Towle about old times. Nobody could see us under the smoke of our pipes. Arthur was a stoker, and we once served on the same destroyer. Afterwards I had to walk around to get some fresh air into my faculties before driving home. Tomorrow, we'll go arm in arm, though, you and me together. I can't have the love of my life feeling neglected.'

'I'll never feel that, Sailor.'

A piece of grit seemed to irritate his eye. 'Even so, it's only when I'm with you that I can be sure of not seeing it.'

'Seeing what?' She couldn't be certain whether he meant a spectacular musical comedy, or a queen walking the Bloody Tower with her head under her left arm.

He smiled the question away. 'Something that's finished and done with.'

'Tell me about it.' The pain seemed too much for him. 'But don't, though, if you don't want to.'

'There's nothing to tell. It's so far in the past it's not worth the candle.'

She put an arm around his shoulder. 'Just as you like, Sailor.' If there was so much to talk about that he couldn't then there wasn't. When he had to, if ever he did, she would hear whatever it was. They stayed up till midnight with their arms around each other, seeing the video and drinking from the bottle he'd brought.

He came back one day and unloaded six tins of paint from the car boot. 'We're going to decorate the house.'

Trestles were borrowed from Bill and Edna, and Sailor hoisted himself up to transform the walls into a shining scape of white. With his cap on and pipe going, he came down to lay newspapers over carpets and furniture. Ann, in shirt and jeans, did the woodwork of cupboards and skirting boards, wondering why she had waited so long to have the house re-done. 'Now we can see each other, Sailor.'

'Even the cat,' he laughed, wiping the end of Midnight's long tail with a rag soaked in turps.

In the garden he got out of his seat to dig a bed and weed the borders, though his energy seemed diminished. A trellis fence screened them from neighbours, and at the lower end clouds showed above the roof tops. He had built a feeding board for the birds, and collared doves drove sparrows from the peanuts. They rarely flew away when Sailor walked out. She watched him talking to them. 'What do you say to each other?'

'We have a chat,' he grinned, 'about the oceans we've crossed. We compare notes.'

He gazed at the sky, a battle with the west wind imminent, clouds distorted as if into shapes he needed to see. Midnight lay in a hump on his knees and he stroked him into a purr, another black cloud under his control.

Craving a swallow at the bottle, or wanting to read the newspaper, his knees parted slowly to let the cat fall. He filled his pipe as if putting shreds of his soul into it, then puffed out shapely billows of smoke.

When the weather was bad they picked away at the puzzle of Nelson's last battle, Ann listening to Sailor's stories as if she hadn't already heard them, wanting to know what happened next in those half forgotten. He assembled a patch of the main deck, while she worked at the glowering French ship that had given so much slaughter.

'We'll need a month of Sundays, but we're getting there.' His remark signalled a break from the gloom of billowing cannon smoke behind the *Victory*'s deck. He reached for glasses and a bottle from the sideboard.

They played games of draughts, alternated by tots of whisky and mugs of tea. Sailor drooped in the armchair and slept. She wondered about the travels of his dreaming mind, and one afternoon he came out of sleep with skin like pale clay, dull eyes looking but not seeing. 'Oh,' he moaned, 'I'm glad I'm back.'

She held his hands. 'Of course you are, Sailor. You're with me. But where did you go?'

The old smile was distorted by uncertainty. 'I wish I could put a name to it. All I know is I don't like being there. I'm in a boat, you see, and the alarm bells go. The ship's sinking and the sky's all dark. The flashes could be guns or lightning, because there's no sound. It never bothered me when I was young, so why does it now?'

He tried to shut his past from her. If she knew everything she would love him more, but if she never knew anything more about him she wouldn't love him any the less. Maybe it was only the war which tormented him. She hoped so. His medals were in a case on the mantelshelf, and she had seen the paper with his name written there, telling what they were for: 'In the Service of the Principles of the Charter of the United Nations; Korea; the Defence Medal; the Pacific Star; the Africa Star; the 1939–1945 Star.'

'You're all right now, Sailor.' Tears on her cheeks said she couldn't be sure. 'Nothing bad can happen while you're with me.'

'Don't worry, love.' He stroked her face. 'We'll be all right. You're the queen, and I'm the king. That's the only thing as matters.'

The pain of her spirit, so hard to endure, was dulled by a drink of whisky. 'It's the best thing out for lessening life's little obstacles,' he said.

You had to believe him, for who knew better? He must have fought through many obstacles in his life, and keeping the memories in watertight compartments was his way of making the pain bearable. Perhaps not talking made them worse, but dousing their pain with alcohol brought her and Sailor closer than if he had relinquished his guard and told all that gnawed at him.

Sidney's prize carriage clock was no longer in its place on the living-room shelf, and she stared at the space as if to make it come back. It was plain they had needed the money, and Sailor had sold the clock that he knew was precious to her, because how else had the whisky that he brought back every day been paid for? His savings must have finished long ago.

The thought that he might be out of the house so much because he had found another woman almost caused her to faint. She couldn't wait for him to fall against the kitchen door, but put on her coat to go out and look for him.

The slow bus seemed to be sliding backwards, her emotions melting into that pitch of jealousy which she had been too unknowing to suffer with Sidney. He wasn't in The Black's Head, and she didn't find him in the Radford pub, either. She imagined herself either one step behind or one in front, weeping because she didn't know whether or not she was being a fool. On her way home she bought supper at the chip van, and Sailor was waiting at the house.

'Thank God.' He held her for a kiss. 'I thought you was gone for good.'

'How could you think such a thing?' But there was a lightness in his tone. 'Have you been in long?'

'Ten minutes,' he said.

She spread fish, chips and saveloys, sliding the pan into the oven. 'Where did you go? I looked everywhere.'

'I was in The Jolly Higglers.'

She hadn't gone there, but she couldn't have called in every pub in Radford. 'Were you?'

'You don't believe me? I was talking to a chap as deals in cars, and I sold him my old banger for a hundred quid. He's taking it away tomorrow morning. I don't drive much these days, and it's only good for the knackers' yard. Anyway, it'll help our finances along.'

She sat before him. 'What have you done with the carriage clock, though?'

He paused from filling his glass. 'I've hidden it.'

'You wouldn't tell me lies, would you, Sailor?' She looked into his eyes. 'You didn't sell it, did you?'

He reached for her hand. 'I love you too much to lie. I suppose you'll think me a bit touched, but I didn't like such a valuable timepiece being kept on the shelf for anybody to see and carry away as soon as they broke into the house.'

She was ashamed at having called him a liar. Even if he had been she shouldn't have said it, and he wasn't, which made it worse. 'Come on,' he said, 'I'll show you.'

He pulled a shoe box from behind cloths and tins of polish jumbled in a cupboard under the stairs, showing her the clock in the bed of a yellow duster. 'Maybe I am barmy. The notion does occur to me at times, but so many houses around here get broken into that I had a funny feeling somebody would nick it. I like to follow my instinct, as I did when I fell in love with you and asked you to marry me.'

'And I'll always be glad you did, Sailor. I can't think of a better man than you.'

When supper was heated to a tolerable crisp in the stove he fetched a bottle of whisky from behind the settee, which he had hidden as a surprise on coming in, and they laughed at a slyness made innocent only because he wanted to make her happy.

*

She flooded what was done of the puzzle with light, and saw that it hadn't much increased. A completed frame hemmed the conflict in, but she longed to see the picture finished, in the hope of finding something about her and Sailor. When it was done she wouldn't be able to use the table, but she couldn't bear the thought of breaking it up after years of slotting every piece together. 'That would bring bad luck on us,' she told Sailor.

'I sometimes think the best thing would be to burn the whole lot,' he said. 'I'll never want to see it again after it's done.' He assembled a glimpse of clear sea. 'Look at this space for lost souls, though.'

'I like it,' she said. 'It's so much part of you. We'll fasten every piece onto some sticky Cellophane and have it framed. It'll look nice on the wall above the fireplace.'

'Anything you like.' He pounced on another bit of the sail. 'Your wish is my command.'

'It's looking wonderful.' Both were happiest at such moments. 'We're really getting on.'

The face of Roman numbers was plain to see when unwrapped from the cloth. The key stopped unmistakably against the barrier of being fully wound, minutes clicking healthily as if measuring her life and Sailor's from its snug hiding place. She knelt on the floor to feel its weight, knees sore on standing up and life itching back.

The cloth wrappings dropped from her fingers, and for a moment her heart seemed to stop. She couldn't see the clock with the eyes God had given her. Or the devil of a timepiece had grown legs and gone walkabout, sending out rays saying come and find me. She pulled everything onto the carpet but it still wasn't there. Sailor had found a new hidey-hole, and she already heard him making a joke of it. His mind might be unfathomable, but he wasn't the sort to play a game without good reason, in which case she wouldn't let the matter worry her, and saw no point asking where the clock had gone.

Whenever the vision of any clock moved across her eyes she searched every cranny, as if exploring the house for the first time, which made it easier not to let Sailor know the clock wasn't where it should be. Even so, it was nowhere to be found, and from deciding to say nothing so as not to spoil his fun in thinking she hadn't twigged its disappearance, she said when he came out of the bathroom looking fresh from his wash: 'Sailor, I can't find that carriage clock anywhere.'

His embarrassment showed as usual by a firework crackling of knuckles. She couldn't feel regret at Sidney's heirloom going west, and didn't care that she would never see it again, but had asked without intending to.

He faced her across the table. 'I suppose it's time I told you. I owed a big bill at the off-licence, and when I showed him the clock he agreed to take it in exchange. Otherwise he would have had me in court.' He sat as if waiting for a sentence of doom. 'I'm sorry, love.'

'I wish you'd asked me.'

'I should have done. I don't know why I didn't.'

First the car, and now this. Money had to come from somewhere for their drinking. Nobody could afford to go at such a rate. She laid a hand on his wrist, unable to bear the least sign of his misery. 'I'd do anything for you, Sailor. You know that, don't you?'

He nodded. They were silent, like two thieves caught out instead of one. Speculating as to who was the biggest made her smile, which gave him hope. She would rather not have known, and searching for an explanation as to why she had brought the matter out made her laugh.

The sculptured fixity of guilt on Sailor's face dissolved. 'There's only one thing to do, if that's the way it takes you. The pubs'll be open in ten minutes, and it'll be nice sitting there to forget our troubles, if that's what they are.'

To prepare them for the walk he took a half-gone bottle from the top of the television and poured two powerful drinks. She liked his style, and his timing, and the first sip of whisky was as welcome as if she had been waiting for it all day.

On their way to the pub it was no longer necessary to keep up with his pace, and she even adjusted hers so that he could stay level. He sat in his usual corner, little framed hunting scenes on the wall behind, pipe well chimneying. His arm lost its slight shake after the enabling liquid of the first strong bitter had gone down.

People who had known him from his caretaker days called out: 'Hello, Sailor, how are you? Still at that titty-bottle, I see!'

Knowing himself to be a waymark of their ordered lives lit his eyes back to a hundred watts. He only nodded, however, not wasting words, though he liked being popular. What man didn't, Ann thought, or any man at all, come to that. Some greetings were so brazen she wondered whether he had known the woman before meeting her. Still, such attention only increased his value in her eyes, and the esteem for her in his, and she knew that the more esteem he felt for her the more he loved her, which made the love between them as perfect as any could be.

Walking home hand in hand she stopped to kiss him beneath the corner sodium, not caring what anyone might think. A feeling of carefree youth had come back to her on living with Sailor.

'I love you.' He relaxed his embrace. 'I can go through the shoals and the shallows with you.'

One day he went out on his own and was away longer than usual. The sky was black with a threat of rain, and streetlights came on as he reached for the gate latch. He sat in the armchair as if he would never get up again.

She stroked his face. 'I wish you wouldn't overdo it, Sailor. You aren't as young as you were.'

'I know. I walked too far.'

'Where did you go?'

He yawned. 'To damn near Strelley and back. When I get going it's hard to stop.'

'That's miles away.'

'No buses went by, and when I was near home three shot by.'

'If I'd been with you I'd have called a taxi.'

'It's all right, love. I'm better now I'm back with you.'

She followed him down the spirals and discovered it was where she wanted to go. If he pawned or sold their possessions it was only because she had always wanted to do the same. All that mattered was for two people to use them so that they could live the way they wanted. Love wasn't love unless you could break free of the crushing pressures inside yourself.

She kept a glistening sort of order in the house, everything spick and span, as if to spite Fate at her surrender to the way it said she should live. Energy came from she didn't know where as she pushed the Electrolux in and out of the bedrooms. A green cloth suitcase with a number stencilled across in black lay at the bottom of the wardrobe. She lifted it, to suck dust from the corners. What he kept inside she didn't know. Her own papers were stowed in a cigar box of Sidney's which she kept on her dressing table. Now and again she threw away old bank statements and cheque stubs, or took out cashpoint and credit cards when they were short of money.

She swilled dishes and cutlery, and stowed everything in its place until she felt exhausted. By the time Sailor came down from the mists of sleep, she had cooked the breakfast he was so fond of, and put biscuits and coffee out for herself.

'I eat so much of a morning,' he quipped, 'that you'd think I was going to be hanged.'

'Except it's almost midday,' she smiled, 'so it's a bit late for that.'

He took the empty plate to the sink, looking around before

lighting his pipe. 'The place is as clean as a new pin. I don't know how you do it, my love.'

'I have to,' she said. 'I like it that way.'

'Same here. Squalor would be the death of me. You get a horror of it after a life on the mess deck.'

He went for a walk, so she put on the front-room light and gazed at the jigsaw, finding it hard to pick from the multitude of pieces. About a third was done, and the ominous French ship was taking shape through smoke and bloodshed. A chair eased her aching back, and she wasn't sorry to lose the overall view.

Dabbling among the blue-grey of the upper right she found three pieces to slot in. Then she stared, discouraged at what was yet to be done, though glad they had accomplished so much. The mast of the *Victory* was reassuring in its girth. Sailor had assembled it in earlier days, his face like a child's while it came together. She smoothed a finger up and down, as if there were no curving interlocking lines and she was carressing three-dimensional wood.

He made no mention of her progress, but sat in his usual armchair by the fire. 'You look as if you went a long way,' she said.

'I did, but not too far from you, and that's what keeps me going.' After a silence he turned to her. 'I saw a face I had to leave behind.'

His fear alarmed her. 'What face?'

'I can't explain. I just want to rest, love.'

If there was more to his walk than was hinted at she would only find out by following him, but would die of shame if he turned and saw. On the other hand maybe the act of doing so would prove her love.

Whisky cooled his tea, and she reached for the bottle to pour some in hers as well. 'Eating and drinking will wake me up.' He drained his cup, and took a piece of cake. 'Do you believe in God?'

Such a question could only be answered by saying yes.

'Why?'

'I've got to,' she said.

He relished another fill of potent tea. 'What sort of a chap do you think He is?'

'I don't know. How could I ask?' The talk disturbed her. 'But I'm sure He'll look after us.'

He stroked Midnight, who jumped down, sensing his unease. 'I think He's got it in for me.'

'Why's that, Sailor?' She couldn't bite her tongue and keep silent. 'Is anything wrong with your life?'

He altered tack, her question warning of further turmoil. 'I'd just like to be able to make you happier.'

'I'm as happy as I want to be, and it's all because of the way you care for me.'

'I get this ache up my left arm.' He lifted it, let it fall. 'It might be rheumatism.'

'You should see a doctor.'

'It comes and goes.' He splashed more whisky into his cup. 'But this puts the melters on it.'

She would believe in God a little less if He had it in for Sailor. 'Still, you should call at the doctor's,' though she knew he wouldn't, and hoped her heart would go bang before his, a massive cardiac explosion landing her in the middle of nowhere for ever and ever.

Blue veins pulsed on the back of his hand. 'I will. But if God has it in for me I can't say I blame Him. If I'd been Him I would have killed me years ago.'

Silence was the only way to question him. She stroked his face, a drop of clear water falling onto her hand, and he fell asleep before she could ask.

He only came alive in the morning after getting at the bottle. Nor did she feel part of the world till the first strong drink had gone down. Neither said much after it had. The lines of walls and windows sharpened as the liquor took effect, and whoever felt like it stood up to make breakfast.

Through the mist of her apparent wellbeing Sailor sat with smouldering pipe, looking as young as ever. In the hours that passed he told matelot stories in a clear voice, Ann not caring that they'd been heard before. The ghost that threatened him was harmless while he talked. After tea they sat drinking till going to bed at eleven, by which time two bottles had gone dry.

He rubbed a hand across his eyes as if to order the thoughts behind. 'It gets worse, and I don't know why that should be.'

She hoped he wouldn't say, as if any revelation would be too late. 'What does?'

'It's eating me to death. I'm starting to see them everywhere. I know it wasn't my fault, but that don't help, though I had to live through it.'

To tell something dreadful about herself might have comforted him, but all she could do was listen, pulling Midnight onto her lap for comfort. 'I don't know what you mean, Sailor.'

'It's my first wife I'm talking about. She did it on me a few times, though I was no angel, either. We had a daughter, a wonderful girl she was, and then my wife told me she was somebody else's. She let me know in such a way that I could see a mile off how true it was. I'd loved Melanie for ten years as my own kid, but she had been put into my wife by somebody else. I went mad. That sort of thing's murder land.'

Ann didn't know whether her face went flour-white or blood-orange red at the certainty that he had killed his wife, and that that was his appalling secret.

For a smile he managed a bleak jack o' lantern grimace. 'No, my love, I never touched her. It was too big a blow. I'd take nobody's life. Nor have I ever gone in for hitting women.'

She wished there was some way of stopping him, because what did anything from the past have to do with the way they lived now? His blue-glow eyes looked ahead, as if he was telling everyone in the world because he could hardly bear to let her know, or recall it himself. 'You should have told me before, Sailor.'

'How could I?' He turned to her, and she felt close again. 'I couldn't bear the sight of her, so I lit off. Not long after, she killed herself, and left a note saying it was because of me. I'd ruined her life. I was the worst person she'd known, the worst in the world. That's why I couldn't tell you. Nothing she said was true, but with a person like that you've got to take the responsibility. If I'd told her I'd forgiven her for what she did she might not have done it. It didn't occur to me. Even if I didn't mean it, I could have said I forgave her, then maybe she wouldn't have gassed herself.'

'I'll never believe it was your fault, Sailor.'

He didn't hear. 'If I couldn't believe that, I might live in peace for the rest of my life. But let me go on, because you haven't heard the rest of it yet. Though Melanie wasn't mine I never held anything against her. And she was my daughter by the time I'd brought her up. She left home at eighteen, and I saw her a time or two. She was happy enough. We got on so well she said she'd come and live with me when I left the Navy.'

'That was nice,' Ann put in.

He looked at rain making tracks down the garden window, unable to face her. 'She did the same thing as her mother, took pills and killed herself when she was twenty. She did it out of the blue, just like that.' His glass was empty, and he leaned towards her, his expression as dead as if he'd had no rest from the day he was born.

'You can't say it was your fault.'

'I've got a conscience, though. The sharks were set on me, and they won't let go.'

He had never been altogether hers, but at this moment he belonged to her more than he ever had, more than she could have thought possible. 'It does no good to torment yourself.'

'I know, and I feel a bit calmer for telling you. I did want to let you know about it on the day we were married, but I couldn't

ALAN SILLITOE

bring it out. Troubles shared are troubles doubled, in any case.'

'They wouldn't have been, not with me.' Troubles shared are proof of love. 'And what if they are?'

She decided from now on to check what liquor was brought into the house, and when he came back with an off-licence plastic bag of new supplies she asked where the money had come from. 'We can't afford to go on drinking at such a rate.'

'Never you mind about that, my love. We're managing very well, as you can see. We'll be all right, as long as the rent gets paid.'

'That's because I take it straight out of the pension every month.'

'I bless you for that, but leave the rest to me.'

They tried to drink less, but two bottles were finished all the same, levels going down like sand in an egg timer. When Sailor fell out of his chair and lay full length before the fire he was hard to rouse. Bringing the story of his wife and daughter into the open had made things worse, a despairing thought she found impossible to endure while heaping blankets over his body so that he wouldn't be cold in the night.

She rested her ear on his chest to find out if he was breathing. How daft to think he's dead. His body shuddered, a heartbreaking sigh from deep inside. Midnight's furry weight warmed her knees when she sat in the next chair knowing that before long she would get up and pour herself another drink.

Her credit card had gone from the cigar box, so it was obvious where the money was coming from. A smell of frying bacon filled the kitchen, Sailor singing with sleeves rolled up as he stood by the stove. Fearing the edict he knew must come, the ditty faded. She put two slices of bread in the toaster. 'We've got to stop drinking, Sailor.'

His cheeks were purplish, hands shaking as he pushed the spatula around the pan. 'Just as well stop living. Nobody knows how long they've got on this earth, and if I don't drink I won't last as long as if I do.'

Her look made him alter his mind. 'That can't be so.'

He set eggs, bacon, sausage, fried bread and tomatoes before her. 'You may be right. We'll give it a try.'

She carried two large bottles of water from the supermarket to pour into their glasses. 'It's time we had another go at the puzzle. It'd be marvellous if we could get to the end.'

'I've been trying for years, but I was waiting to finish it with you.' He was smiling with pleasure. 'Come on, let's get cracking.'

They had never fitted so many at one time. He completed the main deck of the *Victory*, and found the sail that was to become Nelson's shroud, while Ann put together the uneven line of marines. 'Now for the mizzen starboard tackle,' he said.

He looked better after the nap. At moments she felt the hardship of resistance, and looked around for a drink, hands shaking no less than his. She caressed a glass, but wouldn't be the first to give in, the struggle so consuming that she no longer bothered to clean the house.

Sailor came back from a walk, a half-bottle showing from each pocket. He put them unopened on the sideboard, and lay back in his chair. She sat by him on the arm. 'What happened, Sailor?'

'I turned a corner at the top of Hillcot Drive, and saw one of 'em.'

'Who?' She dreaded the answer.

'Melanie looked at me from over a hedge, and the blood stopped in my veins. She was wearing a blue frock, and smiling like she used to be when she waited for me to come home after months at sea with a present. But she screamed, terrified. Her mother was there as an old woman, and she never was one. She came out of the door and tried to pull Melanie inside. I walked away as quick as my legs would take me. I didn't care in what direction I made distance. They'll chase me into the grave. Sometimes it's all right for weeks. Then it hits me again. It gets worse.'

'Maybe it'll go away,' though she didn't see how it could, because as he talked she was seeing them herself, a flash of both by the kitchen door, doll-faces glaring at her with loathing.

He stood, pale and unsteady. 'I'll be in the front room, doing a bit at the puzzle.'

He took the terrors with him, as if they were built into his broad shoulders. She found him asleep, a few pieces in a clenched hand. She caressed him, then punched and pleaded till a half-opened eye made a window of light into his soul. 'Come on, Sailor, let's get you upstairs.'

The manoeuvre took half an hour, but she hoped he would stay in bed for as long as it took to bring him peace. The time she sat by him couldn't be measured. Talking more about his curse would break the spell, she hoped, and it seemed to, for after three days in bed he walked almost normally to the pub, wearing his cap and the indestructible duffle coat, and using the stick Sidney had hiked with in his youth.

'Smoke, noise and beer smells are my natural element after sea water,' he smiled on opening the door. It had become hers as well, the one atmosphere in which she and Sailor could be alive together. 'This'll drive the sickness out,' he said when they sat down to the first drink. 'I've never known it to fail.'

They lay side by side in bed, and the terrors came into his dreams. He didn't tell her, but she knew they did because they spilled into hers as well. Melanie and her mother sat in a deep armchair in the lounge of The Tummler Hotel. Ann saw the high chairs from the back, and on turning to look saw their bloody and decaying faces. The room wasn't the same because bales of straw were scattered among grey cobwebs, and Sailor was hanging from a beam, but still living, his body turning and turning as if a high wind was blowing, at which gyrations Melanie and the old woman began to laugh.

'What's the matter, love?'

She grasped him. 'I was having a bad dream.'

'Seemed like a nightmare the way you screamed. But don't cry. You're all right now. You're with me.'

'I'm sorry I woke you.'

'I'm glad you did. That's what I'm here for. But go to sleep now. You'll be all right.'

In the morning Sailor was comatose and could hardly breathe, but he got out of bed and came down for breakfast, a lifetime's drill helping him to live. 'You'll have to see the doctor,' she said, but knew he wouldn't when he reached for the bottle even before eating.

The cat scratched to go out and do its business, and so, putting away the temptation of another drink, she opened the garden door to follow. Teddy shouted in argument with his mother, and the echoing smack of a hand which must have come from his father set him on a long wail of rage and protest.

Evening clouds formed a hose for letting down rain. She hoped the ululation of a car alarm wouldn't waken Sailor, who said they reminded him of danger signals on a ship. A white sparrow perched at the nuts finished gorging then flew off with one in its beak.

The end of the June day turned chilly, and she sat mindlessly till the first drops of water told her it was time to go in. Annoyed at the smell, she assumed Midnight had messed before being let out, though he had been a well-behaved cat, ever since Sidney had put its kitten's paws into a pat of lard so that it wouldn't forget where it lived.

In the front room Sailor's head had fallen among bits of the puzzle, hands loose over both arms of the chair. The car alarm stopped, and Midnight mewed as if his tail was trapped. Bending close, she saw that Sailor's eyes were open, tear marks on his cheeks, a bottle half empty on its side.

Her hand and his damp forehead grew cold together, while Midnight played 'in and out the window' around her ankles, his mewing as loud as a baby's cry. 'What shall I do, Sailor?' Unable to do anything, she yearned for him to tell her while holding the icy hands.

She screamed in the garden as if to get her heart going again. Edna was putting rubbish in the outside bin. 'Whatever's the matter, duck?'

'It's Sailor.' Rain spattered the overgrown lawn. 'I've got to use your telephone.'

The Pakistani doctor told her what anyone would have known. 'What was it?' she said, standing by the door as if to stop him leaving.

'Liver, heart, everything. We'll know later.' It was Friday evening so he said she could call at his surgery for the death certificate on Monday. He clicked his bag shut and went away.

She reached for the bottle, and sloshed out a glass. That would have been Sailor's advice. 'Wouldn't it, Sailor?'

'You'll stay with us tonight, duck,' Edna said. 'We've put Teddy on the parlour sofa, and he thinks it's a great adventure because that's where the hi-fi is. And we had to promise he could see the body.'

Bill scarcely credited that the doctor had helped so little. A vein at his temple turned dark with anger. 'You mean he just told you Sailor was dead, and then pissed off?'

Sailor wasn't with her anymore, so it didn't much matter. 'Yes.'

'We'll have to call the undertakers first thing tomorrow.' Edna took the bottle from Ann, and emptied the brew into a flowerpot. 'You shouldn't drink so much. It'll rot your guts. It'll kill you, just like it's done poor old Sailor.' She swept the pieces of the jigsaw into a cloth bag. 'I allus knew this would happen, him coming back night after night with bottles sticking out of his pockets.'

They spread two eiderdowns on the table and laid the body down. Edna cleaned up the mess and covered Sailor with the largest sheet in the house. 'I know what to do because I helped a woman with my mother when she died.'

There wasn't even enough spare change to buy a bottle of beer, every wallet, purse and pocket empty, but she found supplies all over the house, mostly half bottles in crannies of the wardrobe and under the beds, or behind the linen shelves, with a nip or two still left in each. Two boxes of chemical wine tasted so sour she slopped them into the toilet, wondering when he could have brought them in. An almost full bottle of White Horse, hidden in the fuse box cupboard by the back door got her through the funeral without falling down.

Edna filled in forms to get the interment costs settled by the DHSS, and Ann signed with a quivering hand. She was looking after herself but not, Edna saw, very well. 'I don't know what I'd do without you,' Ann said, alone with the cat after five years married to Sailor.

Edna spread papers from the cigar box and Sailor's case over the floor. 'It seems you're knackered, duck,' she said on going through them. It was a blessing Sailor had died when he did, she explained, otherwise she would have been living in a cardboard box under a bridge somewhere. 'And just look at these gas and electric bills: they haven't been paid for months. He's left you in a bottomless pit, and no mistake.'

Her credit card with a limit of five hundred pounds had been overdrawn by fifteen hundred. Letters from the bank asked for repayment but, stranger still, another letter of a later date offered to lend her more, at which Edna broke into a long choking laugh: 'Bloody effrontery! Would you believe it?'

Ann stared into space, then smiled at Sailor's audacity of overdrawing her account to the tune of fifteen hundred quid.

'It's bloody villainy, really,' Edna said, 'though I suppose we should be grateful he was the sort who saved every bit of paper.'

Ann felt she must defend Sailor's good name, even so. Only one suit was left out of five that once hung in the wardrobe, and she had long ago noted his precious Japanese tea service missing, as well as the walnut-cased clock from school.

'He even got rid of that teapot we brought you from Turkey,' Edna said. Pawn tickets cascaded from an old wallet, and a wad of betting slips fell out of a box. 'He's left you in a real bleddy fix.'

'There's no money left then to pay anything?' She had never doubted that he had got the money from somewhere for their life of Riley, and tears fell at the thought of Sailor not seeing how she appreciated such open-hearted behaviour in doing his best to make both of them happy.

'Don't cry, duck, it wasn't your fault.' Edna took her hand. 'You're up to your neck in it, but the debts of the dead die with them, so let the bank whistle for their money. They can't get blood out of a stone. You've got to promise not to drink anymore booze, that's all.'

'This is when I need it most.'

Edna unfolded her arms and picked up the mug of coffee. 'I shan't come and see you again if you don't pack in the rat poison.'

'I like it.'

'So do I, now and again. But you've got to stop. You can if you want to. Me and Bill will help. One good turn deserves another. You looked after our Teddy while we was on holiday when nobody else would.'

'I'll do the same again if ever you want.'

'Not if you don't get off the drink. You won't be capable. Think what it did to Sailor. Two bottles a day, you tell me. He must have been a man of iron to last so long. You'd have been in your bury-box as well in another few weeks.'

He had died when he did in order to save her, she would like to think. 'Sailor was looking after me, as well.'

At the supermarket Edna kept hawk-eyes on what Ann put in her trolley. 'I'm not a young girl,' she said. 'I can look after myself.'

Edna sniffed, a hand pushed over her face in disbelief. She rummaged by the till and found whisky under cat food and packets of frozen peas. Not without a tussle she put it back on the shelf. 'I told you, no booze.' She couldn't keep an eye on her every minute. 'You can have four tins of shandy a week, that's all.'

Ann replaced two half-bottles of rum that Edna hadn't found. 'I don't want anything.'

She got up from the settee. The days were longer but the nights flashed by. She didn't dream about Melanie and her mother anymore. Maybe Sailor had taken them away. She didn't even dream about him, and found that strange. But he was present every moment of the day.

She'd had little booze since the funeral and, looking back on a month of nights, wouldn't taste it again. Tears fell from her thinning face as she shook the thousand pieces of the jigsaw puzzle back onto the table. Call me Sailor, he had said, in a voice never to be forgotten. His smile during however much time was needed to put it together would show her what a villain he had been to leave her in such a state, but she was getting enough from the DHSS to manage. She didn't know whether she would glue each piece firmly till it could be framed and hung as they had talked about, or scatter the completed picture broadside into the fire, hoping to see Sailor one last time among the flames.

Alan Sillitoe

The Loneliness of the Long Distance Runner

Smith is an incorrigible and defiant young rebel, inhabiting a no-man's land of institutionalised Borstal. Watched over by a phlegmy sunlight, as his steady jog-trot rhythm transports him over an unrelenting, frost-bitten earth, he wonders why, for whom and for what is he running. The film of the story, starring Tom Courtenay, has cult status.

Evocative, realistic and superbly written, the other stories in this collection introduce us to, among others: the war-veteran Uncle Ernest who resorts to the oblivion of the beer pump to fill the passage of empty, loveless days; the schoolteacher Mr Raynor who relies on voyeurism to reward his exasperated, solitary existence.

'Sillitoe writes with tremendous energy, and his stories simply tear along.'   *Daily Telegraph*

'A beautiful piece of work, confirming Sillitoe as a writer of unusual spirit and great promise.'   *Guardian*

'Graphic, tough, outspoken, informal.'   *The Times*

'All the imaginative sympathy in the world can't fake this kind of thing. It must have been lived in, seen, touched, smelled: and we are lucky to have a writer who has come out of it knowing the truth and having the skill to turn that truth into art.'
                                                     New Statesman

ISBN 0 586 09241 2

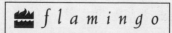

Alan Sillitoe

Saturday Night and Sunday Morning

Working all day at a lathe leaves Arthur Seaton with energy to spare in the evenings. A hard-drinking, hard-fighting young rebel of a man, he knows what he wants and he's sharp enough to get it. And before long, his carryings-on with a couple of married women are part of local gossip. But then one evening he meets a young girl in a pub, and Arthur's life begins to look less simple.

Alan Sillitoe's classic novel of the 1950s is a story of timeless significance. The film of the novel, starring Albert Finney, transformed British cinema and is much imitated.

'That rarest of all finds: a genuine no-punches pulled, unromanticised working-class novel. Mr Sillitoe is a born writer, who knows his milieu and describes it with vivid, loving precision.'

Daily Telegraph

'His writing has real experience in it and an instinctive accuracy that never loses its touch. His book has a glow about it as though he had plugged it in to some basic source of the working-class spirit.'

Guardian

'Sillitoe has written a stunner. Miles nearer the real thing than D. H. Lawrence's working-men ever came.' *Sunday Express*

'Very outspoken and vivid.' *Sunday Times*

'A refreshing originality.' *Times Literary Supplement*

ISBN: 0 586 09005 3

flamingo

Alan Sillitoe

Life Without Armour

The autobiography of the early years of one of the greatest English writers of the twentieth century.

'A marvellous escape story. Throughout the book, Sillitoe is in a state of constant excitement and impatience for life to begin.'
New Statesman & Society

'A modest, unassuming and decent book, best where it tells self-mockingly of Sillitoe's early literary efforts, but chilling also in its brief account of his childhood.'
ROBERT NYE, *Scotsman*

'Few writers have come quite so far on such unpromising fuel. An absorbing book, not only for its portrait of a pre-Welfare State slum childhood, but for its angle on the position of working-class writers.'
D J TAYLOR, *Independent*

'Sillitoe's autobiography is the more impressive for being told in a simple, almost biblical voice: the voice he was in search of all those years, trimmed to the essence and peculiarly his own.'
Observer

'A cheery story, something rare in any sort of biographical writing nowadays.'
Sunday Times

'*Life Without Armour* is indeed an extraordinary book.'
Mail on Sunday

ISBN: 0 00 638430 7

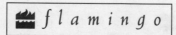

Alan Sillitoe

Collected Stories

From one of the most distinguished English writers of the twentieth century comes an impressive collection of his greatest short stories.

'No-one who cares for good writing and honesty of purpose will want to be without a copy. Sillitoe's work is distinguished by its honesty, the clean cut of its narrative line, the authenticity and congruence of its detail. The thirty-eight stories put together in *Collected Stories* strike me as the best part of Sillitoe's life's work, and worthy to rank with the finest things done in that difficult form.'   *Scotsman*

'As a short-story writer he is on the fringe of the V S Pritchett class, along with the justly admired (but unjustly more admired) William Trevor. It is time the magnitude of Sillitoe's achievement was more widely recognised.'   *Daily Telegraph*

'*Collected Stories* show him at his best. Alan Sillitoe writes effectively and poignantly.'   *Mail on Sunday*

'As his *Collected Stories* show convincingly, Sillitoe is, at his best, a master of the genre ... Tense, compact and gritty, they speak out with a voice that one recognises at once, with gratitude, as wholly truthful.'   *Evening Standard*

'Shows a writer who understands the art of the short form.'
Hampstead & Highgate Express

ISBN: 0 00 649306 8

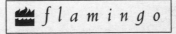 *flamingo*